Treasure Under the Tree

Palmyrton Estate Sale Mystery Series

S.W. Hubbard

Published by S.W. Hubbard, 2021.

This is a work of fiction. Similarities to real people, places, or events are entirely coincidental.

TREASURE UNDER THE TREE

First edition. October 18, 2021.

Copyright © 2021 S.W. Hubbard.

Written by S.W. Hubbard.

Chapter 1

A ship has run aground in my backyard, thirty miles inland from the Jersey shore.

A pirate ship, inflatable, bouncy. Water to be supplied by two lawn sprinklers.

My husband Sean and I are half an hour from total bedlam, when fifteen preschoolers will descend to celebrate the fourth birthday of Lo Griggs, nephew of my assistant, Ty. I'm not the craftsy type, but Sean has tapped into his inner Martha Stewart, stringing red and black paper streamers, drawing pirate faces with eye patches on helium balloons, and hanging a big yellow parrot pinata from the lowest branch of our maple tree.

He's had lots of kiddie birthday party practice with his nieces and nephews, and he longs to do the same for our own kids.

So far, no prospects on that front.

"Betty's here," Sean announces, holding the back door open for Ty's grandmother, who's lugging two shopping bags of supplies.

"Hello, Audrey baby." She drops the bags and pulls me into a warm embrace as if we haven't seen each other for months, when, in fact, she visited the offices of Another Man's Treasure Estate Sales just yesterday afternoon to confer on last-minute party plans.

Grandma Betty releases me and heads out on the lawn. "Oh, my, my—would you look at that bouncy boat! Lo is going to love this." She sticks her head into the various portholes and tests the bounciness of the gangplank slide. A big grin splits her face, and she clasps her hands to her heart. "Ty was right to order this. Our little man is going to have a wonderful birthday party! And you were so kind to let Ty set it up here."

"Our pleasure," Sean says as he staggers out of the house with a cooler full of juice boxes and soda. He's not saying that to be polite. Sean has been as excited about this party as the birthday boy himself. And we have the perfect day for it. The May sun beams down on our yard, not too hot, no clouds in sight.

I smile and nod hoping to stay off the touchy topic of the bouncy boat. Ty first spotted this model last fall in the backyard next to an estate sale client's home. He's been plotting to get one for Lo's springtime birthday ever since, but he faced two obstacles. First, the lack of backyard in which to set it up; and second, the fierce opposition of Lo's mother, Charmaine. Although Charmaine appreciates Ty's devotion to Lo, she doesn't care for the way Ty spoils the child.

And apartment-dwelling Charmaine hates accepting favors.

I had vowed to stay out of the epic bouncy-boat-or-not battle, but Sean torpedoed that by proactively assuring Ty and Charmaine that we'd love to have Lo's fourth birthday party in our backyard. Ty leapt on the offer, and Charmaine recognized she'd been out-maneuvered.

"Where's Charmaine?" Betty asks as she begins setting up pirate-themed paper plates, napkins, and party hats on the folding table.

"On her way," I explain. "She's picking up the cake at the bakery. And Ty will arrive at two with the birthday boy."

"I hope those two aren't still fussin' at each other," Betty says. "A party is meant to be happy."

"I think Charmaine conceded on the bouncy boat as long as Ty promised not to buy Lo a BlastMaster as his birthday gift." BlastMaster is THE hot toy of the moment among older kids, but as a four-year-old only child, Lo is blissfully unaware. Ty, on the other hand, longs to buy his nephew the pricey toys he himself never had as a child.

"Oh, Lawd! I gotta agree with Charmaine there." Betty wags her head as she unpacks her shopping bags. "Lo don't need no fancy ee-lec-tronics to have fun. Why, yesterday that child played for two hours with a stack of cardboard boxes I had set out for recycling. Those boxes were a castle, and a boat, and a school, and a treasure chest."

Charmaine enters the backyard through the gate from the driveway in time to hear Betty's report. "That's what I keep telling Ty, but he won't listen."

This puts Grandma Betty in a tight spot, as she hates to side with Charmaine against Ty. Ty is her deceased daughter's only child, while his half-sister Charmaine shares Ty's father, a man Betty has no use for. If you're tracking DNA, Lo is not technically Betty's great-grandchild. But Betty lives by the heart, not microbiology, and she adores Lo. "Well, girl—you know Ty just wants to give our little man a childhood where he never comes up short for anything."

Uh-oh. We're heading into rocky terrain here. Charmaine is a single mother, but she works hard to give Lo everything he needs. BlastMaster does not make the list of essentials. Before Charmaine can snap back, I grab her elbow and steer her toward the house. "I think we should keep that cake in the fridge until we're ready to serve it. Can you help me rearrange stuff to make space for it?"

Charmaine stomps into the kitchen with me and bangs the cake box on the counter. "I am so tired of arguing about my child's birthday party. Lo is not deprived." She tosses her long braids and furrows her brow. Her skin is the same rich brown as her son's. She's a pretty woman, but not very approachable when she's looking so fierce.

"Of course, Lo's not deprived," I reassure her. "He's smart and happy and well-adjusted." To end the debate, I stick my head into the fridge, where I find some decaying leftovers that can be tossed and shove some condiments to the rear. Then I turn to Charmaine and hold out my hands for the cake.

She passes it over, but her face is still contracted with annoyance. "Look, I know there's going to come a time when I'll have to spend money to get Lo the shoes and jeans and computer games he'll want in order to fit in with the other kids. But that time hasn't come yet. And I don't see the need to rush it."

Our conversation is cut short by the sound of a car door slamming, followed by a high-pitched squeal of joy. "A pi-watt ship!" Charmaine and I make it back into the backyard in time to see two little sneakers disappearing into the vessel. A few seconds later, Lo's delighted brown velvet face pops out of a porthole. "Mommy! Audee! Sawn! Look at me!"

In a flash, Charmaine's grumpiness dissipates. She smiles at her brother and mouths "thank you."

And the party takes off. The moment the clock strikes two, a steady stream of Lo's pre-school classmates and their parents arrive in our backyard. Sean pumps his favorite kiddie music Spotify playlist through the wireless outdoor speakers. Betty sets out the fried chicken, mac and cheese and potato salad. I offer drinks, while Charmaine discreetly referees some toddler takedowns.

The party is in full swing when a tall, muscled Black man with silver at his temples arrives. I feel Grandma Betty stiffen beside me. It's Marvin Griggs, Ty and Charmaine's father and Lo's grandfather.

Charmaine's face lights up. "Daddy!" They embrace, Charmaine enthusiastic, Marvin a bit reserved. "Lo, look who's here."

"Hi, PawPaw! Look at my boat!" Lo waves his grandfather over, but Marvin must pass Ty to reach his grandson. The two men shake hands, more like business acquaintances than father and son. But at least they're speaking.

Betty's usually smiling lips are pressed into a hard line. Over fifteen years have passed, but Betty still thinks Marvin's arrest and imprisonment is the reason her daughter lost her will to fight the cancer that killed her. "Marvin, you better fix yourself a plate. I'm about to put this food away before it goes bad."

I nudge Marvin toward the kids and fix a plate of food for him myself. The party has been going so well; I don't want any explosions now. Marvin hugs Lo awkwardly. I can see he wants to join in the fun with the kids but doesn't know how to go about it. I watch as Sean comes over to rescue him, handing him a beach ball to toss to the kids as they come down the slide. Sean is so good at knowing exactly how to keep the kids engaged without overstimulating them into a frenzy.

A mother sinks into a lawn chair next to me with a blissful smile. "This is great! Austin will sleep like a rock tonight."

Another mother agrees. "Heaven! My son's birthday is in February, so we always have to throw an indoor party. But you can't choose when your kids will be born!"

Or if they'll be born. Sean and I would happily accept a February birthday for our child. In fact—I do some quick mental math—if I got pregnant this month, our baby would arrive in February. But what's the likelihood our rigidly programmed sex schedule will result in a hit this cycle? It hasn't worked the last eighteen months we've tried.

The squeals of the kids interrupt my pity party. Sean lines them up in front of the pinata, being careful to space them out so they don't clobber one another. The backyard grows a little blurry as I rail for the millionth time how unfair it is that a man who enjoys kids as much as Sean does can't conceive his own.

The parrot pinata proves impervious to the kids' puny swings of the wiffle-ball bat, so Ty hauls off and whacks it like Sammy Sosa and the candy spills to the ground. During the ruthless scramble for loot, Charmaine carries out the cake. We all move into singing Happy Birthday, and Lo blows out the candles. Then the birthday boy gets to open his presents while his friends practice envy-control. Finally, Lo distributes the goody bags, and the party officially ends.

After all the little guests and their parents have left, and the adults are enjoying a beer, Ty goes out to his car and returns with a large box wrapped in yellow, green, and purple dinosaur paper.

Charmaine's eyes narrow. "That better not be a BlastMaster."

There's no need for Ty to answer because Lo has the paper shredded in seconds, revealing a Tonka excavator. The little boy waits impatiently as Sean uses a combination of engineering skills and brute force to release the toy from its packaging. "Tank you, Uncle Ty," Lo shouts when the toy is finally liberated.

Ty crosses his arms across his chest and mutters under his breath. "Imma get him a BlastMaster for Christmas. Ain't nobody can stop Santa Claus."

Chapter 2

We awake on Sunday to a gray drizzle. The generator that pumps hot air into the bouncy boat has been unplugged, and the pirate ship lies crumpled on the grass as if it's been pillaged by a rival gang of rogue sailors. The decapitated parrot head swings gruesomely from the maple tree, and the helium balloons have lost their lift and roll aimlessly across the patio, their pirate smiles smeared by the rain.

"Guess we should have cleaned up better yesterday," Sean says as he looks outside.

"The rental company will be here soon to collect the boat," I tell him. "Let's get the balloons picked up and look for any candy packages in the grass before I go get Ethel." Our dog spent yesterday with my dad and his wife so she wouldn't bowl over any little children, and they wouldn't poke her eyes out. Once she returns, Ethel will follow her nose to any spilled treats in the yard, and I want to avoid a trip to the vet caused by eating candy, wrappers and all.

"Right," Sean agrees although he makes no move to go outside. His hands are jammed in his pockets, his gaze focused somewhere far beyond our back fence.

I come up behind him and slide my arms around his waist. "I've been thinking that it might be time for us to fill out some adoption applications. The process will take a while, and we can keep trying while the agencies interview us."

We agreed in principle that we were open to adoption when we first learned about Sean's low sperm count. All those months ago, the prospect of adoption seemed theoretical. Now, after a year of infertility treatments, it feels much more real.

But we want to be parents.

"Yeah. You're probably right. It's just...." Sean cannot meet my eye. I suspect he feels that starting the adoption process is admitting failure.

His failure.

I'm afraid to go near the touchy subject of his challenged masculinity, so I take a different path of reassurance. "Look at how much Betty loves Lo even though they're not biologically related," I remind my husband.

"Hey, I love that little guy, too." Sean smiles, buoyed by the prospect of a kid as great as Lo waiting for us somewhere in the world.

I hug him tightly. The uncertainty of trying and failing to get pregnant every month is killing me. Starting the adoption process is the right move. It's tangible. There will be a definite end in sight, even if it's a long way off.

———————⦁———————

At my father's condo, Ethel flings herself onto me, covering my face with kisses and wagging her entire rear end. "I know you got plenty of treats and love here, missy, so don't try to make me feel guilty for a 24-hour absence."

"She didn't ask about you once." My father gives me a peck on the cheek. "Ethel's very grateful to have escaped all those childish ear pulls and eye pokes, aren't you girl?"

To validate my father's claim, Ethel runs to fetch the giant new Nylabone her grandparents have bestowed on her.

"How was Lo's party, dear?" Natalie asks as she fixes tea and cookies for our visit.

"Fun, exhausting...sad."

Natalie lays her soft hand on my shoulder. "I worried that a party full of kids and parents might be hard for you."

"The kids didn't bother me. It's watching Sean have so much fun with the kids and then seeing him so dejected today that's breaking my heart." I stop stirring my tea and make eye contact with Dad and Natalie in turn. "I told Sean I thought we should start the adoption process now."

The two of them nod. Neither is the type to offer a dramatic reaction to news, no matter how momentous. But I think I detect a hint of disappointment in my father's eyes. Or maybe I'm just projecting my own unease onto him. "I mean, we'll still keep trying to get pregnant, but adoption takes a while—our friends, Peter and Noreen, have been working on it for months—so we probably shouldn't procrastinate any longer."

My father is relentlessly logical. But he also longs for a grandchild—one without fur, that is. "By all means, start the application process. But if you're going to keep trying to get pregnant, it seems to me you should be trying a new approach. Because doing the same thing—"

"—over and over and expecting different results is the definition of insanity." I finish my father's favorite expression for him. God knows, I've heard him say it often enough. "But we've already tried everything our doctor has recommended. And I've done research—a different doctor would do all the same things. We're at a dead end."

"A different *traditional* doctor, perhaps...." My father steeples his fingers and gets the look he gets when the chessboard unexpectedly reveals an unseen path to victory.

"Your father's been seeing an acupuncturist lately." Natalie sets homemade Snickerdoodles before us. "She's helped him quite a bit with his balance issues."

Given the severity of the stroke he had five years ago, my father has made remarkable progress with physical therapy. But his right leg still drags, and he needs a cane to guard against falls.

Dad sits up straighter. "I walked all the way around the block yesterday without my cane."

"Acupuncture? You?" My father has two gods: math and science. Acupuncture falls into the quasi-spiritual, magical realm that he firmly rejects.

"One of the fellows in my Tai Chi class recommended his acupuncturist. I've gone as far as I can go with the neurologist and the physical therapist, so I figured I had nothing to lose." Dad gets out of his chair without a struggle and walks a lap around the living room to demonstrate his improved mobility. I must admit, he seems to be lifting his right leg more smoothly than usual. Could it be psychosomatic?

"But how does it work?" I study him suspiciously. "You don't really believe there's some mystical energy source flowing through your body, do you?"

My father purses his lips and tilts his head before he answers. "I don't know if I agree with Qi, the explanation given by Chinese medicine. But even Western medicine has come to acknowledge the effectiveness of acupuncture. Often, we know that things *do* work before we know *why* they work. Ship captains knew that eating oranges prevented scurvy long before science discovered vitamins."

"So you're just rolling with it?" He's been my father for nearly forty years, but he still has the power to astonish me.

Dad smiles. "Yes. I'm rolling with acupuncture, and I think you should, too."

"But wouldn't Sean and I both need to go?" As Dad and Natalie are well aware, Sean's low sperm count is the cause of our fertility problem.

"Yes, but if you go first, I bet you can persuade Sean to follow. And Min-Wei says both partners' bodies must be in perfect harmony to create new life, so she'll help you, too."

I choke off the impulse to remind him babies are often conceived through rape and one-night stands and other less-than-harmonious encounters. Dad is trying to help, and he's right—we have nothing to lose. It's not like acupuncture is dangerous.

"They wouldn't put the needles, uh, you know..." I cringe at the thought of Sean's most valued resource being used as a pin cushion.

"Nothing to fear." Dad holds up his hand to dismiss my concern. "They don't jab the needles directly into the site of the problem."

I turn to Natalie. She's a retired nurse-practitioner and the source of all my medical second opinions. She's smiling in that beatific way she uses when she's offering reassurance. "Your father has made such remarkable headway since he's been visiting Min Wei. He returns so relaxed. If nothing else, she'll help you manage all the stress you've been experiencing."

I drink my tea and eat my cookies. And when I leave with Ethel, I have a pale green business card printed with some Chinese characters and a name: Min-Wei Ling, Licensed Acupuncturist.

Chapter 3

Isabelle Trent, Palmyrton's most successful real estate agent, starts talking the second I pick up the office phone on Monday morning. "Darling, I need your help with a house I've got listed in Palmer Estates. It's got great bones, and the roof, plumbing and HVAC are all in top shape. But I've had it for three months with barely a nibble."

I'm suspicious. Isabelle moves houses faster than Shoprite moves toilet paper before a blizzard. "It's not a hoarder house, is it? You know I won't touch those." I still have the occasional nightmare from my experiences working in Harold the Hoarder's house.

Ty overhears me and starts shaking his head and waving his arms like a ref calling a runner out at home plate.

I put the call on speaker and Isabelle's voice broadcasts through the office. "No, no—nothing like that," Her voice stays light and breezy. "Indeed, Mrs. Aronson's housekeeping is impeccable."

"So...?"

Isabelle sighs. "Some of her decorating choices are...er...unfortunate."

"Hoo, boy!" Ty mutters. "If Isabelle says it's unfortunate, it must be sca-*ree*."

"Yeesh," Donna agrees. "Unfortunate is worse than *quirky*."

"Even worse than *highly individual*," Ty concurs.

Ty and Donna are just as familiar as I am with Isabelle's Realtor-ese. "Unfortunate in what way, Isabelle?" I demand.

"Oh, darling," Isabelle's cheery optimism slips. "I really can't describe it. You have to see it. I need someone to help me think outside the box on this one."

What can I say? Isabelle has thrown a lot of work my way over the years, and she's become a friend, too. The least I can do is take a look at this house. "Okay, I'll meet you there. But I can't promise we'll do a sale if the stuff is so awful no one would want it."

"You're a businesswoman, and so am I." Isabelle's brisk tone returns. "We'll find a way to make this work for both of us. 375 Partridge Crescent. See you there at four."

And she hangs up.

Ty points a long finger at me. "Imma come with you."

"No need," I protest.

He folds his arms across his chest. "I'm comin' so someone can say, 'N. O.' "

"If Ty's going, I'm not missing out," Donna chimes in.

I know when I'm beaten. "Fine. An end-of-the-day field trip."

Palmyrton has several high-end neighborhoods, each built at different points in the town's life cycle. The grand Victorians in the historic district were built when Palmyrton was a get-away location for rich New York City industrialists. The huge McMansions of Palmer Summit popped up during the stock market boom of the early 2000s. But the gracious homes of Palmer Estates fall between those two extremes. They were built right before the Great Depression to house a prosperous Palmyrton-based upper middle class of doctors, lawyers and bankers. Those were the days when every well-to-do family had a live-in maid, so many of these gracious center hall colonials have back staircases and a small bedroom tucked behind the kitchen. The brick, stone, and clapboard houses all sit well back from the street, shaded by stately maples, oaks, and beeches. Each house is different—some have verandas, some sunrooms, some screen porches—but they all blend harmoniously. Certainly, the houses have been updated over the years, but there have been no tear-downs, no monstrous modern additions.

"I love this neighborhood," Donna says with her nose pressed against the rear passenger window. "I'd move here in a hot minute."

"Better plan on winnin' the lottery, then. You can't touch a place here for under 750K," Ty warns.

Ty is right. The price he quoted is for houses on the smaller end of the spectrum with no recent updates. The big five-bedroom houses with third floors finished as nanny suites and upgraded chef's kitchens can easily fetch two million. No wonder Isabelle is eager to get the house on Partridge Crescent sold.

I make a right onto the cul-de-sac, and we begin looking for the house. "Three-seventy-one, three-seventy-three—" Ty points ahead. "There it is—the big stone house."

"Ooo—I love that porch," Donna gushes from the back seat. Indeed, the house is very attractive and well-maintained, with a gray stone façade, a red front door, and a circular driveway. There's a rather ornate flower urn in the half-moon of lawn that the driveway wraps around, but other than that, the house blends in with its neighbors. My mood brightens. Surely, we could run a successful sale here.

The three of us exit the car and march up the front steps. Once we're on the porch, we see the outdoor furniture: two wicker chairs with fan-shaped backs big enough to make them into his-and-hers thrones, a wicker settee with red and purple cushions, and a life-sized bronze statue of a naked warrior carrying a horizontal spear from which dangles a serving tray suspended by chains. In a bow to modesty, someone has tied a silk scarf around the warrior's loins.

Donna peeks under the wrap. "Hey, baby. You can wait on me any time."

Before we can say more, Isabelle throws open the front door. "Audrey, darling—thanks so much for coming."

Isabelle, blonde hair perfectly coifed, looms over me in her trademark stilettos. Barefoot, she's tiny, but those shoes help her project authority.

As does her unflappable demeanor.

We follow her into a large, square foyer from which rises an elegantly curved staircase. The stairs, carpeted in blood red wool embossed with gold fleur-de-lis, are illuminated by a crystal chandelier as large as the one in *Phantom of the Opera*. The foyer wallpaper, rose and red flocked velvet, pulses from the walls.

Ty turns a pirouette. "Whoa."

"That's a lotta red," Donna offers.

"Indeed." Isabelle marches past a chinoiserie commode depicting an epic battle of the Ming Dynasty and leads us into the formal living room.

Just as much gold. Red replaced by green.

Chartreuse. Lime. Emerald.

Sedate sage? No way.

"So the homeowner embraces color," I say.

"Beige is not in Mrs. Aronson's vocabulary," Isabelle admits. "The dining room is blue. The study lavender." She lifts the corner of a violently patterned green area rug with the tip of her black patent leather pump. "But the floors are in perfect condition and two of the three bathrooms are tiled in white and black." Isabelle's shoulders slump. "The third is a devastating shade of puce."

"Wow, it's like the love child of Marie Antoinette and Elton John in this room." Donna shields her eyes as if she's gazing into the sun, not a rococo mirror.

"Yeah, we got a definite Versailles vibe goin' on." Ty drags a finger along some gold leaf on the ormolu mantel clock. Then he frowns at some sequined throw pillows on the lime velvet chaise. "With some late seventies disco thrown in."

Donna wanders over to a life-size statue of a Greek goddess—Artemis? Aphrodite? Donna strokes the goddess's arm. "What's this made of?"

From where I'm standing, the statue looks like solid marble, but Donna hugs it and lifts it right off its plinth.

We all laugh. "I guess she's papier mache," Donna says. "I wonder where she came from?"

"What's the old lady like?" I'm finding it hard to conjure up an image of the person who assembled this riot of colors and styles.

"She's quite delightful," Isabelle declares. "Just determined in her belief that the house will sell better furnished as it is. Believe it or not, she's got another home decorated just like this one in West Palm Beach. She's planning to move there full time now that her husband has passed. Right now, she's living in a hotel downtown while the house is on the market. She doesn't like being here when potential buyers come through."

"And you haven't had any offers for this house at all?" I ask.

"Oh, a couple low-balls from people who appreciate the value of the location. But Mr. Aronson instructed his wife on his deathbed not to accept a penny under a million-five. He was a shrewd businessman."

"And you think you can get that if we empty the place out?" Donna asks.

"I stand a chance with white walls and the rooms staged with conventional furniture. Like this," Isabelle lifts her hands in dismay, "no way."

I put my hands on my hips and shift my gaze from Ty to Donna. "What do you think, team? Can we sell this stuff?"

"We got any ho'houses on our customer list?" Ty asks.

Ignoring his smart mouth, I turn to Donna. "Remember that guy who was a prop master who came to the Chalmers sale? Do you have him marked on our database?"

"Of course," Donna says. "Let's invite him and tell him to bring all his friends." She prowls around the living room. "You know, some of this wouldn't be bad on its own. It's the combination of so much of it together that's...."

"Off-putting," Isabelle supplies one of her trademark euphemisms. I suspect Donna had been about to say, "hideous."

I drop to my knees to examine the inside of a black lacquer cabinet. "This is genuine art deco, not a reproduction."

Donna removes a green and orange silk flower arrangement in a gilt-rimmed vase from the top of the cabinet. "Yeah, this could be really pretty in a sleek, uncluttered room."

Ty has wandered into the dining room. "Whoa! Hold up, hold up."

I follow the sound of his excited voice and find him standing in front of a mural-sized oil painting of two Black men—one old, one young—playing chess in a city park, against a backdrop of colorful storefronts and brownstone apartments. Three little girls jump rope under the watchful eye of a grandma leaning out a second-floor window. A young man sprawls on a front stoop daydreaming, while two women push strollers, one with a baby, the other with a bundle of laundry. The painting is incredibly detailed, right down to the iridescent feathers on the pigeons at the men's feet.

"This is a Nathaniel Thurman." Ty points excitedly at the black scrawl of the artist's signature in the bottom corner of the painting. "The Studio Museum in Harlem is planning a retrospective of his work next year."

"Really?" Isabelle steps closer to the painting. "I do like it, but that one fellow seems a little fierce as a dinner companion. Mrs. Aronson told me the artist's uncle was a longtime employee at her husband's factory in Hillside."

Ty has become quite the expert on 20th and 21st Century African American art. In fact, he's even bought a few pieces. "Can you afford to acquire this one, Ty? It might not fit in your apartment."

"Ha! This is probably worth a cool thirty grand, Audge. I was just talking with Carter about Nathaniel Thurman last week." Ty's usually laconic voice speeds up in excitement.

"Carter Lemoine is interested in this artist?" Now Ty has my full attention. Carter Lemoine earns his living as an expert in 19th century decorative arts for Christie's auction house, which is how I first met him. But his true passion is the art of underrepresented cultures, and he and Ty have become unlikely friends in their pursuit of contemporary African American art. Carter's enthusiasm for this artist validates Ty's zeal.

"Carter always says there ain't nuthin' like dying to drive up the value of an artist's work, and Thurman didn't just die. He disappeared under tragic circumstances." Ty lectures as he paces back and forth in front of the large painting. "Next year will be the seventh anniversary of his disappearance, so his heirs will be able to declare him legally dead. There's a lot of speculation about what that's going to do to the value of his work." Ty pauses and cocks his head. "And there's also rumors that he might reappear in time for the retrospective."

"Reappear?" Donna rearranges her mane of black hair up in a scrunchie, a motion she goes through when she's thinking. "Reappear from where?"

"Thurman had mental health problems." Ty taps his temple. "Depression, bipolar, stuff like that—and like a lot of people, he used drugs and alcohol to deal with it. Since he liked to paint pictures of street life, whenever he was struggling, he'd go off for a while and live with the kinda people he painted. When he checked out six years ago, that's what everyone thought he was doing. But then he never came back. By the time anyone officially reported him missing, the trail was cold. There was a big article about it in *Art Scene*. So maybe he died or committed suicide and his body was never found. Or maybe he's still out there."

"Wow!" Donna and I say in tandem.

"Quite a story," Isabelle agrees.

"Will this painting be included in the sale?" I ask. Suddenly, I'm a lot more enthusiastic about this job.

"We'll have to discuss it with Mrs. Aronson when she arrives. But my impression is that she's already taken everything she wants to keep from this house." Isabelle glances at her phone. "I'm expecting her here in about ten minutes. We need to come up with a strategy. I think if we could persuade her that you'll find good homes for all of this—"

"Ty will do it," Donna assures her. "He's really good with old people. My Nonna Sophia is crazy about him."

Isabelle looks dubiously from Donna to me.

Ty laces his fingers together and stretches his arms until they crack. "Leave it to me. I'll convince her to have a sale."

Chapter 4

While we're standing around the living room talking, a gargantuan aqua Cadillac pulls into the circular drive. Moments later, we hear the front door open, and Pearl Aronson enters the room.

Her love of color extends to her person. Mrs. Aronson's bouffant hairdo is dyed an extraordinary shade of boiled shrimp; her deeply tanned, walnut brown face shows off coral lips, electric blue eyelids, and hot pink cheeks. She's wearing a purple velour jogging suit with a silver metallic stripe down each leg, and fuchsia and green sneakers. At about four foot ten, she resembles Dr. Ruth Westheimer colorized by Lo with a box of brand-new crayons.

"Hello, everyone! You must be the estate sale organizers Isabelle has been telling me about." Pearl beams at us with her bright white dentures. "What do you think of my home?" She extends her arms to take in the magnificence surrounding us. "My sweet Irving and I lived here for fifty-three years."

"Fascinating," I say.

"I can tell every item was selected with love," Donna adds.

Pearl grasps Donna's hand. "Exactly! My Irving never denied me anything."

I'm thinking ol' Irv could have denied her access to Sherwin Williams with no harm done.

Ty steps up and introduces himself. "I was just admiring the Nathaniel Thurman painting in the dining room, ma'am. Could you tell me more about it?"

Pearl lays a wizened, diamond and ruby encrusted hand on Ty's arm. Her skin is so tanned, the two of them are practically the same color. "Oh, what a sharp eye you have! The painting is called *Your Move*. Come, I'll tell you all about it."

And they're off. Ty bows his head over her tiny frame, listening to her every word, murmuring questions in his deep voice. Pearl explains that the painting depicts a scene of street life one block away from their factory in Hillside. "See, there's a part of the sign on the factory up in the right corner. And that's the bodega where Irv bought his coffee every morning, and the basketball court where the young men like you played every afternoon."

Ty squints at the artwork and points. "I'm guessing, but is that man going into the bodega your husband? I know Thurman liked to paint people he knew into his large works."

"Aren't you smart! Yes, that's Irv." Pearl pats Ty's arm. "I own another Thurman painting in Florida, but this one is my favorite. I wish I could take it with me to Palm Beach." Her smile fades. "But it's just too big. I have nowhere to hang it."

Ty steps back to take in the full view of the painting. "I love it too, Mrs. Aronson. We could help you find the right home for it."

Mrs. Aronson turns her walnut shell face up to Ty. "You can call me Pearl."

Donna grins at me as Ty and Pearl leave the dining room for the study, passing from our sight. She pulls out her phone to check the time. "He should have this wrapped up by five, five-fifteen at the latest." We're both confident enough of Ty's success that we begin taking photos of some of the items in the living room.

Isabelle paces with her lips pursed. "Mrs. Aronson can be quite firm in her opinions. But I know she's eager to get back to Florida. Most of her New Jersey friends have relocated there now."

In under twenty minutes, we hear laughter in the hallway. Then Ty and Pearl reenter the living room.

"I do believe you're right, Ty." Pearl gives Ty's arm an affectionate squeeze, then turns to face me. "So, when can you start?"

Donna shoots an "I told you so" look at Isabelle, while I sit down and review the contract with Mrs. Aronson. I explain that she can take anything she wants from the house, but once we sign the contract, everything must remain in the sale. And I tell her that we will get the painting appraised and set a minimum price for it. If we don't sell it during the sale, we'll move it to a gallery for them to sell.

"I'll have my lawyer look it over," Mrs. Aronson tells me. "But pencil me in for the weekend before Memorial Day weekend."

Looks like we have a new job, one that we can make profitable if we can bring in the right customers.

On the way back to the office, Ty is in a pensive mood, gazing out the car window as if the streets of Palmyrton are as unfamiliar as those of Lima or Zagreb. Meanwhile, Donna chatters in the back seat, giving me a blow-by-blow description of her plans to promote the Aronson sale on social media. Soon, she becomes absorbed in composing a Facebook post and quiets down.

I tap Ty's knee. "You okay?"

He startles. "Yeah, fine."

"What did you say to Mrs. Aronson to convince her to have the sale?"

"Didn't say much. Listened, mostly."

Sitting quietly. Smiling, nodding, agreeing, asking the occasional question. This is how Ty closes a deal. The technique works because he's genuinely interested in what people tell him. Unless, of course, they try to bullshit him. Which Mrs. Aronson clearly did not do.

"But why do you think she changed her mind about emptying out the house?" I press. I'm curious about the psychology at work.

"I think Isabelle took the wrong approach talking about how the house has to be all neutral to get the best price. Pearl felt like she and Irv were gettin' erased." Ty makes a scrubbing motion with his hand. "I put it to her different. Told her the sale would be sending little bits of her and Irv out into the world. That made all the difference."

I take my eyes off the road long enough to give Ty a smile of gratitude. "What else did Pearl talk about?"

"Her husband. The house. They liked to throw big parties. Bring all kinds of people together." Ty smiles, but not the big grin he usually offers. "They once invited all the most important couples from their synagogue to a party with Nathaniel Thurman and all the artists and musicians he could round up. Pearl said they figured it would do both groups good to see how the other half lives."

When we stop at a light, I twist to look at Ty. "You seem kind of...wistful...when you talk about Pearl."

"Nah." Ty gives himself a little shake. "It's just...a lotta the old people we meet in our work are at the end of the line, not enjoying life anymore. Pearl and Irv were still havin' fun, and then—boom—he keeled over from a heart attack not long after he sold the factory. I woulda liked to have met him. Sounded like a sharp old dude. Plus, I feel bad about making fun of her decorations. Pearl likes to make a splash with everything she does. Gotta admire that."

"We'll try to send her stuff on to other party animals. Face it—anyone who buys that lime green chaise is going to be a fun-loving person."

Now Ty's real smile breaks out. "That's what I told her. There's a lot more parties out there, just waitin' for your stuff to brighten 'em up."

Once we're back at the office, Donna and Ty head for home, but I settle at my desk to check my emails and tie up a few loose ends. The first email that catches my eye is from the Family Builders Adoption Agency, the agency our friends Peter and Noreen recommended. They attached an application we must complete, and then we'll be scheduled for an interview.

I take a deep breath. This is real. We're moving in a new direction.

The next email in the queue is from Min-Wei, the acupuncturist. "I'm sorry I missed your call. Here is a link to my on-line appointment scheduler. I have so enjoyed working with your father, and I look forward to meeting you soon."

I stare at the message for a full minute. Going to the acupuncturist while simultaneously moving forward with the adoption process feels like being engaged to two men at the same time. Don't I need to commit one way or the other?

My finger hovers over the keyboard and I click on the link. Min-Wei has an open slot tomorrow afternoon. I take the appointment. It couldn't hurt to go and check her out, right?

Chapter 5

"**D**amn!" Ty tosses his phone onto his desk in disgust.

"What's wrong?" Ty's remark didn't seem directed toward me, but I'm looking for any distraction. He doesn't answer me—just picks his phone up and punches in numbers with a scowl.

I should be elated because Mrs. Aronson signed her contract this morning, but I'm tired and restless today after spending the last two evenings working on the adoption application with Sean. Even with the guidance of Peter and Noreen, the process is overwhelming. In addition to the logical questions about our health and finances and careers, there are probing questions that require us to plumb our emotional depths and consider issues about parenthood we hadn't thought about much. Will we raise our child in an organized religion? How will we deal with a congenital health problem? Is there anything that would cause us to decline a particular child?

We skip over some questions, the way we skipped over the hardest questions on the SAT years ago, figuring we'll come back to them later. But we won't be saved by a ticking clock—all these questions must be answered eventually.

And then we have to write our adoption statement, the piece that will go into our portfolio to persuade a birth mother to give us the privilege of raising her child. It was a feat of salesmanship neither of us felt able to handle late last night.

Sean had snapped the laptop closed at ten-thirty. "This isn't fair. It seems like novelists and journalists and ad copywriters will have a leg up in this section. But that doesn't mean a cop and an estate sale organizer wouldn't be better parents."

When we went to bed, we both lay silently in the dark. I'm pretty sure our thoughts were the same: there are no hoops to jump through when a couple has a biological child.

Ty bangs his phone on the desk a second time.

"What in the world is going on with these calls you're making?"

This time, Ty answers my question. "I've called three different stores and checked five websites and none of them has a BlastMaster in stock."

"You're already shopping for Christmas? It's not even Memorial Day."

"You can't wait on this thing." Ty leans back in his swivel chair to lecture me. "BlastMasters sell out as soon as they're delivered. And there's some kinda Chinese computer chip shortage, which might slow down their manufacturing for months."

"Can't you put your name on a waiting list?" Donna asks.

"I tried, man. But these stores don't wanna bother with the headache of a list. They know they can sell out in minutes as soon as they announce they got some BlastMasters in stock. So I gotta call and check every day. It's like playin' the Lotto."

Ty returns to speed-dialing, and Donna and I exchange a glance over his head. We both think his obsession with getting this toy for Lo is nuts. The kid doesn't even care about it.

Will adopting a child make Sean and me behave in crazy ways? Will we go overboard to prove our love? When you're having a biological child, no one forces you to think about anything. But the bar is higher when you adopt.

After Ty hangs up on yet another BlastMaster call, I've had enough. "Shouldn't you be working on getting the Thurman painting appraised and finding a gallery for it if it doesn't sell at the sale?" I ask him with a raised eyebrow.

Ty looks at the clock on the wall. "Can't call New York galleries before ten in the morning," he protests. "But don't freak—I'll start right now."

"So how well did Pearl know Nathaniel Thurman?" Donna asks. "Did she mention his mysterious disappearance when you were alone with her?"

Ty holds up a finger while he leaves a voice message for a gallery. Then he answers. "We didn't talk so much about Thurman himself. I got the impression Pearl only met him in person at that one big party. I think Irv knew him pretty well, though."

Donna's hands hang suspended over her keyboard. "I'm going to post all over social media about this painting. Maybe Thurman will see our messages and make his grand reappearance at our sale. Wouldn't that be cool?"

At the end of the workday, I head out to my acupuncture appointment. The clinic is on the first floor of an old house on the edge of the historic district. Melodious wind chimes tinkle in the breeze as I mount the stairs to the porch. When I push open the front door, a lovely aroma of lavender and mint greets me. The reception area is empty, but a calligraphy sign on the desk urges me to take a seat. There are no magazines, just a fish tank where some colorful koi swim languidly.

I resist the urge to entertain myself with my phone and let my gaze follow the circling orange and white and red fish. I'm agreeably zoned out when a petite Chinese woman enters the room through a soft green curtain.

"Welcome, Miss Audrey. I am Min-Wei." She bows her head slightly and smiles.

She takes a clipboard from the desk and sits beside me. "I will ask you a few questions about your health and the reasons for your visit today. And then we will begin."

I tell her about Sean's and my struggle to conceive. Min-Wei doesn't offer a strong reaction to anything I say, just responds with a nod or a gentle exhalation of breath. She doesn't judge, doesn't offer opinions or solutions. After all the well-meaning advice I've received over the past year, I find talking to Min very soothing.

Soon, she leads me into the treatment room, a space filled with recliners and massage tables. Soft, Eastern music plays, and the lavender mint scent lingers in the air. The patients in the room lie extended, some on their backs, some on their stomachs. I don't want to stare, but I shoot curious, quick looks at the fine needles poking from necks and knees and foreheads and feet. No one looks uncomfortable; indeed, most seem to be dozing.

I take my place on a recliner and Min runs her cool, soft fingers over my skin. When she picks up her needles, I decide to shut my eyes as I always do when I'm getting a shot.

Minutes pass and nothing happens.

I open my eyes to discover I've got fifteen needles sticking out of me. I didn't even feel them go in. Min leaves my side and goes to check on her other patients. I watch as she plucks needles from one sleeping patient and gently nudges him awake.

He sits up, stretching and smiling.

Then Min leaves me and the rest of her patients in the cool, dimly lit room. Soon I feel the irritations of the day, the week, the month drift away from me. I'm coasting, free from worries and intrusive negative thoughts.

The next thing I know, I hear Min's gentle voice. "Wake up, Audrey. It is time to return to the world."

Surprised, I look down at my body. All the needles are gone. I feel so deeply relaxed that I have to summon my muscles to lift me out of the recliner.

"I will see you on Wednesday," Min says, and I agree without debate. I don't even care if this treatment cures infertility; I simply want to keep feeling this mellow.

Even as I drive home, I'm floating in a sublime cloud. As soon as I find Sean on the patio, I launch into an enthusiastic sales pitch, describing my experience at Min's clinic. "You have to try this." I pull out my iPad. "I'll make you an appointment right now."

"Whoa, Audrey—slow down." He frowns at his phone. "I've got a busy week coming up."

"Sean, please. Just do it. Don't think of acupuncture as a fertility treatment. Think of it as the antidote to fertility treatments. Everything we've been doing for the past eighteen months has been so demoralizing, so dehumanizing. We've been poked and prodded and drugged and scheduled. The doctors don't even look at our faces—we're just pieces of meat rolling by on a conveyor belt. Even without the needles, being with Min is so restorative. She made me feel like a person, not a condition."

Sean knows I'm not given to flights of fancy. He studies me for a moment, then nods and hands me his phone with this week's calendar cued up. "Go ahead and sign me up."

Chapter 6

Attending your own estate sale can be compared to watching vultures pick over your own body. For this reason, we always advise clients to spend the day of their sale elsewhere.

Pearl Aronson, however, is not one to accept the received wisdom on estate sales, decorating, or any other matter. Shortly before we are ready to open the doors of Partridge Crescent for the first day of the sale on Friday, Pearl arrives in the aqua Caddie and ensconces herself on one of the big throne chairs on the front porch. Today she's wearing teal and purple leggings, a long teal sweater, and purple and silver sneakers. "Don't worry. I'll move when someone buys the chairs," she assures me cheerfully.

A long line of early birds has already formed. Because of the legendary parties Pearl and Irv hosted over the years, many neighbors and friends and members of her synagogue have arrived to say goodbye to Pearl and the house, and to buy something as a memento of the Aronsons' hospitality. So Pearl sits on the front porch waving to the crowd like Queen Elizabeth at the trooping of the colors.

"She looks like she's enjoying herself," Donna says as she peeks through the side light in the foyer where we are preparing the check-out table.

"Hmmm. Let's hope she stays cheerful when customers start haggling over prices." I've seen sales turn ugly when homeowners insist something should be sold for more than its marked price, or worse, when they want to give an item away to a friend. The terms of our contract forbid this. Once the homeowner has removed the items she wants to keep, everything else must remain ours to sell.

"Thought you said you and Pearl and her lawyer went over the contract line-by-line." Ty drops a big box of supplies at our feet.

"I did. And she's sharp as a tack. Still, once emotions enter into the sale..." I shake my head.

"I don't think we have to worry," Ty assures me. "Pearl is giving all the money from this sale to charity. She and Irv never had kids, and she says Irv's

25

nephews don't need the cash. I think she came here today to say good-bye, that's all."

Given that it's now minutes to show time, all I can do is hope that Ty is right.

We open the doors, and the hordes pour in. After nearly twenty years in this business, I should no longer be surprised that the weirdest items often sell first. In the first half hour, the naked bronze butler, whom Donna has christened Buck, goes home with an excited gay couple who own a bed and breakfast in Lambertville. A folding screen depicting the x-rated abduction of Persephone by Hades departs with a mild-mannered Classics scholar. And a three-foot-tall gilt vase filled with real ostrich feathers is snapped up by an insistent woman whose husband knows better than to protest.

Then two young men in topsiders and polo shirts carry the papier mache Aphrodite to the check-out table. "She's gonna look awesome at the frat house," one tells me.

Donna winces as they exit. "I hope Pearl doesn't hear where that's going," she says.

Seconds later, Pearl pops her head into the foyer. "You sold Aphrodite!" she exclaims with a grin. "Those boys told me they're putting her in their frat house. She's the goddess of sex." Pearl winks. "She should be happy there."

Since Pearl is clearly not offended by Aphrodite's fate, Donna keeps the old gal talking. "Where did you get her, Pearl?"

"She was a prop in a show I performed in years ago."

"You were an actress?" Donna asks, clearly impressed.

"Not an actress like Meryl Streep," Pearl confides. "I was a performer. I used to do song and dance and comedy routines as part of a troupe that toured all the big Catskill resorts in the fifties." She breaks into a little soft-shoe in her silver sneakers. "The Borscht Belt, they called it. Jewish families from New York City and New Jersey all vacationed there every summer."

"How exciting," Donna gushes. She loves hearing stories of women who had eventful youths since her own was very tame.

"It was fun for a time," Pearl says. "But I was pushing thirty and hadn't had my big break. I met Irv when I was performing at Grossinger's, and he was vacationing with his family." Pearl smiles dreamily at the memory. "What a summer that was! I had a big solo number singing a tune from *Mame*, and I fell in love with Irv."

"After you got married, you quit performing?" Donna asks.

"Yes, I couldn't be a good wife and keep touring." Pearl grins. "But it was fun while it lasted. Most of the big, old hotels in the Catskills that catered to Jews have closed now. Grossinger's is gone and so is The Concord." Pearl gets a wistful, faraway look in her eyes. "A few of the smaller places have repurposed themselves as family camps. Water slides and ziplining—that's what folks want these days. No more song and dance revues."

Pearl's tiny shoulders slump for a moment, then she snaps back into good cheer with a clap of her hands. "No point in whining that life isn't the way it used to be, right?" She pivots when the front door opens. "I'm heading back out to the porch to look for more of my friends."

Donna smiles fondly at Pearl's retreating figure. "She's got a great attitude."

After that flurry of big sales, we settle into selling small tchotchkes to the neighbors. "I'm worried about that green and gold area rug in the living room," I say to Donna. "If we don't sell it, it's going to be hard to give away."

"Yeah, even Sister Alice won't take that," Donna agrees.

We donate items that don't sell to charity, and Sister Alice, who runs a community outreach center in Newark, always has someone who can use a set of dishes with an ugly pattern or a bedside table with a water-ringed top. But her clients don't live in homes that would accommodate a twelve-by-twenty area rug even if they weren't fussy about the garish pattern.

"Maybe the movie prop people will take it." Donna accepts five dollars for two ornate teacups and saucers and wraps them in newspaper for their new owner. "I'm expecting them around noon."

As the front door opens and closes, we catch glimpses of Pearl chatting happily with customers coming and going. So far, Ty is right—the old gal isn't causing any trouble. Far from being distraught, she appears to be having a lot of fun.

At noon, Ty descends from the second floor helping an antiques dealer carry a Renaissance Revival dresser that threatens to crush Ty if either man takes a false step. I rush to the foot of the stairs to direct them. "Three more steps...two...one. You're on the level now."

Muscles bulging, Ty carries the dresser to the checkout desk. The antiques dealer spots something else he might want in the living room, so Ty hangs out with us for a moment. "Things are moving slow but steady upstairs." He mops his brow. "Good thing about this sale—there's no jewelry to shoplift. Pearl is keeping all that. Only getting rid of her winter clothes."

"Yeah, no need for a down coat in Palm Beach, but selling a neon orange one in size 4 petite will be a challenge," Donna says.

Ty moves to the front door and waves to Pearl. Then he returns to Donna and me. "Any sign of those two art buyers?"

Donna shakes her head. "No one who asked about the painting or looked like they were from a gallery—you know, skinny and all dressed in black."

Ty rolls his eyes at the stereotype. "I told them both to ask for me. But I guess it's possible they slipped in, looked at the painting, and left." He jams his hands in his jeans pockets. "I really want to sell that painting here. We'll get a bigger cut of the proceeds."

I pat him on the shoulder just as the antiques dealer returns with the or-molu clock. "They might still come tomorrow. It would be nice to sell the painting ourselves, but we knew it was a long shot." Ty shrugs off his disappointment and helps the antiques dealer carry his treasures out to his van. Two more highly individual pieces of Pearl's life are out the door.

Ty has just returned upstairs when the prop master and his assistant sweep in and announce themselves. I would have known them even without the announcement since they look nothing like residents of suburban New Jersey. The lead guy is about six-four and maybe weighs 130 pounds soaking wet. The world's skinniest jeans cover his heron legs, and long, pointy black oxfords encase his feet. As a woman who prides herself on her excellent spatial relations, I'm flummoxed by the laws of physics that must have been broken for him to get those huge feet through those narrow pants legs. His assistant is a gender fluid person with a thin, dark moustache, red acrylic fingernails, and fake eyelashes that look like twin centipedes.

Both have green hair.

Well, they should like Pearl's living room.

Donna springs into action to show them around. "Push the rug," I mutter as she leads them off.

I soon hear cries of, "Fabulous! Just what we need for the off-Broadway play!" and "Oh. My. Ga-a-wd! Perfect!" That kind of enthusiasm means I'm making more full-price sales. I'm starting to feel that this sale will be quite profitable even if we do have a larger than usual quantity of items that must be trashed. I hope Pearl isn't planning to return all day tomorrow because the final hours of a two-day sale are sad even for me. That's when the picked over remnants of the homeowner's life plead to be taken home like a three-legged pit bull at the pound.

With Ty working the second floor and Donna guiding the prop buyers, I'm flying solo at the check-out table in the foyer when I hear a huge commotion out on the front porch. Shouting, squealing, exclaiming—low voices and Pearl's high-pitched one. Happy or upset? I can't be certain.

I've got three customers lined up to buy and a cash box I can't leave unattended, so I keep my ears peeled for trouble. Just as I'm finishing with the last customer in line, tiny Pearl with her pinkish hair and coral lips enters the foyer leading a contingent of three Black men: one in his seventies and two around Ty's age. She looks delighted.

"Look who's here!" Pearl pulls the two youngest men forward as if they're toddlers, not linebackers. "These are Nathaniel Thurman's two great-nephews. They came to see their *groys feter's* painting before someone buys it."

The two young men glance uneasily at the red and pink flocked wallpaper and the chandelier whose dangling crystals nearly brush their heads. Their faces clearly indicate they think they've stumbled into some brightly colored alternate universe. "Where's Ty?" Pearl asks me in a voice loud enough to carry. "I want him to tell these fellas all about where the painting is going if it doesn't sell here."

Before I can text him, Ty comes trotting down the stairs, and Pearl begins a round of introductions. It seems the oldest man in the group, Eugene, is the long-time employee at Irv's factory who was the artist's uncle. Ty shakes hands all around, and he and Pearl lead the men into the dining room. Luckily, Donna soon returns with the prop masters and their selections, so I trail after the group of Thurman's relatives.

I arrive in the dining room to hear Ty explaining that due to the painting's large size, professional art movers will remove it from the wall on Monday if it doesn't sell this weekend and transport it to the New York gallery handling the sale. "We've set a minimum price for selling it here."

One of Thurman's nephews frowns. "You think some random housewife," he glances at a middle-aged lady considering Pearl's candelabra, "is gonna come to this house and want to buy that painting?" Implied but unspoken are the words "some *white suburban* housewife" and "that painting *of Black, urban street life.*"

Ty answers patiently. "Yeah, it's not likely someone will wander in off the street and want to buy this. But we've invited certain collectors to come see the painting here, and if it doesn't sell this weekend, then we move it to the gallery."

Eugene, the artist's uncle, steps up close to the canvas. He lifts his hand toward it, and I notice Ty wince, but the old gentleman stops short of touching the painting. "See this here? This guy lookin' in the trash can is Nathaniel. He always painted himself into the background of every picture. And this old man walking into the bodega is Irv— he got a big kick outta that. And over in the corner is the edge of the factory building. See how the words on the sign are cut off?"

The two young nephews stare stone-faced at the painting. Are they bored? Unimpressed? Annoyed? Or simply concealing their emotions?

"Who are the chess players?" one of them finally asks.

"There's a tiny little park at the intersection—just a couple benches and two stringy trees for shade. Back in the day, the chess players were there playin' every day, even in winter. Nathaniel loved talking to them. Said chess was another type of art."

My father would certainly agree with that. Now that he's retired from teaching college math, he devotes himself to introducing young kids to the joys of chess. For the first time, I pay close attention to the chess board in the painting. "This is a famous attack—the Smith Morra gambit," I say pointing at the player playing the white pieces.

Everyone turns and looks at me.

"I play chess." I smile sheepishly for horning into the conversation. "Do any of you play?"

They all shake their heads and murmur no. One of the nephews turns to Ty. "Who gets the money when you sell this?"

"Mrs. Aronson owns the painting, so she gets most of it," Ty explains. "The gallery and us, the estate sale organizers, will get a percentage."

"And the artist gets nothing?" the other nephew says with an edge of belligerence in his voice.

"He got paid when the Aronsons bought it," Ty says. I can tell he's also got his back up.

The nephews still look like they think their uncle got cheated.

"Look, if I sell my car to you," Ty points to the first complaining nephew, "and you turn around and sell it to him," he points to the other nephew, "I don't get more money from that sale, right?"

The young man scowls as if Ty's logic shouldn't apply to his situation.

Eugene looks uneasy. "I brought you boys here because I thought you'd appreciate seeing your uncle's work. I didn't invite you to create trouble."

But the taller nephew isn't backing down. "I don't see the point of this painting. Why paint a picture of people just sittin' around wastin' time?"

His brother nods in agreement. "We've been working summers at the factory since we were sixteen. We're both in college now. Our mother wouldn't allow us to hang on the streets like that."

"The title of the painting is *Your Move*." Pearl speaks for the first time, and the sound of the firm voice coming from the tiny, elderly body startles the men. "You must consider the title *and* the image when you speculate about the meaning of the painting."

Then Pearl pivots in her shiny purple and silver sneakers and returns to her front porch throne.

Chapter 7

Day Two of the Aronson sale has a totally different vibe than Day One. Mrs. Aronson has wisely decided to stay away, so there's no high-spirited receiving line on the front porch. The weather is chilly and damp, the customers cranky and itching for bargains. Most of the best—or at least, the most unique—items have been sold, and what's left is a mishmash of Pearl's enthusiasms: vivid cushions and throws, a menagerie of animal statues, geometrically shaped side tables and ottomans, lamps and mirrors designed to dazzle.

I drive hard bargains wherever possible even though I've told Donna I'll get rid of the green living room rug for a buck. Ty has brought the few remaining items down from the second floor, and we consolidate the sale into the living room, study, and kitchen. Pearl freely admits to never cooking, so all we must sell from the back of the house are her extensive collections of fancifully shaped glasses (mermaid champagne flutes, anyone?) and her assortment of vivid Mexican, Thai, Nigerian, and Guatemalan serving bowls and platters.

"Have fun with these," Donna says as she accepts five bucks for a twelve-piece set of faux snow-capped old-fashioned glasses and a penguin-shaped cocktail shaker. "I wanna go to that party," Donna says wistfully as she watches the twenty-something girls who bought the set giggling over the cocktail recipe book they found stuffed inside the penguin. With only two hours to go, someone finally buys the living room rug. Whew!

By two-thirty, no one has entered the house for the past half-hour and we send out for pizza, which we eat while sitting in the foyer. Ty devours four slices, gathering strength for the clear-out that awaits us. We talk strategy: what should go to the dump, what can go to Sister Alice and Goodwill, what might still sell.

And of course, there's the painting. The three different art collectors who came to see it during the sale all left without making an offer. I suspect the painting's monumental size is limiting the market. It now seems certain the art movers will have to come on Monday to transport *Your Move* to the gallery. Our commission on the eventual sale will be halved.

32

Ty checks his phone yet again. "Supposedly, I got two more guys comin' to look at the painting today. They should have been here hours ago." He scowls. "Could at least text if their plans changed."

Ty pops the last crust of pizza into his mouth just as two forty-ish men walk through the door. Hilariously, as Donna predicted yesterday, they're both thin and dressed entirely in black. "Hi," the taller of the two says as he raises his eyebrows at Ty. "I'm looking for Ty Griggs."

Embarrassed to be caught slacking, Ty jumps up. "Hey—really glad you made it. We're winding down for the day here. But that means you can see the painting with no one else around to distract you. Follow me."

Donna and I smile as the men head through the living room toward the dining room with Ty talking enthusiastically about the history of the painting. "Maybe we'll make this final, big sale after all."

Soon their conversation is just a low, distant murmur. But a minute later, I hear an anguished scream.

Ty.

I jump up and run for the dining room. Surely, those two guys aren't dangerous? Ty is bigger and stronger than either of them. But Ty sounded like he'd been hurt.

I round the corner to see Ty on his knees with his face inches from the painting while the two prospective art buyers stand back looking like they're witnesses to a ten-car pile-up on the Turnpike.

"Ty, what's wrong?"

He turns his face up to me, his eyes wet with tears. "Someone vandalized the painting."

My gaze goes to the spot he's pointing to. Sure enough, one of the minor figures in the background of the painting has been blacked out. It looks like someone used a Sharpie to draw a black rectangle over the figure.

Why?

One of the prospective buyers finds his voice. "This is a fabulous work of art. What a tragedy that it's been defaced."

The other guy makes eye contact with me. "Any idea how it could have happened?"

Ty struggles to his feet, but he's still too distraught to speak.

The gut-punch of the destruction is receding in me, replaced by a cold analysis of the situation. "It doesn't seem to be a casual attack just for thrills, like when a punk keys a car or spray paints a building. The person took the time to very neatly black out that one character in the painting."

Ty massages his temples. "I'm trying to remember what figure was there. There must be some meaning to it."

I hold up my hand. "Figuring out why will be a long process. Let's start with when and how."

Chapter 8

By the time the police arrive, Ty, Donna and I have worked out a timeline for when we last saw the painting intact. Yesterday afternoon when Thurman's uncle and nephews were here, the painting was certainly perfect. After they left, at the end of the day, Ty helped a buyer carry out the dining room table and chairs. The man commented on the painting, so Ty remembers explaining it and pointing out details. After that customer departed, we locked the doors and spent half an hour straightening up the house, marking down prices, and generally getting ready for Day Two of the sale.

I explain all this to the two patrolmen who arrive, but I can see I'm not getting through to them that a valuable piece of artwork has been damaged. Possibly even destroyed, if an art restorer can't fix the defaced area. They look at me like I called to report a ruined paint-by-numbers landscape I was trying to unload at a garage sale.

One uniformed officer asks me a series of questions then writes laboriously in his notebook after each answer. "The lady who owns this house is moving, right? And she doesn't want that painting anymore? And you were trying to sell it, but no one bought it?" He exchanges a glance with his partner as if to say, "what's the big deal?"

I've had enough of dealing with these two and do what I should have done from the get-go: call Sean. Fifteen minutes later, a detective arrives and sends the patrolmen off.

And we start all over again with the questions. "So the painting was definitely undamaged when you locked up last night?" Detective Sanchez asks.

"Yes, but...." In the past hour, several puzzling scenarios have sprung up in my mind. "You see, we were in the house after we locked the doors to customers, but we weren't in the dining room because we moved the few remaining items in that room into the living room to consolidate the sale."

"And then we went upstairs and carried everything from up there down here to the living room and the study and the screen porch," Donna explains.

"So it's possible someone could have slipped in while we were working. The door between the kitchen and screen porch was unlocked."

Sanchez nods. "But that would've been risky, no? And the vandal would have had to know how you operate to realize he could have some time alone in the dining room."

Ty nods. "Good point. But you said it looks like he didn't break in at night."

Sanchez has already walked through the house looking for signs of a break-in and found nothing. "No signs of forcible entry. But we'll need to confirm exactly who has keys to this house. Apart from you, of course."

We told him that when we opened the house for the sale this morning, the glass French doors between the living room and dining room were still closed, and the sign we posted saying "no entry" was undisturbed.

"But the French doors weren't locked?" Sanchez clarifies.

I shake my head. "We didn't have a key. Donna just looped a rubber band around the two handles to discourage people from opening them. That's usually enough although, God knows, customers can be persistent if they want something."

"And the door from the kitchen into the dining room was blocked with a big cabinet that hasn't sold," Donna adds.

Sanchez pauses in his note-taking. "But if you were still trying to sell the painting, wouldn't you want people to go into the dining room?"

"We knew we wouldn't sell it to some casual passer-by," I explain. "We invited some art enthusiasts specifically to come. That's who Ty was showing the painting to when he discovered the damage."

"But during the sale today, you were all in and out of the living room, and you could see the painting through the glass French doors, correct? You didn't notice the damage then?"

"Yes, we could see the painting, but we just glanced in at it. We would've noticed if it had been slashed or something," I pace up and down in the foyer as I speak. "But this damage was near the bottom, and you don't notice it much if you're looking at the painting from an angle."

"But it's very obvious when you're standing right in front of it," Ty adds miserably.

"So you believe the painting was most likely attacked during the day today when you were busy elsewhere in the house?" Sanchez asks.

"Yes, because there were some stretches with very few customers in the living room. The vandal could've slipped into the dining room and done the damage in a matter of minutes."

"Even though it was done carefully, methodically," Sanchez clarifies. "How many people would have known that painting was in the house?"

Ty lets out a low whistle. "Lots. Everyone I specifically invited to come and look at it, plus all the people who went through the house on Friday."

"And I posted about it extensively on social media," Donna adds.

"A lot of the people who came to the sale were friends and neighbors of Mrs. Aronson," Donna explains to the detective. "In fact, three guys—who worked for Mr. Aronson and were related to the artist came to see the painting on Friday afternoon."

Sanchez raises his eyebrows. "Wouldn't you say that's significant? Do you have their names?"

"The painting was fine when they left, and none of them came back today." Ty's voice rises in irritation. "So how could it be anything to do with them?"

Donna slinks back in her chair but she defends her theory. "I didn't mean them specifically. I know those particular guys didn't come back. But one of them could have mentioned the painting to someone else. I mean, they came specifically to see it, so it makes sense they'd talk about it when they left."

"I guess." Ty taps a pencil on his knee. "There's a reason the vandal blacked out that one figure in the painting. I just haven't figured it out yet. I can't remember exactly what's there."

"Wait—didn't you take a picture of the painting to send to possible buyers?" Donna asks Ty.

Ty slaps his forehead with the heel of his hand. "Of course. Man, I'm so blown away by what happened, I can't even think straight."

Ty forwards the photo to me so we can enlarge it on my iPad. Then we all squeeze around the screen looking at the section of the painting that was vandalized. Ty's long, dark finger touches a figure on the screen. "It's this dude who's blacked out."

The character is a young Black man sprawled out on the front stoop of a row house. One long leg is extended over two steps while the other is bent with the foot flat on one step. His head is tilted back, and he has a dreamy expression on his face.

Detective Sanchez squints at the photo. "Is he supposed to be passed out? Like drunk, or stoned?"

"Could be," Ty says. "Or maybe he's daydreaming...enjoying the sun...looking at something across the street. Something not shown in the painting."

"He looks normal to me," Donna says. "Why would anyone choose to black him out?"

"Thurman's uncle said that sometimes he painted real people that he knew into his paintings, and sometimes he created characters who were composites of different people," Ty says as if he's thinking aloud.

Sanchez scratches his head. "So maybe this guy is a real person who didn't appreciate being in the painting and decided to erase himself?"

"This is one of the last major works Thurman painted before he disappeared," Ty says. "It's about six years old."

"So this character looks to be late teens, early twenties. He'd be close to thirty now. Did you see any tall, lean thirty-year-old Black men at the sale today?" Sanchez asks.

Donna shakes her head. "Most estate sale shoppers are older—people interested in antiques and collectibles. A few younger women into kitsch and vintage clothes. A few families looking for cheap furniture and toys for their kids. Young Black men are unusual."

Ty nods. "Unusual enough that I'd notice if someone who looks like me walked through the door."

Detective Sanchez rises. "I'll need a list of all the art buyers you invited, plus those relatives of the artist and former employees who visited."

"I'll send you the names of the art buyers, Ty says. "But you'll have to get the names of the other guys from Mrs. Aronson. She's staying at the Palmyrton Crossings Hotel."

I extend a restraining hand to the detective. "Let me break the news to Pearl Aronson. I feel responsible."

Sanchez nods hesitantly, cutting me a break because I'm his colleague's wife. "You can come with me, I guess."

Chapter 9

"Don't blame yourself," I pat Ty on the arm as we drive to the Palmyrton Crossroads Hotel where Pearl is staying until the house sells.

"I feel like I would if I let Lo get hurt when I was supposed to be watching him."

"The painting looks bad right now, but we won't know how serious the damage is until the art restorer examines it." Ty has called Carter Lemoine to get a recommendation for a restorer, so we're prepared with information and a plan to solve the problem.

Ty scowls. "You can be sure the vandal didn't use those washable markers that Charmaine gives to Lo."

"Art restorers must have all sorts of tricks up their sleeves. I've read about them being able to strip away an entire painting that was painted over an old master. Fixing this can't be impossible." I say this to be reassuring, but the knot of tension in my gut grows as every block we travel brings us closer to a showdown with Pearl Aronson.

Ty's phone pings repeatedly as we cruise away from Pearl's residential neighborhood. I have to focus on navigating the traffic in downtown Palmyrton, but Ty gives me updates as he answers texts and emails. "People are contacting me about buying the painting," he says with rising excitement. "The news is out about the damage, and all kinds of buyers I never heard of are interested now." He taps back responses. "This is insane. The defacement is making *Your Move* famous."

Maybe there's a silver lining to this awful cloud. The Palmyrton Crossroads, a grand old hotel right on the town green, looms into view. It's got a doorman who wears a uniform with gold braid epaulettes and a lobby filled with fresh flower arrangements. I'm too cheap to spring for the hotel's valet parking, so I find a spot at a meter and Ty and I walk the last two blocks.

He's still agonizing, despite the uptick in interest for the painting. "I just can't understand why. Why would anyone want to destroy a work of art?"

"Maybe Mrs. Aronson will have some ideas." I smile at the doorman and usher Ty to a grouping of chairs near the elevator where we see Detective Sanchez waiting for us. Ty texts Pearl that we're here, but she still doesn't know why we've asked to meet with her.

The Pearl Aronson who meets us in the lobby of the hotel is a different woman than the one we saw at the sale on Friday. As soon as the elevator doors open and I see her walking toward us, I can tell something is wrong. She looks smaller, frailer—even her pinkish-orangish bouffant looks flatter.

Ty hurries over to her when she appears to sway while walking around a cluster of businessmen. Reluctantly, she takes his arm. But she doesn't look so delighted to see him.

Once Ty delivers her to a chair, Detective Sanchez introduces himself and between the two of us, we explain what happened. Ty shows her pictures of the damage on my iPad, and she looks at it briefly, then turns her head with a wince. Even though she was ready to sell *Your Move*, I can see this wanton destruction pains her.

Detective Sanchez takes over, peppering Pearl with questions about who had keys to the house and who knows the painting is there.

Pearl gives one impatient shake of her head. "Irv didn't believe in passing out house keys. Even my cleaning lady doesn't have one. And I certainly didn't hide one under a flowerpot." She narrows her eyes at the detective. "Anyone who's visited my house for the past six years could have seen that painting. But that's just my lady friends and my canasta group. I don't entertain the way I used to since my husband passed." She makes a shooing gesture with her hands. "I don't want my friends disturbed. I don't want the police involved in this. You can go."

Sanchez shoots me a look before responding to Pearl. "If you plan to make an insurance claim, you'll need a police report on the crime."

Pearl draws herself up as tall as she can in the over-stuffed easy chair. "There's no crime. It's some *meshuggeneh* thing. There's no insurance. I don't need the police."

"But...." I sputter.

Now Sanchez looks irritated. "This is a property crime. If Mrs. Aronson doesn't want to pursue it..." He shrugs and stands up.

"That's correct. I don't want to pursue it." Pearl struggles to push herself out of the deep chair, but the poor soul can't manage without help because she's so short. Ty doesn't offer a hand.

Sanchez nods to me and I follow him a short distance away. "Seems like she knows who did it and doesn't want to press charges," Sanchez says. "Nothing we can do. It's her choice."

I thank him and return to Ty and Pearl. Ty is leaning forward, speaking in an intense, low voice. "Do you have any idea why someone would do this, Pearl? Why would he choose that particular figure to cross out?"

Pearl's gnarled hands tighten on the arms of her chair. "How should I know why a crazy person does what he does?"

I join the conversation. "It doesn't strike us as a crazy action. That perfect rectangular black block drawn over that particular figure in the painting. It seems quite deliberate."

"Nonsense." The creases in her wrinkled face deepen. "People are off their heads these days with the drugs and the, the...." Again, she struggles to rise and fails.

Pearl is a lousy liar. She knows why this happened, but she doesn't want to tell us. Is she protecting someone? I suppose that's her prerogative. But she seems nervous, uneasy.

I change tacks. "We've found an art restorer who can come to examine the painting on Monday and tell us what it will take to fix the damage, and then—"

"No." Pearl speaks firmly but evades my gaze. She keeps her eyes focused on the registration desk across the lobby.

"What do you mean, no?" Ty asks. "The painting has to be restored—it's a valuable modern masterpiece." His voice becomes more agitated and incredulous. "To leave it like that is like, like...refusing to take an injured person to the hospital."

"Another Man's Treasure has insurance to cover damage that occurs when we're holding a sale," I assure Pearl, in case she thinks she's on the hook for a huge restoration bill.

"I don't want it fixed." Pearl twists the big diamond ring on her knobby finger. "I've changed my mind about selling it. I'm going to, to...put it in storage."

"But I have people interested in buying it," Ty protests. "And a gallery lined up where it could get even more exposure."

"Ironically, news about the attack has increased interest in the painting," I explain.

"News?" Pearl's electric blue eyelids lift in dismay. "What happened to my painting has been on the news?"

"Not the TV news," Ty explains. "But two potential buyers were with me when we discovered the damage. And I asked a friend to recommend an art restorer. I guess they all talked to other people, and now the New York art world is starting to buzz about this painting."

Pearl chews some of the coral lipstick off her lower lip. "I'm not selling it. The estate sale is over. The house is empty. Let's settle up and move on."

I shoot an uneasy look at Ty. Normally, I don't sweat the small details with clients, but Pearl's decision stands to cost us thousands of dollars. "Pearl, the contract you signed with me stipulates that you can't withdraw items from the sale. You're committed to letting us sell this painting."

Her eyes shift from left to right. Pearl can't say she didn't understand the contract since she reviewed it line-by-line with her lawyer. If she'd changed her mind about some sentimental item or a small piece of furniture, I wouldn't be such a stickler for the rules. But the opportunity to sell *Your Move* was the main reason I agreed to take this job. It's the single most valuable item in the house, and selling it will add at least three grand to the bottom line of this sale. And with interest in the painting growing, that number will probably go up.

With great effort, Pearl pushes her small body out of the deep chair. "I still own the painting, and I refuse to give you permission to have work done on it." She turns to face the long walk back to the elevator. "My lawyer will be in touch with your lawyer."

"Pearl, wait!" Ty jumps up to follow her, but the old woman lifts her right hand to ward him off.

Ty knows better than to cause a scene in a public place. He stands helplessly and watches the old gal shakily make her way across the lobby.

Chapter 10

I direct Ty into the hotel bar. We can both use a drink.

And just in case the booze isn't enough, I'm heading to the acupuncturist later today.

"What just happened there?" Ty asks as he sips his cognac, the drink he always orders in stressful moments. "Instead of being angry about the damage she seemed..." Ty lifts one hand, unable to produce a word.

"Scared. To me, she seemed scared."

Ty ponders this. "Yeah, maybe. She's a tough old bird, so she didn't act like I'd expect a frightened elderly lady to act. I mean, she sent the cop away like a boss. But Pearl was definitely twitchy. What happened to the painting seemed to be, like, a signal to her. A signal that she shouldn't sell."

"She's had that painting hanging in her dining room for nearly seven years. Who would care that she wants to sell it now?" I use my swizzle stick to poke at the lime wedge in my drink. "And what hold do they have over Pearl?"

I watch Ty's gaze skim the long, polished mahogany bar, the avuncular bartender, the sedate faux fox-hunting prints, and I suspect what's going through his mind. Pearl's money gives her entrée to this comfortable, safe world. Who would dare threaten her here? But she and Irv seemed to run with a more diverse crowd in their married life. For starters, Irv's factory is in a rougher, working-class town. And to hear Pearl tell it, she and Irv enjoyed pushing their upper-middle-class Palmyrton friends into contact with artists and other characters from a grittier background.

"Pearl has plenty of money and no kids to worry about." I venture a theory. "But she's still devoted to her husband's memory. Maybe old Irv had some shady connections."

Ty picks up my train of thought. "Maybe Pearl's worried about dealing with those characters all on her own."

"So she's going to put the painting in storage." I rattle the ice cubes in my gin and tonic. "What purpose does that serve?"

"That's what's killin' me. That painting deserves to be seen, to be enjoyed. And what if she sticks it in some cheap self-storage unit?" Ty shudders. "Heat...cold...humidity...dirt—it'll be totally ruined in a year or two."

Ty's phone chirps and he glances at the screen. "Look at this—another offer to buy the painting. If I had this kinda action on Friday, the painting would've been sold, and we wouldn't be sittin' here."

"That proves the old adage that all publicity is good publicity." I wave off the bartender offering us another round. "Do you think all this interest stems from the two guys who were with you when you discovered the damage? Do they know that many buyers?"

Ty shakes his head. "Not just those two. I think the interest is coming more from me reaching out to Carter Lemoine to find an art restorer. He put out a call, and now everybody's buzzin.'" Ty throws back the dregs of his drink. "Seeing these opportunities to sell *Your Move* slipping through our fingers—Ugh!" He pounds his heart with the side of his fist.

"So what are we going to do about it?" I ask.

"What can we do? Turn it over to Mr. Swenson and let him duke it out with Pearl's lawyer." Ty's head droops over his empty glass.

I throw cash down on the bar. "No one wins once the lawyers get involved. Our best bet is to figure out what's scaring Pearl. If we can set her mind at ease, maybe she'll go through with the sale."

"Yeah. Yeah!" Ty gathers enthusiasm for the project. "Where do we start?"

"I say we start with Nathaniel Thurman's uncle. He's the one who knows about how the artist put real people into his paintings. And maybe he even knows something about Nathaniel's disappearance."

"You think he'll know the identity of the young guy sprawled on the stoop?" Ty asks. "You think that matters?"

"It's the logical place to start." I slide off my barstool. "If anyone knows, it'll be him. The problem is, how can we track him down? Did you get his full name? Is he Eugene Thurman, or is his last name different than his nephew's?"

"Different. I can't bring it to mind right now. But don't worry—it'll come to me. And I remember he said he lives near the factory in Hillside. I'll head over there tonight and ask around."

Immediately, I get worried. "Maybe I should come with you."

Ty gives me a long, silent look. Then he starts to chuckle. "Audge, a forty-year-old white lady's really not going to be a big help where I'm plannin' to go."

Chapter 11

By the time Ty and I part ways in downtown Palmyrton, it's already pushing seven, and I have to rush to make my acupuncture appointment. I arrive breathless and more than a little dewy with perspiration.

Min Wei smiles her enigmatic smile and invites me to recline. She runs her smooth, cool fingers across my forehead and flutters them over my wrists. "I think you have had a stressful day, yes?"

Ruined a painting...lost thousands of bucks...annoyed the police and my client—yeah, you could say a little stressful.

I simply nod.

"I will add some needles for the tension in your head and neck," she assures me. Min sets about her work inserting needles, and this time I watch. She inserts a needle and I actually feel a knot uncoil in my neck.

However it works, it sure is effective.

But at this session, when Min leaves me to let the needles do their work, my mind hasn't entirely stopped racing. Despite my effort to unwind, I find myself thinking of Nathaniel Thurman's disappearance. Was his family as devastated by his unknown fate as my family was when my mother disappeared on Christmas Eve? Could his long-ago disappearance have something to do with the present-day damage to his painting? I'll have to get Sean to help me find some details of the original investigation.

The thought of asking for my husband's assistance turns my mind in a different direction. Sean had his first appointment here at the acupuncture clinic yesterday and came home as mellow and converted to the process as I did. I smile as I think of how his description of his experience here led to a very enthusiastic exploration of one another's needling points. We should do that again tonight. I smile as I drift off on a lavender-scented cloud.

Maybe that's how acupuncture works to cure infertility.

———⬤———

When I get home, I find Sean unpacking containers from our favorite Thai take-out. He asks me for more detail on what happened with Detective Sanchez and Mrs. Aronson, but I don't want to lose the buzzy glow I've got going from my acupuncture session. I push his hand away from the reheat button of the microwave and slide my other hand under his shirt. "We can talk and eat a little later, no?"

He grins and follows me upstairs. Now that we've let go of our obsession with sperm motility and ovulation cycles and put our family-building faith in acupuncture and adoption, sex has become fun again. So what if we don't eat dinner until nine? It's good to feel this primal hunger for each other again.

When we finally dig into the pad thai and basil chicken, I give Sean an update on all that's happened since the sale ended, including my various theories about why the painting might have been defaced. "What can you find out about the original investigation into Thurman's disappearance?" I ask. "Did the Hillside cops even make an effort to find him?"

"I'll see what I can find out," Sean says. "But don't be too hard on my Hillside comrades. The disappearance of a middle-aged man with drug and mental illness issues doesn't stir up the same urgency as the disappearance of a toddler from a playground, no matter what town you're in."

I rub my bare foot along his shin. "But you'll check for me on Monday?"

"Yes, dear."

After dinner, despite the late hour, I can't resist a quick Google search on Nathaniel Thurman. His Wikipedia page provides the basics. He was born in Newark and lived most of his life in towns in New Jersey, with some forays into Brooklyn and Manhattan. He disappeared when he was forty-five and would be fifty-two now (if he's still alive). He briefly attended the Pratt Institute to study painting but left before graduating. He came to the attention of the art world with a painting he did for the SoHo restaurant of a celebrity chef. After that, he had several successful gallery shows. The profile lists the galleries and Thurman's agent. It sounds impressive, but I don't know enough about the Manhattan art world to be certain. Under a subhead entitled, "Personal Life", the profile describes Thurman's periodic struggles with mental illness and addiction.

Next, I read an interview Thurman did with an art blogger. Here, the artist's voice and personality really come through. He talks about how he's inspired by "the courage and beauty of everyday living." He describes his love of street life.

"My people come alive outdoors when they leave the confines of their crowded apartments. My people don't have a bedroom with a door that locks. They don't have a backyard with trees and grass where the neighbors can't see them. Privacy is a foreign concept. They have the street. The sidewalk. The stoop. The basketball court. The bodega. This is where I find my people's stories. So this is where you'll find me."

Chapter 12

On Monday, Sean comes home from work full of news about the old investigation into Thurman's disappearance. Despite my suspicions that the cops didn't put much effort into finding the missing artist, Sean assures me that the case file is extensive and well documented. We put Ethel on her leash and go out for a walk while Sean tells me what he's learned.

"Although Thurman did paint some smaller pieces, his favorite style was to do big canvases with very detailed scenes of everyday life in his community. So naturally, he needed a big studio space. He couldn't afford some trendy, arty neighborhood and he liked to be close to the scenes he painted, so he used this abandoned warehouse space in Hillside." Sean pauses while Ethel pees at the corner to let all the other dogs know this is her block. "But here's the thing—Thurman didn't rent the space. He squatted there. The space has great natural light, and in the winter he used propane heaters to keep warm."

"That sounds like a fire waiting to happen." I wave to our elderly neighbor but decline to stop for a chat. I want to hear what Sean has to tell me. "Did anyone hassle him for being there?"

"Apparently not. Even the cops couldn't figure out who owns the property. The taxes haven't been paid in years, and the town can't find a buyer. According to the file, the beat cops in the neighborhood were aware Thurman was using the top floor, but he was the least of their problems. The ground floor was used by addicts and hookers."

Ethel stops to sniff a decorative stone wall where the neighborhood chipmunks are known to congregate. "So did the detectives consider that one of those low-lifes could have killed Thurman?" I ask.

"Yes, they interviewed them as best they could—it was a rotating cast. But Thurman was kind to these people...painted them...gave them money when he had it. They had no reason to hurt him, and if they did kill Thurman, they probably wouldn't have been sharp enough to cover up the crime. So the detectives mainly considered them witnesses, not suspects." Sean tugs Ethel away from the wall, tiring of the endless wait for a rodent to appear. "Of course, they were unreliable witnesses because no one could agree upon the exact day when they last saw Thurman."

"I heard he had drug problems. Didn't he also share drugs with these people? Or buy from their dealer?" I ask.

"Thurman was bipolar and would have these bursts of creativity during his manic phases. He'd try to extend them or bring them on by taking stimulants: cocaine, Ecstasy, meth. The addicts in the building were all on heroin. That wasn't Thurman's drug of choice. The detectives knew all the local dealers and had a good idea of who supplied Thurman, but they didn't suspect him of involvement. Thurman wasn't in debt to him."

"Where did Thurman live?" I ask as we lead Ethel past the home of her sworn enemy, Puddles the schnauzer.

"That's the reason his disappearance wasn't reported immediately," Sean says. "Thurman had been living with a girlfriend off and on for over a year. But they had one of their periodic breakups, and he started sleeping at the studio and showering and eating at his sister Gloria's home. Sometimes he'd come and go when Gloria and her family were out, so he wouldn't bother them. That's why Gloria didn't start to worry until more than a week passed without contact. She figured her brother was either at the studio or with the old girlfriend."

Puddles senses Ethel's presence on the sidewalk and begins hurling himself at the picture window. We can see him bounce off the window, roll down the back of the sofa visible through the drapes, and pop back up again for more hysterical barking. "I could watch this all night long," Sean says. "But maybe we should get Ethel outta here."

Ethel lifts her nose in the air and marches down the sidewalk, too dignified to respond to Puddles' provocations. I follow, deep in thought. "So once Gloria got worried and called in the cops, what did they do?"

"Followed standard operating procedure for all adult missing persons. Checked all activity on his phone—calls were all routine, to people he knew well. The last call was on the same day he withdrew a hundred bucks from his bank account and charged a ten-dollar lunch to his credit card. That's also the last day he was spotted in the neighborhood, buying a soda at the bodega on Fuller Street. Thurman didn't own a car, so they checked with local taxis and checked the CCTV tapes at the train station. Found nothing. Went to his studio and found all his painting supplies and a half-finished painting. There were clothes there, but the sister couldn't tell what, if anything, was missing."

"So the cops just gave up looking for him?" I'm as indignant as Ethel when we pull the discarded half-slice of pizza from her mouth.

"No, they didn't give up." Sean gets agitated defending his crew. "There was no sign of foul play. No suspicious transactions. No beefs Thurman had with anyone. The sister said she sensed he was cycling into a depression, maybe because of the breakup, or maybe because the painting wasn't going as well as he hoped. And he had gone off the grid once before. Slept under a bridge with an encampment of homeless people and returned two weeks later to paint a bunch of pictures from the experience. So his family was holding on to hope that he checked out to, you know, recharge his creative batteries or whatever. But he's been gone nearly seven years."

"Wow." We finish our loop of the neighborhood, and our snug house comes back into view. How comfortable and secure we are here! I try to imagine what it would be like to work and even live in an abandoned building shared with addicts and hookers. Thurman lived in poverty while he was creating, and now that he's gone, his paintings are becoming more and more valuable. No wonder his nephew is aggrieved about the sale of *Your Move*.

Ethel tugs to return home, eager to take up her spot under the kitchen table for human dinnertime. "Surely if Nathaniel were alive, he would've contacted his family to let them know he was okay. So maybe he did kill himself." I shiver. "Such a great talent lost to the world."

And now, one of his masterpieces has been defaced. It makes me even more determined to get the painting restored and find it a worthy new owner.

Chapter 13

The next morning, I come to the office and share everything I've learned about Nathaniel Thurman's disappearance with Ty and Donna. While I talk, I work on the financials from the Aronson sale. Despite our success in unloading some strange items at full price, we had to accept some hard bargains on the second day of the sale. Without the commission from the painting, this will be a below-average sale for Another Man's Treasure. So when Ty tells me he managed to track down Thurman's Uncle Eugene in Hillside and that he wants to pay a visit, I don't quibble.

Ty and I decide to combine a trip to Newark to drop off a van full of donations to Sister Alice with a visit to Eugene in nearby Hillside. He drives the van while I answer some emails and make some business calls.

Whenever I look away from my phone, I notice a sneaky, Cheshire cat half-smile playing on Ty's lips. Finally, I can't resist teasing him. "What are you daydreaming about? Some cute girl you met last weekend?"

Ty snorts. "Hell, no. None 'a that."

"Well, something's making you smile while you drive, and it's certainly not the scenery," I say as we pass a junkyard heaped with rusting cars.

"When I was hanging out in Hillside looking for Eugene, I picked up a lead on where to buy a BlastMaster. New shipment's due soon."

"Ty, Ty, Ty—why is getting this toy for Lo so important to you?"

He taps his long fingers on the steering wheel as we pause at a light. "When I was in second grade, the big toy that year was a Shell Shocker. It was this radio-controlled thing that transformed from a ball to a monster and you could make it roll right over stuff that it ran into. I wanted one so-o-o bad. I wrote my letter to Santa Claus, told him I didn't want nothing else but that. I worked real hard on bein' good so he'd have no excuses not to bring it for me." Ty stares straight ahead and grips the steering wheel as he talks. "Me and my friends talked about how we'd have battles with them after Christmas once we all got ours."

I can see where this story is headed. Second grade is the year Ty's father first went to prison. "But Marvin went to prison and your mom was struggling and you didn't get a Shell Shocker," I say to make the story easier for him.

"My mom was off her head with worry, so Grams took over Christmas. She went to Walmart and the Shell Shocker was eighty bucks and there was another remote control toy that looked the same to her and was only thirty, so she bought that," Ty explains. "Then to cheer me up about my dad being gone and my mom being so distracted, Grams kept telling me what a good boy I was, and how Santa was going to do me right."

Ty arches his back in the driver's seat. I can see he is far, far away from the Garden State Parkway. "I'll never forget how excited I was when I woke up on Christmas morning and saw the big box under the tree. And then I ripped off the paper and..."

He can't continue.

As a girl who got educational toys for Christmas every year instead of the glittery trash she craved, I can totally relate. But I've gotten over it. I'm still not clear on why Ty hasn't recovered from this disappointment.

"But Lo doesn't even know about BlastMaster. He's not going to be disappointed when he doesn't get it," I point out, employing my best logic.

I should know that logic isn't what's called for here.

Ty keeps his eye on the rearview mirror as he changes lanes. "Second grade was the year I lost my dad, but it was also when I lost my trust. I realized there wasn't no Santa Claus. That moms and dads and grandmas could lie. That friends would drop you if you didn't have the right stuff."

I want to hug him, but that's not possible when we're careening down the highway at seventy miles per hour. "Everyone learns those hard lessons eventually, Ty," I whisper with my hand on his knee.

He shakes it off to tap the brakes. "Guess you could say BlastMaster is more than a toy to me. It's a symbol, the way a Thanksgiving turkey is a symbol for having plenty to eat." Ty suddenly realizes where we are and exits the highway with a screech. "Now I'm in a place where I can protect Lo. And I'm gonna do that as long as I can."

Chapter 14

A quick visit with Sister Alice is always rejuvenating. The sturdy nun is ageless with her saggy corduroy slacks and iron gray, bowl-cut hair. Her eyes light with anticipation as she trots to the back of the van to see what we've brought her. She accepts a gilt Roman goddess lamp and an elephant-shaped ottoman without passing judgment. "Oh, and look at these delightful pink curtains," she says, hugging four panels of Pepto-Bismol colored satin to her chest. "I know a little girl who'll be thrilled to have these."

"So Pearl and Irv have spread their joy to Newark," I say to Ty while waving good-bye to Sister Alice through the van window.

Ty purses his lips. "I'd be happier if Pearl would spread a little joy to our bottom line and let us sell that painting. Let's see if Eugene can help us with that."

Fifteen minutes later, we locate Eugene's well-kept row house on a hit-or-miss block in Hillside. Eugene's left-hand neighbor has a neatly mown patch of lawn and sedate beige curtains in the front windows, while his right-hand neighbor has a tangle of weeds and trash blocking the short path and a red blanket pinned over the front window. Ty has to drive to the end of the block to find a parking space big enough for the van. When we get out, a group of young men on the corner eyes us up and down. If I'd been alone, I wouldn't make eye contact and would keep walking. Ty returns their gaze with a frank assessment of his own: touch my vehicle and you're dead. Then he turns and escorts me down the cracked sidewalk to our destination.

Eugene Caldwell opens the door as soon as we knock. His face lights with pleasure. "Come on in. It's so nice to see you again. Did Pearl send you?"

"In a way," Ty answers vaguely.

Luckily for us, Eugene is of the age where he welcomes all visitors without questioning their provenance. He escorts us back to his tidy kitchen where he insists on making us a cup of coffee. "I'm sorry I don't have any cookies to offer you. When my wife passed two years ago, I stopped keeping sweets in the house." Through the doorway to the dining room, I spy a Nathaniel Thurman painting on the wall. It's much smaller in scale than the one in Pearl's dining room, but the bold colors and strong brushwork mark it as a Thurman.

Making and serving the coffee seems to help Eugene dispel his nervous energy. Does he suspect why we're here? I sit back and wait for Ty to make the opening remarks.

"Mr. Caldwell—"

"Call me Eugene." He sets three mugs on the yellow flowered tablecloth and sits down with us.

"Eugene," Ty begins again. "I got some bad news. *Your Move* was defaced last weekend, sometime between when we closed up for the day on Friday and the end of the sale on Saturday."

Eugene's face draws down in a frown. "Whattaya mean, defaced?"

"Someone blacked out one of the figures in the painting." I pull out the iPad to show him the before and after close-ups of the damaged area. Eugene's mouth drops open and he rubs his eyes.

"You told us that Nathaniel put some real people into his paintings, so we were wondering if you know who that young man is." Ty taps the iPad, and the reclining man's face fills the screen.

Eugene's eyes dart back and forth, like he wants to look anywhere but at that screen. "Why you care about that? He's not the one who hurt the painting."

How can he be so sure, unless he knows who and where the man is?

Ty offers a reassuring smile. "We just want to get the painting fixed, and then we can find it a new owner—maybe a collector or maybe a small museum—who would appreciate it the way it should be appreciated."

Eugene leans back in his wooden chair, squinting at Ty. "You sayin' Pearl don't appreciate that painting?"

"No, no. It's just...well..." Ty glances at me, unsure of how much we should confide in Eugene.

"Pearl has suddenly shown some, er, reluctance to sell the painting," I explain. "She wants to put it in storage."

Ty spreads his hands. "And then it would be lost to the world. That seems like a shame to me."

Eugene nods slowly. "Why'd Pearl change her mind?"

"We don't know," Ty says. "She seems nervous since this happened. Instead of being mad that the painting was damaged, she seems kinda scared. So we thought if we could figure out why the painting was defaced, maybe we could persuade her...."

Ty trails off uncertainly. Laid out to a stranger, our mission seems a little far-fetched.

Eugene stirs his coffee for a protracted period. Finally, he speaks. "I dunno about persuadin' ol' Pearl. Once that woman has her mind made up, ain't nobody gonna change her. But I'll tell you this. The boy in the painting is dead. So he can't have had nuthin' to do with hurting *Your Move*."

I'm shocked to hear this. "He's young. How did he die?"

Eugene turns to face me. "How do young men die on these streets? He ran with the wrong crowd. Didn't work an honest job. Got killed for his efforts."

"Was his killer caught?"

Eugene shakes his head. "Huh-uh. I don't know who killed Darnell Peterson, but there's plenty who do know. They just not talkin'."

"Nobody wants to snitch," Ty says.

Eugene sips coffee that must now be tepid. "They afraid."

Ty and I exchange a glance. If the young man in the painting was killed by gangbangers, then blacking out his image could have been done as a warning, or a reminder. But why send that message to Pearl? And how would gangbangers in Hillside know about the painting hanging in Pearl's Palmyrton dining room?

"How long ago did Darnell die?" I study the daisy pattern in the tablecloth, not wanting to seem overly interested.

"Hmm. Right around the time Nathaniel disappeared."

Could the murder and Nathaniel's disappearance be linked? I continue to probe. "Would Pearl and Irv have known Darnell?"

"Nah. Irv was always willing to give young people from the neighborhood a job. I recommended different people to him over the years, and he always found them work. But I don't think Darnell had any interest in working in a factory. He wanted to be a big man." Eugene's mouth twists in disapproval. "And you see where that got him."

"How well did Nathaniel know Darnell?" Ty asks. "Did he try to encourage him to stay outta the gang life?"

"Oh, Nathaniel would talk to anyone and everyone. That doesn't mean he *knew* them." Eugene laces his fingers together. "I think he put Darnell in that picture because he saw him as...what's the word? Nate told me once..." Eugene furrows his brow in concentration. "An archetype! That's it. See how Nate painted Darnell layin' back and lookin' up at the sky? He was one kid who stood for al-l-l the young men with big dreams but no real ambition and energy to make the dreams happen."

Ty hangs on Eugene's every word. Perhaps he sees his younger self in Darnell. Perhaps he's thinking how narrowly he escaped Darnell's fate.

"Did Nathaniel have kids, Eugene?" I ask to break the silence. "Or are his nephews his only survivors?"

"Nathaniel didn't have kids of his own. Because of his, er, spells," Eugene touches his temple, "he thought he wouldn't be a good husband or father. But he loved his nieces and nephews, and he was real good to them."

"So he had more than the two you brought to see the painting?" Ty asks.

Eugene launches into a complicated explanation of Nathaniel's family tree. "My sister—that's Nate's mother—has passed, and her girls, Gloria and Patrice, each have two kids. The boys I brought to Pearl's house are Gloria's sons. Patrice has a girl and a boy, but they live down in Maryland now."

We all jump when we hear the front door open and close again. "Uncle Gene? I brought you some chicken and greens I made yesterday," a female voice calls. "Where you at?"

"Here in the kitchen," Eugene answers. "I have company."

A large woman in her forties with a friendly smile and no-nonsense eyes enters the kitchen. I can see her accepting Ty's presence but puzzling over me. "Hi, I'm Gloria." She extends her hand and Ty and I both jump up to shake it while Eugene performs the introductions and tells his niece about what happened to *Your Move.*

She listens as she bustles around the kitchen unpacking the food she brought for her uncle. When Eugene gets to the part in the story where he describes Darnell being blacked out of the painting, Gloria freezes. She pivots from her position in front of the fridge and stares at us. "What's that you say?"

Ty holds out the iPad so she can see for herself.

Gazing at the damage, Gloria's face transforms. Her brisk competence dissolves, replaced by hurt and loss. "Another piece of my brother taken away from me," she whispers. "When will it end?"

"Gloria wanted to come with us to see the painting at Pearl's house, but she had to work." Eugene pats his niece's hand to console her. "They got mandatory overtime at the factory these days. Can't ask for time off. It's not the same as it was when Irv owned it. Glad I retired when I did."

Gloria swallows hard. "At least my boys saw it. They used to love spending time with Nathaniel. But seven years is a long time for young people. I worry they're starting to forget him."

"So you used to work for Irv and Pearl and now you work for the new owner?" I ask Gloria.

She concedes this fact with one sharp nod and returns to straightening out her uncle's refrigerator. Several almost empty condiment containers hit the trash.

"Pearl told us Irv used to go into work even after he sold out," I say. "Did he agree with the changes the new owners made?"

Gloria makes a face, and I'm not sure if she's reacting to moldy leftovers or my question. "Lev and Yuri didn't pay any attention to Irv. They were glad when he died."

I trade a glance with Ty. Could that have something to do with why Pearl seems frightened? "Did Nathaniel ever work at the factory? Is that how Irv met him?"

Gloria gives a laugh that's more like a bark. "No, factory work wasn't Nate's bag. Irv knew Nate from the neighborhood. Irv talked to everyone, just like Nate did. In that one way, they were like two peas in a pod."

"Could Irv have known Darnell?"

Gloria whacks a plastic container against the side of the trash can to dislodge the contents. "Why you askin' so many questions?"

But Eugene jumps in to answer his niece. "They say Pearl won't sell the painting since it got damaged. She wants to put it in storage. Something spooked her, they think."

Gloria continues to eye us suspiciously. "Why does that matter to you?"

I incline my head toward Ty, hoping the explanation will seem more convincing coming from him.

"We stand to make some money off the sale, that's true," Ty conceded. "But *Your Move* needs to be restored. It shouldn't get shoved into storage and forgotten. And all the publicity around the damage has stirred up new interest in your brother's work."

With that last statement, Ty has Gloria's attention. "How so?"

"The art market is fickle. Artists fall in and out of fashion. This publicity, even though it's for something bad, has brought Nathaniel's work back to the front of art buyers' minds." Ty spreads his hands. "And there's also some crazy rumors on social media that maybe this is some kinda sign that, well, your brother is coming back. And that's getting the market even more riled up."

"That's foolishness!" Gloria begins scrubbing Tupperware at the sink, slamming the clean ones into the drainer with ferocity. "Nate's not coming back, and it's cruel to say he is."

"You think he's dead?" Ty asks as gently as he can.

Gloria spins around. "He has to be. Why else would he stay out of touch for so long? But the police never made any effort to find out what happened to him."

"Putting aside the rumors and gossip, we'd just like to find a way to persuade Pearl to restore *Your Move* and sell it," I say. "Do you have any idea why seeing Darnell's figure blacked out of the painting would make her change her mind about selling it?"

"No idea." Gloria dries her hands and looks pointedly at her watch. Ty and I rise to leave.

"Didn't you know Darnell's older brother?" Eugene asks Gloria as we leave the kitchen.

Her face hardens. "Haven't seen him in years."

"Is he the kind of person who might do something like this?" I ask as she follows us to the door.

"He's the kind of person who'd stick a knife in your eye." She lets us out of the house and closes Eugene's door sharply behind us.

Chapter 15

Ty and I pass out of the small yard and head down the sidewalk toward our van. "Kind of an odd dynamic there, wouldn't you say?"

Ty nods. "Gloria wanted to get rid of us. Seems like Darnell was a sketchy character, and she's doesn't like his connections."

"And she has no use for the new owners. Lev and Yuri—sounds like they're Russian."

The circle of young men still stand on the corner, and Ty nods to them in acknowledgement as we get into the van. He seems somber as we begin the ride home. I wait for him to tell me what's on his mind, but nothing comes.

After his third sigh, I ask what's bothering him.

"I'm thinkin' some cold thoughts, Audge. Real cold." We stop at a red light, and he faces me. "We always say 'follow the money,' right? Who stands to gain from what's going on in the art market?" Before I can speak, he answers his own question. "People who already own Thurman paintings."

"But how could anyone predict that defacing the painting would produce that effect?"

Ty passes the ramp to get on Route 78 to take us back to Palmyrton.

"Hey..." I point out the window.

"I figure as long as we're here in Hillside, let's go see the street that appears in *Your Move*," Ty explains.

"Oka-a-ay. You think we can find it?"

"We know it's around the corner from Pearl and Irv's factory. I Googled the address for that before we left."

The determined set of Ty's jaw brooks no argument. I guess we're exploring the streets of Hillside. After twisting through stop-and-go traffic, passing blocks of small storefront churches, bodegas, autobody shops, and carry-out Chinese restaurants, we arrive at a street with a long, four-story building taking up one whole side of the block. In the far corner, on top of the roof is a big sign that proclaims, I A Industries—Clothing Made in America, with a painting of a billowing flag. Over the main door is another sign that reads, Keep Your Eye on Quality, with a big painted eye with long lashes.

Ty points to the sign on the roof. "You can see part of that sign in the painting, so the street should be around the corner to the right."

"I thought that the whole garment industry moved to China and Viet Nam and Bangladesh where they can pay the workers a fraction of what people make here."

"This town used to be full of garment factories. Most of them were driven out of business by cheap foreign labor." Ty speaks with great authority. "But Irv was smart enough to hop on the 'Made in America' bandwagon and position his factory as the patriotic, high-end alternative. They do work sewing clothes for certain specialty brands. Not stuff you buy in Walmart."

"Pearl told you all that?" It didn't seem possible Ty could have elicited so much information from her in their brief conversation before she agreed to the sale.

"Nah, I found an article online about Irv's business. He got profiled a few years back in an article about small scale manufacturing in New Jersey." Ty turns the corner, and we look around, trying to get oriented to the perspective of the painting.

"Look, that's the little pocket park with benches." I point ahead. "But no chess players today."

Ty parks the van, and we get out. Standing on the sidewalk and looking away from the park, we can see the corner of Irv's sign. Across the street is the bodega where Irv bought his coffee. But the other mom and pop storefronts depicted in the painting have changed—some are boarded up, some replaced by sketchy check-cashing establishments and pay-as-you-go cellphone stores. And the sidewalks are not as filled with people as they are in *Your Move*. No children playing; no moms and grandmas watching. In fact, the street seems lonely and dejected, not brimming with life as Nathaniel depicted it.

Has the neighborhood changed in the seven years since the painting was created, or did Nathaniel use artistic license to create the street as he wished it was? I nervously scan the block looking for signs of drug dealers, but even that activity seems to be gone.

Ty points across the street. "Let's go in the bodega and see if anyone there remembers Irv or Nathaniel."

We enter the Speedy Mart, where a large pot of coffee sits scorching on a burner. The market sells lottery tickets, cigarettes, soda, junk food, and in a far corner, wickedly overpriced diapers and toilet paper. Milk, eggs, juice, and anything else remotely nutritious are conspicuously absent. The cashier sits behind a scratched Lucite screen with a half-moon shaped opening for cash to change hands. His pasty white face and pale, squinty eyes are barely visible to us, but his general air of suspicion and hostility comes through clearly.

"Hi!" I step up to the counter with my best "happy to meet you" smile. "We're looking for anyone who knows Irv Aronson or Nathaniel Thurman. I believe they used to shop here."

The cashier tilts his head and scowls. "People come in, go out. Don't know names."

I nod but persist. "Irv used to own the factory around the corner. Short, older gentleman? Silver hair and mustache? Used to come in every morning for coffee."

"Nah. I am working here two months only." He turns his back on me and returns to reading a folded newspaper.

So much for hoping this little market is a slice of Mayberry on an urban street. Ty and I wait until we're on the sidewalk to speak. "Did you hear his accent and see that newspaper?" I ask.

"Yeah. He's Russian, just like the new owners of the factory." I glance back into the store. The cashier is holding his phone to his ear as he looks directly at me.

Chapter 16

Two days after our trip to Hillside, Donna and I jump at the sound of someone trying to kick in the office door. Then we hear Ty's voice. "Yo! Open up!"

Donna scowls as she gets up from her desk. "Hold your horses." She flings open the door. "Did you forget your—"

Ty staggers in with his arms wrapped around a huge, colorful box. "It's Christmas in June! I finally got my BlastMaster!" His face splits with a grin as he sets the unwieldy box on the floor. We gather around as if a rare bird has alighted in our midst.

"What store finally came through?" Donna asks. "Best Buy? Target?"

Ty dismisses these guesses with a snort. "Haven't been in stock there for weeks. I got this baby straight from the docks in the Port of Elizabeth."

My eyes widen. "Ty, is that toy *stolen*?"

He looks deeply offended. "I didn't steal nuthin'. I paid two hundred and fifty bucks for that. My contact has access to a certain number of BlastMasters that are available outside standard retail channels."

In other words, stolen by the suppliers if not by Ty himself.

In the total range of larcenous activities, I suppose purchasing a hot Blast-Master is on the low end of the spectrum, but I still feel Ty should know better. This ridiculous toy has made his common sense fly right out the window.

Donna drops to her knees to study the explosive pictures printed on the box. "It sure looks like fun." She frowns and points to some small print. "Although it does say ages 6 and up."

"Bah! Lo is smart for his age. He'll be good with it. Besides, he'll be nearly five when he gets it at Christmas."

I resist the urge to be strictly mathematical and point out that Lo will be four-and-a-half at Christmas. "Are you really going to manage to hold off giving it to him until December?"

"Have to." Ty jams his hands in his back jeans pockets. "Charmaine gets really pissed when I buy Lo toys every time I see him. Says I'm teaching him to equate love with gifts."

"Charmaine is a good mother." I try to keep my tone neutral.

"I know." Ty scuffs his big sneaker on the worn office rug. "Lately, I've been taking Lo to the park or shootin' hoops with him instead of buying him stuff."

"I bet he loves that even more than a new toy," Donna says, patting Ty on the back.

Ty rolls his shoulders, then snaps into action. "But look how awesome this is! It's got a controller and a joystick and you can switch it into ten different modes. We're gonna have a ball with this on Christmas morning." He picks up the box. "But I gotta store it here, so no one sees it at my place. I'm not even tellin' Grams about it because you know how she talks."

Donna scurries to the far corner of the office and shifts some boxes. "Put it back here, then I'll move this stuff in front of it. That way Lo won't see it in case he comes to visit."

I follow Ty to watch the BlastMaster take up its new home. As he angles it to fit in the space, I notice the colors on the sides of the box are slightly lighter than on the front and top, and one corner of the cardboard is a little dinged. Not that it matters. A kid would never notice such a small detail.

Donna tosses an old bedspread over the box, and she and Ty stack some other items in front of the toy.

I return to my desk. "It's well hidden there. I just hope it doesn't accidentally get donated to Sister Alice."

Ty points his trigger finger at me. "Not funny, Audge. Not funny at all."

———————⊛———————

At dinner, I tell Sean about Ty's BlastMaster. "He won't get in trouble for receiving stolen goods, will he?"

Sean laughs. "That's a hard charge to make stick. The prosecutor has to prove that you knew the stuff was stolen. I doubt law enforcement bothers much with dockworkers diverting a few toys from a big shipment and selling them to friends."

I stab a piece of grilled chicken from the serving platter. "I still don't like it. Ty has lost his mind over this stupid toy. Promise me we'll never do that with our kids."

"No worries. When I was a kid, we each got three toys for Christmas, and we all played with one another's stuff. Nobody got anything big and fancy, but we all had fun."

"Maybe that's what we should write our adoption essay about," I say. "We can talk about how we'll bring a baby into a big, extended family with lots of aunts and uncles and cousins."

"Describe all the parties but leave out all the fighting." Sean winks at me.

"We have to finish the application tonight, Sean. We've been procrastinating too long."

He nods as he chews his cauliflower. "What's the latest with Peter and Noreen's application? Have they heard anything more from the birth mother who chose them?"

After months and months of waiting, Peter and Noreen are suddenly very close to adoption because a young woman in her ninth month of pregnancy has chosen them to adopt her baby. "They're trying to control their excitement because something could still go wrong," I tell Sean.

We subside into silence thinking about the stress our friends are facing. Then my phone rings. "It's Noreen," I announce as I answer and put the phone on speaker.

"Audrey! Our baby was born today!" Her voice shakes with joy. "A healthy baby boy. Eight pounds, two ounces. We're going to call him Lucas."

Sean and I both shout our congratulations. "Is it a done deal?" Sean asks.

"She talked to us this evening. She says she's signing the relinquishment papers in the morning. Then we'll fly to Ohio to pick him up."

"That's fabulous! Are you ready? Do you need anything?"

"We've had the nursery set up for months," Noreen laughs. "You can come visit as soon as we get settled." Noreen begins to cry. "Oh, my god, Audrey. I can't believe how much I love Lucas already. I'm going to share the photo his birth mother sent us."

We ooo and ahh over the photo of a tiny red, wrinkled, bald bundle. Then we say goodnight as Noreen moves to call more friends and family with her news.

Sean feeds Ethel the last bite of chicken on his plate as he begins to clear the table. "Wow. Just like that," he snaps his fingers, "Peter and Noreen are parents."

I keep staring at the photo on my phone. I don't want to say aloud what I'm thinking, but my husband reads my mind as he looks over my shoulder. "He's kinda homely, isn't he?"

I enlarge the photo and lean against my husband. "I bet that red mark on his cheek is from forceps. And I remember Deirdre saying one of her kids had a head that was flat on one side for months. But they're all cute now."

Sean's gaze searches my face. "Will we be able to love the baby we get instantly, like Noreen does?"

"I don't know. It's scary."

Chapter 17

"Audrey, shouldn't you be leaving for your appointment with Mr. Swenson?" Donna says from her perfectly organized desk. Two weeks have passed since our original meeting with Pearl Aronson. As I predicted, her lawyer and my lawyer have exchanged phone calls and letters which have not brought us any closer to resolution. Ty has tried calling Pearl to set up another meeting, hoping a face-to-face chat about our visit to the locale of the painting would bring her around. But she refused to take his calls. Ty went so far as to hang out in the lobby of the Crossroads Hotel to casually intercept her, but he left when he felt hotel security giving him the stink eye.

Consequently, *Your Move* still hangs in Pearl's dining room. Isabelle Trent has hired workmen to "neutralize" the first floor of the house, and now that they've finished painting walls and stripping wallpaper, she's eager to start showing the house. If she gets an offer, the painting will have to go somewhere.

Storage or the gallery? Maybe my lawyer will have some positive news.

"My appointment's on the sixth." I answer Donna without looking away from the spreadsheet on my computer screen.

"Yeah. Today is the sixth."

My head snaps up. "What? No—today's the fourth." I grab my calendar to check. And sure enough, today, Thursday, is June 6th.

I jump from my desk chair. "Good grief! What's wrong with me? I'm living in a cloud."

"Relax. You have time to get there." Donna picks up the phone. "I can call Mr. Swenson and tell him you'll be a little late."

I drag a brush through my hair and grab my tote bag. "Yeah, do that, please. And thanks for reminding me, Donna. You saved my ass."

I arrive at Mr. Swenson's office breathless and spouting apologies. My mild-mannered attorney sits behind his desk with his hands folded and waits for me to settle down. I feel my eyes glaze over as he reviews all the legalities of contract law that have brought us to this impasse, but I know from experience that the thorough and meticulous Mr. Swenson cannot be rushed.

"What's our next move?" I ask when he concludes.

"I suggest offering Mrs. Aronson the opportunity to buy her way out of the contract. What did you stand to make in commission if you sold the painting?"

"Well, it's hard to say for sure. We agreed we wouldn't sell it for less than $20,000, but it was appraised at $25,000. And Thurman's paintings have been increasing in value since the defacement hit the news, so if we sold it today, we might get as much as $40,000."

Mr. Swenson makes a face like he bit into a mealy peach. He hates imprecision. "What is the most optimistic estimate of the commission you could make if you sold the painting today?"

I do some quick mental math. "Eight thousand dollars."

"Fine. I'll ask her lawyer for ten thousand and we'll negotiate down from there."

Wow! I wouldn't have the cojones to do that myself. Mr. Swenson, despite his mousy appearance, has a bullish disposition. "So, she'd pay us what we stand to lose and then she gets to do whatever she wants with the painting?" I clarify.

"Precisely."

"Okay—I guess it's worth a try." I stand and sling my bag over my shoulder. "Let me know how it goes."

"I won't settle without your approval."

⸻ ◉ ⸻

Despite the rocky start, my meeting with Mr. Swenson went better than anticipated. His proposal is a great solution for us financially, but I suspect Ty will be disappointed that this option will allow Pearl to put the painting in storage.

On the drive back to the office, my mind drifts from how to break the news to Ty and back to Mr. Swenson. Thank goodness Donna keeps an eye on my calendar. The thought that I nearly missed this important meeting unnerves me. How could I have been so careless? I'm always on top of my calendar, not only for business but also for fertility tracking. I laugh ruefully to myself. Sean and I really threw the sex calendar out the window this month, too.

Then my hand tightens on the wheel.

I've been two days off all week. I'm near the end of my cycle. My period was supposed to start on the fourth, which I thought was today. But it's the sixth.

My period is two days late.

I'm never late.

My heart rate kicks up a notch.

Stop it, Audrey. You've probably got this date screwed up, too. You need to look at your calendar.

I can't look while I'm driving. Thump, thump, thump—I can feel my heart pounding against the seatbelt. This won't wait until I arrive back in the office. At the next intersection, I pull into an office building parking lot and dive for my phone. With trembling fingers, I pull up my calendar.

As with every month, I've marked my ovulation date with an "o", shaded the days we need to shoot for "maximum exposure" and marked with an x the day 28 days after the beginning of my last menstruation. That day was June 4.

I really am two days late.

Beads of sweat pop out on my forehead. What should I do? I'm as panicky as a teenager, but for the exact opposite reason.

Could this really be it? Could the acupuncture have worked in the first month we tried it? Surely not.

Should I take a home pregnancy test, or wait a few more days?

I should wait. Of course, I should. My period will probably come tomorrow. I put the car into gear and pull back out into traffic.

But it's never been late since I started tracking obsessively last year. Not even when I caught that stomach bug and threw up for three days in a row.

I drive two more blocks and the big red and white CVS sign looms into view.

I could.... No, just go back to the office, Audrey.

At the last second, I flick my turn signal and veer into the CVS lot, causing the guy behind me to lay on his horn and flip me the bird.

Sorry, buddy.

Inside the store, I glance over my shoulder as if I expect undercover operatives to follow me into the family planning aisle. Once there, I'm confronted with a dizzying array of products. I read the packages, reject the cheapest brand, agonize between two that claim to detect pregnancy earlier than any other brand, pull out my phone and Google, "best home pregnancy test," and finally settle on one.

Maybe I should buy the number two brand as well, just in case the first one doesn't give me the answer I want.

I grab two pink boxes of different shades and head to the check-out. For once, I'm happy to do self-check-out away from the prying eyes of the clerk, and I escape quickly with my purchases.

Back in the car, I pause to think. I can't do this test in the office bathroom. I can't emerge, either devastated or elated, sit back down at my desk in front of Donna, and pretend nothing has happened. She knows me too well; I'll never pull it off.

Much as I love Donna, I don't want her to be the first person to know my big news.

If there really is big news.

No, that honor belongs to Sean.

So I text Donna and tell her I'm heading straight home. Yes, the meeting went well. No, nothing's wrong. She sends one more questioning text after that, but I ignore it and head home.

Ethel dances around me as I enter the house. Mom's home, ergo it must be dinner time. "It's only three," I tell her as I march resolutely past her dish toward my ultimate destination.

Ethel follows me into the powder room and sits attentively while I do the deed. "Maybe you won't be an only child any more, Ethel. Are you okay with that?"

Her ears perk up and she tilts her head. Then she lays her nose on my knee and gives a little whine. Either she's wishing me good luck or she's getting really anxious about dinner.

I lay the plastic testing wand on the sink to develop and check the time. 3:05

Three minutes. I have to wait three minutes for the result. What an eternity!

"C'mon, Ethel—let's get your kibble. It won't hurt to eat dinner early just this once." The dog follows me into the kitchen, and I prepare her meal with elaborate attention to detail, mixing in some canned food, sprinkling on some leftover shredded chicken, all the while keeping my eyes carefully averted from the time on my phone.

Finally, I set down Ethel's dish, wash out the dog food can, put the fork in the dishwasher, and look at my phone.

3:08.

My legs turn to jelly. I stumble into the powder room and stand in the doorway looking at the white and pink wand on the sink. I'm going to have to walk over there, pick it up, and stare at the little window.

And if it's blank, I'm going to feel like the biggest fool on the planet.

I take two steps closer to the sink, squeeze my eyes shut, and grab the piece of plastic that contains my destiny.

I take a deep breath and open my eyes.

Chapter 18

Two pink stripes. Pregnant.

My shriek of victory is loud enough to cause Ethel to lift her head from her dish and trot into the powder room.

Once she ascertains that I haven't been assaulted by a slasher, she shoots me an indignant look and returns to demolishing her meal. I lean against the wall staring at the test wand in my hand. Can this possibly be accurate? I decide to repeat the test with the other brand.

This one gives me a pink plus sign.

"We did it, Ethel! We really did it!" I run into the kitchen to confirm the news with the only available living creature in the house. Ethel licks the rim of her bowl systematically before allowing me to lead her in a two-legged dance around the kitchen.

Celebrating with a dog leaves a lot to be desired. I don't want to tell Sean on the phone; I want to see his face when he hears the news. I know that if I call him to urge him to come home early, he'll interrogate me until he discovers the reason why. Texting will be safer.

I'm making dinner tonight. What's your ETA?

Six.

Three-fifteen, and Sean won't be home until six. What am I going to do with myself for three hours?

I check the expiration date on the half-used bottle of multi-vitamins that I always forget to take. Still good for another month. I pop two. I jump on Amazon to order the latest edition of *What to Expect When You're Expecting*. And I call my Ob/Gyn to make an appointment. The receptionist seems utterly unsurprised by my news. Is it my imagination or is she cracking gum? She asks the date of my last period and tells me the doctor can see me on June 15th. The fifteenth! Shouldn't I come, like, tomorrow?

"Can't she fit me in sooner?" I plead.

"Why? Is there a problem?"

Problem? We're talking miracle here. Doesn't the doctor have some slots reserved for miraculous conceptions? "Well, not that I know of. I'm just anxious. It's my first time and I had trouble getting pregnant."

She sighs. "All right. Come on the twelfth at three."

Once my calendar is marked, I set to work making a super healthy dinner with two vegetables and no starches. Brace yourself, baby—there's a whole world of kale and cauliflower headed your way.

Every ten minutes or so, I lay my palm against my perfectly flat stomach. Is there really something...someone...in there? It defies belief.

Finally, Ethel and I hear the rumble of the garage door opening. We run to the back hall to await Sean's entry.

He's used to the dog jumping on him the moment he sets foot in the house but laughs to see me right beside her. He scratches Ethel behind the ears and kisses me lightly.

I pull out of the kiss and grab both his hands. "I have something to tell you."

He arches his sandy brows. Probably thinks I'm going to confess to dinging the car.

Two words don't seem enough to convey the magnitude of this news, but they're all I've got.

"I'm pregnant."

Sean staggers backward a step. "Wha—? How?"

"How? How do you think, silly?"

As the reality sinks in, I hear a note of excitement creep into Sean's voice. "How do you know? Are you sure?"

I whip out the two test sticks: solid forensic evidence.

Sean holds them in his big hands, staring at the stripes...the plus sign...the word: pregnant. A tear trickles down his cheek. I've come to know that his right eye gives in to emotion first.

"We did it," I whisper. This thing that everyone else seems able to do so easily—teenagers and heroin addicts and starving women in war-torn Yemen—this thing that had eluded us.

We did it.

Sean pulls me into his arms, and we rock back and forth for a long time.

Over dinner, we discuss our strategy for sharing the news.

"I think we should wait until I'm three months along, you know, just in case..."

Sean pauses his fork over his plate. "That's not going to happen, Audrey. You're healthy. You won't—"

Neither of us can bring ourselves to utter the word "miscarriage." But it had happened to our sister-in-law, Adrienne. She'd lost a pregnancy in between her two healthy ones, and she warned me that having to tell people the bad news after you'd gleefully told them the good news was a terrible ordeal.

"Besides," Sean says with a grin, "the moment you turn down a glass of wine, everyone will know the reason why."

"True. I'll never keep this on the downlow for three months. But let's just wait until after we see the doctor. Then we'll tell our parents, and the rest of the family, and Ty and Donna."

"Deal."

We return to eating kale.

"Should we call the adoption agency and take ourselves off the list?" I ask. We only recently got on the list after finally completing the essay.

Sean chews slowly, swallows, drinks some water. Is he thinking or choking? "Maybe..."

"You want to hedge our bets?" a note of anxiety creeps into my voice. Did I create this unease by mentioning the possibility of miscarriage?

"No. It's just, well, we could do both, ya know? I mean, I always hoped to have more than one kid." Sean stammers along. "And we might not be able to pull off another pregnancy again at our age. The adoption wouldn't come through for over a year. So..."

"Have one biological child and one adopted?" I know many families are structured this way, but still, it makes me uneasy. "What if..." I hesitate to say aloud what I'm thinking. What if we don't love them the same, treat them the same?

Sean squeezes my hand. "I know it's not so simple. But we don't have to decide right now. Let's just enjoy our happiness. Forget about the adoption agency for the time being. We don't have to take any action at all until they contact us about the home study."

"Right. Will you go with me to the doctor's appointment?"

Sean grins. "Nothing could keep me away." He stands up to clear the dishes and pauses beside my chair. "Do you honestly think the acupuncture worked? Is that why we got pregnant this month?"

I hand him a plate with the last four cauliflower florets I couldn't force down. "No way to be sure. But it is the one thing we did differently this month."

Sean gazes down at his mid-section. "Those little needles super-charged me!"

Chapter 19

Normally, I'd be on tenterhooks waiting to hear the response to Mr. Swenson's proposal to get us our commission without even selling *Your Move*, but excitement over the positive pregnancy test knocks every other concern from my mind. I'm a nervous wreck every time I go to the bathroom, fully expecting my period to start. But it doesn't.

I'm still pregnant.

Amazon delivers my copy of *What to Expect when You're Expecting*, and Sean and I take turns reading passages aloud to each other. I start feeling every symptom the book describes until Sean forbids me to read ahead any further.

Finally, we have our first doctor's appointment, a brief encounter in which Dr. McLaughlin asks some questions, draws some blood, and pronounces me fit for the challenge that lies ahead.

We're stunned by the obstetrician's blasé acceptance of the miracle we've achieved. "We'll see you back here next month for the ultrasound," she tells us.

"Is that when we see the heartbeat?"

The doctor pats Sean on the shoulder. "Yes, Dad. That's when this becomes really real."

After leaving the doctor's office, we head to Sean's parents' house to tell them the news. They're old hands—this will be their ninth grandchild—so I'm not expecting a huge reaction.

But Mary and Joe Coughlin surprise me.

Sean's sensible, no-fuss mother bursts into tears and flings her arms around Sean and then me, while his dad stands shaking his head and murmuring, "a miracle...bless my soul, a miracle."

Then we head over to visit my dad and Natalie.

In the middle of our excited recitation of our success story, my father gets up and leaves the room.

Sean and I stop talking. "What's wrong? Is he sick?" Sean asks.

Natalie smiles fondly at the closed bedroom door. "I think he's a little choked up, dear." She squeezes my hand. "You go to him."

Gingerly, I tap the door and enter. "Dad? Are you okay?"

He is lying on the bed with his back to me, his entire body wracked by sobs. I cross to him and sink to my knees beside the bed, taking his hand in mine. "What's wrong?"

"I'm sorry," he gasps. "I'm sorry for carrying on."

Carrying on is my father's least tolerated type of behavior. I learned at an early age not to carry on when I fell off my bike or didn't get invited to a party or lost my favorite stuffed animal. So I'm astonished to see him so overcome by emotion. I smooth the thin grey hair on the top of his head. "I understand. It's pretty amazing news after we've all been waiting so long."

He struggles to sit up and fumbles for a handkerchief in his pocket. I sit on the bed beside him, rumpling the taut blue quilt. He begins to talk with a shaky voice. "After we lost your mother, I went from being heartbroken to simply being numb. The last six years since we uncovered all our secrets and reconnected have been the happiest of my life. I didn't think I could dare hope for more. But I did want so much for you and Sean to have a baby." He looks at me with bloodshot eyes. "This is wrong, selfish of me to say. But I wanted you to have a biological child because, because...."

Tears slip down his cheeks.

"Because of my mother?" I whisper.

He nods. "I want a little part of her to live on. Despite everything, I still...."

He still loves her. Charlotte. The woman who has loomed over us my entire life. The woman who, when she was my age, was already long gone.

"Don't tell Natalie," Dad says, clutching my hand. "I don't want to hurt her with this unreasonable, irrational desire."

I wrap my arms around him. "I won't tell," I promise. But in my heart, I feel Natalie already knows. Their love, found so late in life, is steady and true. But I guess the irrational passion of youth never fully dies, much to my father's chagrin.

My hand slips to my tummy. Like it or not, a little piece of Charlotte Nealon ticks in there. I hope it's the joyful part that so attracted my father.

Not the dark part that caused us all so much pain.

My father has dried his tears, but he still seems unready to return to Sean and Natalie in the living room. I wait for him to say more.

"Do you think I'll be a good grandfather? I'm not like Joe."

Sean's father is a big man. The little grandchildren climb on him like he's a jungle gym and ride his leg like a horse. The older ones follow his advice on how to swing a bat, how to sink a shot. My father will do none of this. "You'll be a wonderful grandfather. You'll read your grandchildren books, and teach them chess, and show them caterpillars and toads and hummingbirds when you go on walks. And when they get older, they'll bring you their problems and you'll listen. You're a good listener."

Dad gives me a shaky smile.

"Our baby is lucky to have two wonderful and very different grandfathers." I stand and hold out my hand. "Now let's get back to the party."

Dad springs up with surprising vigor. "I daresay Natalie has broken out her secret stash of morning glory muffins. I hope Sean hasn't eaten them all."

Chapter 20

I know that Ty and Donna will have very different reactions to my news, so I want to tell them separately. Ty has been with me longest. We've been through so much together. So he gets the honor of hearing the news first. And the perfect opportunity presents itself when Donna leaves early on Tuesday for a dentist appointment.

With Donna gone, the office settles into a peaceful quiet. Ty is prepping for a sale two weeks in the future, so he's busy firing off emails while I crunch numbers, analyzing our projected income for the next year. I've accepted that I'll probably be utterly useless to Another Man's Treasure for several months, so I'm developing a plan for how Ty and Donna can keep the business running without me.

Scary. But exciting.

"Ty? I need your advice on something," I begin.

He looks up from his laptop.

"If I were out of the office from February through April, would you be able to take the lead on all the sales?"

He scratches his head and squints one eye. "Where you goin'?"

"Oh, I'll be home. Available by phone. Just not here or at the sales." I smile at his confusion and cross the office to stand in front of his desk. "I'm pregnant."

Ty leaps up so fast his desk chair falls over. He grabs me by the shoulders and looks me up and down. "No way. No way! You look just the same."

I laugh. "I'm only in my second month. I have a long way to go."

Ty pulls me into his arms and hugs me so tight I can barely breathe. "You'll be the best mother," he murmurs into my hair.

When we finally pull apart, Ty pulls a tissue from the box on Donna's desk and blows his nose. "Man." He crumples the tissue. "Man, oh man." When the shock subsides, he breaks out some hip-hop moves. "Imma be an uncle again! Oh, baby, I'm yo' uncle. You hear it, I'm yo' uncle."

A phone call interrupts our rowdy celebration. I'm about to let it roll to voicemail, but I answer when I realize it's Mr. Swenson. I wave Ty into silence and put the lawyer on speakerphone.

"Audrey, Mrs. Aronson has accepted our offer."

"The initial offer?" I may be suffering from pregnancy brain, but I don't recall authorizing a counteroffer.

"Yes, the full ten thousand dollars. I admit, I was rather taken aback."

No one does understatement better than Mr. Swenson. The same cannot be said for Ty. "Holy shit! Pearl's givin' us ten K to *not* sell her painting?"

"You can expect the money in your account tomorrow," Mr. Swenson says. "She plans to have the painting moved to storage at that time."

I thank Mr. Swenson for his help and hang up. "Well..." I extend my hands towards Ty. "...a surprising end to an offbeat sale."

"There you go, talkin' like Isabelle. You ask me, the whole thing is freakin' weird."

Weird is right. I can't believe Pearl is so hellbent on getting that painting out of the public eye that she'd pay us our opening offer without even trying to bargain. Why is this outcome so important to her? "I know you're disappointed about the painting going into storage still damaged," I tell Ty, "but I don't think we had much choice."

"This is best for the business. After all," he points to my belly, "we got a baby to put through college." Ty pulls out my desk chair. "You should be sittin' down. And no more carryin' heavy boxes or going up and down stairs a million times. And no breathing in mold in basements, you hear me?"

I laugh, but I suspect he's putting on this little schtick to cover his pain at the sad end of *Your Move*. "The painting will come back on the market someday," I assure him. "Pearl's heirs won't hesitate to sell it."

Ty purses his lips and nods. "Probably true. After all, they're still finding statues from ancient Rome buried in farmers' fields and paintings looted during the Holocaust in people's attics. I guess we gotta hope *Your Move* gets found in a self-storage unit in New Jersey after Pearl dies."

Ty performs a gravity-defying stretch. "I can't complain. I got to see a great painting close up and meet people who knew the artist personally." He peeks over the stack of boxes in the corner. "And that trip to Hillside got me Lo's BlastMaster."

Five Months Later...

Chapter 21

"Ugh," I rest my hand on my huge stomach. "Heartburn. I should never have had that pumpkin pie."

"I'll get you some seltzer," my sister-in-law Adrienne offers.

"Or would you rather have ginger tea?" Deirdre asks, hovering over me in her kitchen. The Coughlin women are cleaning up after Thanksgiving dinner while the Coughlin men watch football. Normally, I'm outraged by this division of labor, but this year, I've been forbidden to lift a finger so it would be churlish to complain about sexism.

"Congratulations!" Deirdre's neighbor has popped over, and she smiles at my baby bump. "Do you know if you're having a boy or a girl?"

"One of each. We're having twins. Their names are Thea and Aiden."

Her jaw drops and she clutches her hands over her heart. "How lucky! They'll be best friends forever."

Every time I tell someone this news, I relive the moment when Sean and I first saw two heartbeats on the ultrasound. We gripped hands tightly as the technician waved the wand over my belly. "There." She pointed to a tiny blip flashing like a lightening bug, and we grinned with joy. Then the technician said, "oh."

Just that one syllable and fear engulfed us. "What? What?" we chorused. "What's wrong?"

"Nothing's wrong." She smiled at us. "There's a second heartbeat right there. Twins."

Just like that we went from winning the lottery to hitting the Mega Millions Jackpot.

And every reaction since then has been priceless.

Grandma Betty: "Praise Jesus!"

Sean's mother: makes the sign of the cross.

Donna: "I'll get them the cutest matching outfits!"

Dad: "What are the odds of that?"

Deirdre: "Don't panic. I'll find you an extra set of everything."

"How are you doing with your Christmas shopping, Audrey?" my mother-in-law enquires as she parcels out turkey leftovers into ziplock bags.

"Haven't even started. I've been so busy getting through these last few estate sales before the holidays."

Sean's mother presses her lips into a disapproving line. I'm not sure what offends her more—late Christmas shopping or my continued attention to my business.

Deirdre stops scrubbing pots and puts her hands on her hips. "When are you going to start your maternity leave now that the doctor says you'll deliver in January?"

My obstetrician has revised my original February 16 due date. She says I'll never make it to the full forty weeks with twins. She's aiming now for January 15, when I'll be 36 weeks along. "We don't have any sales scheduled between Thanksgiving and Christmas. I'll work on the books from home." I don't mention my intention to pop into the office for a few hours every week just to check on Ty and Donna.

And to get out of the house. Life as a beached whale is boring and a little lonely. But I'm not complaining.

"Well, you shouldn't...."

All the women in the room launch into their favorite pregnancy advice, each contradicting the other. I smile and nod and tune them out. I do plan to start my Christmas shopping tomorrow—one hundred percent online—and I begin mentally composing a gift list.

When there's a break in the tsunami of childbearing advice, I take the opportunity to change the subject. "What do the kids want for Christmas, Deirdre?"

She lifts her hands to heaven. "I don't know what to tell you. All they talk about is that damn BlastMaster. But it's sold out everywhere."

Another tidal wave gathers force. "People are selling them on eBay for seven hundred dollars!" Even extravagant Adrienne is horrified.

"I told my kids, the day your dad spends four hundred fifty dollars over the list price for a toy is the day hell freezes over," Deirdre says. "I'm preparing them now, so they know there's not a chance there'll be a BlastMaster under the tree."

"I'd never buy one on eBay," Sean's mother says. "I read there's a bunch of counterfeit BlastMasters being sold by people online. The box looks the same, but when the kids plug them in, they don't work."

My ears perk up. "Is that real news or just a rumor going around?"

"It's real." Deirdre's neighbor nods authoritatively. "Channel 4 News interviewed a mom and a heartbroken kid who got a fake for his birthday."

I feel queasy and not because of my pregnancy. Ty bought his BlastMaster months ago. Surely his is okay, right?

But he bought it from some dude on the street in Hillside. That can't be good.

"Are the police investigating where the fakes are coming from?" I ask.

My mother-in-law wags her head mournfully. "One of those strange foreign countries."

That means any country that's not Ireland.

"Romania? Albania? Ukraine? Someplace like that," Deirdre says. "Who wants pumpkin pie to take home and who wants pecan?"

Chapter 22

I spend Black Friday afternoon Christmas shopping from the comfort of my sofa while Sean watches more football with his brothers in front of Brendan's ultra-wide screen TV. He'll be maxed out by dinnertime, when we have a date to visit our friends Peter and Noreen to fuss over their newly adopted baby. Lucas is five months old now, and his head is symmetrical, his cheeks round and smooth, and his dome covered with downy blond curls. Sean and I are relieved that we can gush over him sincerely.

Despite our twin pregnancy, Sean is still reluctant to withdraw our adoption application. I suspect he harbors a desire to have five kids, but I'll wager that once the reality of taking care of two sets in, his desire will change. In the meantime, I'm too happy to argue about anything.

I prop my feet up with my laptop on my knees and start shopping. First, books for everyone on my list—we're a family of readers. Next, some treats: a turquoise and amber necklace from Etsy for Natalie, a cozy fleece from REI for Sean, a pair of house slippers with good arch support for Dad, a blouse for Sean's mother that's less plain and sensible than her usual choices. Then the toys: craft kits, board games, Lego sets—I know my gifts won't produce the most squeals on Christmas morning, but I hope they'll be the ones that provide some lasting entertainment on sleety winter days.

With the easy gifts out of the way, I settle into the challenges. First, a Secret Santa gift for the annual holiday gathering of my girlfriends. Ugh—it's so hard to be clever and creative and keep it under twenty dollars. Inspiration isn't striking, so I move on to Ty and Donna. Of course, I give them both a Christmas cash bonus, but I like to add something personal as well. Donna is easy. She keeps up a running line of chatter at the office about things she wants to get to decorate her condo. Every week she agonizes over buying something and then passes it up to wait for it to go on sale.

And then cries when the item sells out.

I find the placemats and napkins she was pining over at Williams Sonoma last week and click "buy". I gloat over the warning "only two left in stock."

Ty is harder. He loves sharp clothes to wear when he goes out on the town, but I'm not hip enough to make the right choice. However, I do know his favorite brands, so I copy links to three shirts and forward them to Ty's cousin Marcus to get guidance on the final selection.

Exhausted from typing my credit card number and PayPal password so many times, I take a break and surf social media for a while. Instagram is full of people's perfectly decorated trees. Too much pressure! I switch over to Twitter.

Oh, no—#FakeBlastMaster is trending. The thread is full of horror stories about people who thought they got lucky and instead got scammed. The tweets are illustrated with pictures of crying kids, broken toys, furious purchasers...and close-ups of the counterfeit box.

Signs to look for—one side is printed lighter than the others.

I massage my temples. Not good. Not good at all.

Quickly, I text Donna because she's the one with her finger on the pulse of social media. *Have you seen all this news about fake BlastMasters?*

Yeah...but don't you worry about it.

How can I help but worry? Ty's heart is about to be broken. I stop texting and call Donna.

She answers immediately with a furtive, "hullo?"

"I'm sorry—am I interrupting your family time? It's just—"

"I'm not with my family," Donna says. "I'm at the office. I just had to come here and check. Oh, Audrey—I'm sure this is a fake one. The box is partly faded like the pictures people have been sharing. What are we gonna d-o-o-o?"

"Maybe he won't hear about it until Monday."

"No, he's already heard. He's on his way over to the office. That's why I'm here. I didn't want to tell you because it's not good for you to worry."

"I'm on my way."

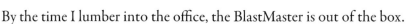

By the time I lumber into the office, the BlastMaster is out of the box.

Indeed, it lies scattered in a million pieces, a victim of Ty's furious stomping feet.

"Imma find the guy who sold me this piece of shit and I'm gonna kill him."

I throw myself in front of the door to block his exit. "Calm down. This stupid toy isn't worth getting arrested over. There's a Facebook page and a Twitter thread where you can post a warning about where you bought your fake so other people don't get burned. That's the best revenge."

"It is not! I don't care what happens to other people tryin' to buy one. I care that now I don't have a BlastMaster to give to Lo on Christmas." Ty's fury echoes around the office. "Knowing that I had this one kept me from trying to find one in a store. Now it's too late. I got nuthin.'"

Donna and I exchange a furtive glance. Only an idiot would be foolish enough to point out that Ty shouldn't have bought this toy on the street in the first place. I take a different approach. "Ty, Lo doesn't even know about Blast-Master. He hasn't been asking for it, so he'll never know he missed out. Buy him something else."

Ty's face is blotchy, his eyes narrowed, his fists clenched. I haven't seen him this angry since he found out Donna's ex hit her. He stands in the middle of the office, breathing rapidly.

"Ty?" Donna begins cautiously. "You didn't promise Lo he was getting a BlastMaster, did you?"

"I...I told him he maybe should ask Santa for it," Ty mutters.

Santa. Who came up with this concept of a guy who will give you anything your heart desires? Things your parents can't afford. Ponies and puppies and monkeys your parents can't house. Just ask the fat man in red! Oh, but there's a catch...if you're good. So now if sweet little Lo doesn't get this stupid toy, he'll think it's because he fell short, is undeserving. I rest my hand on my stomach as I feel the twins kick. Can I opt them out of Santa Claus altogether?

"There's still three weeks until Christmas," I tell Ty. "That's an eternity to a little kid. Lo will change his mind about what he wants ten times between now and Christmas morning. Just don't mention BlastMaster to him again. And listen to the other toys he's talking about."

"Get outta my way, Audge," Ty moves me gently but firmly aside and heads into the cold. "Ain't nobody gonna take me for a fool."

"Killing the guy who cheated you isn't going to get Lo a BlastMaster," I shout after him.

And having his uncle arrested sure isn't going to make anyone's Christmas happier.

Chapter 23

I'm a nervous wreck for the rest of Thanksgiving weekend. Ty only answers a couple of the many pleading texts I send him, but it's enough for me to know that he hasn't given up his quest for revenge on the BlastMaster scammer.

But also enough for me to know he hasn't been arrested.

Yet.

On Monday morning, Ty shows up at the office with a full run-down of his activities.

"I went back to the bar where I met the guy who gave me the lead on the fake BlastMaster. Of course, it's too hot for him there now—he's blown town. Turns out, I'm not the only angry dude lookin' for his sorry ass. So, I got to talkin' to one of the other guys who got scammed. We compared notes on how our deals went down." Ty leans back and links his hands behind his head. "The guy in the bar gave both of us a number to text. The number's disconnected now—probably a burner phone. We both got messages telling us where to bring the cash." Ty pauses and looks into my eyes to make sure he's got my full attention. "We compared our messages and they both had the same, like, errors. 'Bring cash. Put in mailbox. Go around corner. Is waiting the box.'"

I wrinkle my nose. "You expect criminals to text in complete, grammatical sentences?"

Ty leans forward and puts his hands on the edge of my desk. "The message sounds weird—like it wasn't written by an American. I think it sounds like this kid who used to be in my Econ class."

"What? You think a student from Palmer Community College is selling hot BlastMasters in Hillside?" Ty has really lost his marbles.

"No, no—I mean the message sounds like the way this kid talked. He'd always say to the teacher, 'Is right, this answer?' or 'When is test' instead of 'When is *the* test? And this kid was Ukrainian."

"Ok-a-ay. I've heard the fake toys come from somewhere in Eastern Europe, but...." I still don't understand why Ty thinks he's the Hercule Poirot of Blast-Master investigations.

"The guy at the Speedy Mart had that same accent. We thought he was Russian, but a Ukrainian accent sounds the same. And the nasty guys who bought Irv's factory? I called Eugene and he says they're Ukrainian."

"New Jersey has a lot of immigrants, Ty—we're the most diverse state in the country. And immigrants of one nationality tend to settle close together. So the fact that there are Ukrainian criminals in the same neighborhood where there are Ukrainian-owned businesses isn't all that surprising."

Ty purses his lips and bobs his head. "We'll see. We'll just see where this leads."

I cradle my belly with both hands, my new reflex to worrisome news. I don't have the emotional bandwidth to worry about Ty right now. I'm pregnant. It's Christmas. I'm planning for my maternity leave. "Ty, please, I'm begging you—if you have suspicions, report them to the police."

"I'm not confessin' to the cops that I bought a black market BlastMaster." His voice rises as if I suggested he tell the TSA screener at airport security he's got two guns in his carry-on.

"Oh, please—thousands of people have bought these fakes. The cops aren't going to arrest everyone who was conned. And you bought yours months ago. You must've been one of the first victims. Maybe that would help the police." I reach for my phone. "I'm going to ask Sean if the police have some sort of tip line set up to collect leads."

"You do what you need to do." Ty jumps up and heads for the door. "I'll do what I need to do."

I decide to wait until dinnertime to ask Sean about the tip line. He's eager for me to start working from home, and if I tell him that Ty has been at the office getting me agitated, he'll up the pressure. The weeks between Thanksgiving and Christmas are always slow, and I spend them running end-of-the year financial reports, preparing for tax season, and lining up sales for January.

All tasks that I can easily do from home.

But I prefer working here.

I look around at my surroundings—I no longer even notice the water stain on the ceiling and the flaking paint above the front door. Scooting around the pile of junk awaiting dispatch has become second nature although more challenging now that I have a beach ball attached to my midsection. The AMT office is a dump, but it's my dump. My cozy, reassuring dump. I suppose I won't miss it when I've got two infants to care for, but I'm in no hurry to abandon the place to sit in my house all alone.

As if to demonstrate the benefits of working at the office, a text from Isabelle arrives.

I'm right around the corner. Can I drop by?

I tell her I'd love to see her and then start worrying about the mess surrounding me. After three good pushes I manage to get myself out of my desk chair and lumber around to the visitor's chair, where I dust some crumbs off the seat and move a pile of folders from the end table. As long as I'm upright, I might as well put on the tea kettle.

After a light tap at the door, Isabelle enters. I notice her eyes widen before she speaks. "Hello, darling. Don't you look blooming!" She moves to hug me but can't figure out how.

I laugh and settle for a hand squeeze. "I know I'm shockingly huge. Have a seat—I'm fixing us some tea."

Isabelle shrugs off her elegant overcoat. "I haven't seen you for a few weeks." Accepting the mug of tea, she scans me up and down. "Are you feeling okay?"

"I feel great."

Isabelle puts on the dubious expression I see when clients tell her they'll be able to declutter their homes without assistance. Clearly, she doesn't think any woman with a sixty-inch waist could possibly feel well. I have no idea if Isabelle has ever wanted children. At forty-two, her biological clock is ticking, but so far as I know, she doesn't even have a serious boyfriend. Isabelle has never confided much about her personal life.

She crosses one slender leg over the other, letting her high-heeled pump dangle. "I'm here because I'm positively flummoxed by this Secret Santa gift we have to buy for the holiday party at Lydia's. How can I possibly buy a gift without knowing who it's for?"

The five women attending the party are all very different. It's hard to imagine one gift that would be equally appropriate for intellectual, disheveled Roz and immaculate, practical Isabelle. "I think the gift exchange was Madalyn's idea. Maybe we should each buy a scented candle, sit in a circle, and it pass it to the left."

"I can see you're no further along with this than I am." She glances at her phone, which rarely stops vibrating, but declines the call. "I suppose I'll have to wing it."

I smile because Isabelle's the least wing-y person I know. She has a plan for all life's emergencies, from water in the basement to bats in the attic. "I think Madalyn came up with the gift exchange as a fun party activity. Buy something we can all laugh at."

Isabelle throws her hands up. "You're adding more pressure, Audrey. Now I have to find a gift that's both universal and entertaining."

"To be honest, gift-giving makes me anxious, too. I want to get the people I love something thoughtful and a little extravagant. But one person's thoughtful and extravagant is another's weird and useless."

Isabelle's mouth twitches with a rueful smile. "You must've seen the electric corkscrew my college roommate sent me last year."

"You're not alone. Every estate sale I've ever run is full of unused gifts that clearly missed the mark." I shift in my chair, in the never-ending struggle to find a position where the babies aren't pressing on my bladder. "A good gift sends the message, 'I know you. I get you.' So when we get a bad gift, it makes us feel like we're not really seen by the people who are supposed to love us."

This conversation has grown awfully philosophical. I try to lighten it up. "What are you doing for Christmas?" It dawns on me that I have no idea if Isabelle has family nearby. I could invite her to come to our place on Christmas day. Sean and I are making dinner for Dad and Natalie.

"I'm going to Grand Cayman. I always take a beach vacation at Christmas." Isabelle stands and reaches for her coat. "It's the slowest time of the year for real estate."

My question seems to have scared her off. Isabelle doesn't say if she's traveling alone or not, and I don't ask. Another mystery. There's one more thing I want to know before Isabelle leaves. "I see that you finally got your price for Pearl Aronson's house. Have the new owners moved in yet?"

"Last month. They waited until the painters scraped all that red flocked wallpaper off the foyer walls." Isabelle shudders. "It took weeks."

"And Pearl has moved to Palm Beach?"

"She must have. She didn't even stay for the closing. She departed Palmyrton as soon as the painting went into storage." Isabelle ducks into our rest room to rinse out her mug but keeps talking. "However, she called me last week. Left a message that she needed to ask me something."

"Oh?"

Isabelle sets her mug next to the tea kettle and turns to face me. "Why are you so interested in Pearl? I thought her payment to you was a fair solution."

"I'm not complaining about the money," I assure Isabelle. "I just can't stop wondering what caused her to insist on putting the painting in storage."

I know that Isabelle is just as much a student of human nature as I am. She has to be in order to do her job as well as she does. She's good at perceiving the small, unspoken fears that keep people from committing to a house purchase. And she knows that both buyers and sellers will sometimes latch onto a perceived injustice to torpedo a deal. I watch my friend as she ponders my question.

"I think it might have something to do with Irv, with doing what Irv would've wanted. That's why Pearl was so stubborn about the asking price for the house even though she didn't need the money—she was following his wishes." Isabelle holds her hands palms-up. "Irv died suddenly, and that made Pearl realize she also could go at any time. I guess she doesn't want to reunite with Irv on the other side and find out he's mad at her."

"So what did Pearl want to ask you?" I persist.

"We haven't connected—I called back and got her voicemail."

"Well, find out before the party at Lydia's," I tell Isabelle as she heads to the door. Getting up to escort her out seems above and beyond the call of duty.

She laughs with her hand on the doorknob. "You're incorrigible, Audrey. I would think impending motherhood would slow down your mystery-solving impulses."

"Pregnancy doesn't kill a woman's curiosity."

Chapter 24

After dinner, I tell Sean an edited version of Ty's experiences tracking down the scammer who sold him the fake BlastMaster. "He met another person who also bought one and they compared notes. Ty suspects from the wording of the text messages they both received that the counterfeiters are Ukrainian. Who should he call to report it? Do the police have some sort of tip line?"

"This isn't a case for the local cops. We're just handling the fall-out from angry victims," Sean explains as he scrolls through the TV channels. "The FBI handles investigations of counterfeit goods."

"The FBI! How would Ty go about contacting them?" I can't imagine looking up a phone number for the FBI and telling whoever answers I have a lead on a fake toy.

"I can find him the contact person. From what I hear, the Feds really have a big investigation going on. The market is flooded with thousands of fake Blast-Masters, and the company that makes the real toy is furious their brand is being undermined."

"So when Ty bought his back in June, maybe it really wasn't a matter of dockworkers diverting a few toys from a shipment."

Sean stops clicking the remote. "Good point. Maybe the scammers were testing the waters five months ago. Now they've got the counterfeiting operation in full swing."

"Can Ty call the FBI tip line anonymously? He's worried he'll get in trouble with law enforcement for buying a hot BlastMaster."

"Nothing to fear," Sean assures me. "Hell, there are plenty of guys I work with who got sucked into buying one. Most of them knew full well the transaction wasn't legit. In fact..." Sean looks down and mutes the sound on the TV.

"What? Don't tell me you bought one?"

"No, but for one crazy moment, I was tempted." Sean looks at me sheepishly. "For Terry's kids. You know Terry and Alison struggle every Christmas."

Sean's brother Terry is perpetually in and out of work, leaving the support of the family to his long-suffering wife. Sean and his siblings do what they can to help make life easier for the kids. "So you were going to buy Terry's kids a BlastMaster? You know Deirdre's and Brendan's kids want one, too."

"I know. But the others will have a happy Christmas no matter what. Terry's kids...well, there's always so much stress in their family. I thought maybe...."

"You could buy them a morning of joy?" I snuggle into the crook of my husband's arm. "What made you decide not to go for it?"

"I listened to the other guys buzzing about getting a deal on BlastMaster. Bring cash...wait for a text...be prepared to drive off at a moment's notice to pick it up. It sounded too sketchy to me."

"Your instincts were correct. Ty also knew the deal was sketchy, but he went ahead and bought the toy anyway back in June. Now he's mad as a hornet."

"Because he lost two hundred bucks—that would bother me, too."

"It's more than the money. He blames the scammers for diverting his attention from getting a real BlastMaster. He started looking for one back in May. If he had kept calling the legit stores every day, eventually he would have hit on a day when they got a new shipment. Instead, he was impatient and got burned."

"Twenty-twenty hindsight," Sean observes. "He needs to let it go."

"Agreed. I told him the best he can do now is contribute to the effort to catch these guys. I'll let him know you said he has nothing to fear by coming forward."

Sean clicks off the TV and picks up a book. "I'll send you the FBI contact info as soon as I get to the office tomorrow."

"What happens when someone calls a tip line?" I figure I'd better know as much as possible to persuade Ty.

"There's a low-level person screening the calls, weeding out the crackpots, asking preliminary questions. If you say something interesting, they flag it up to a higher ranking investigator."

"Do you think the fact that Ty bought his fake way back in June would be significant to the FBI? He must be one of the first to get scammed. His purchase must've been the beginning of the counterfeit operation."

Sean arches his eyebrows as he finds his place in *We are Legion*. "Could be."

As promised, Sean texts me the FBI contact info by the time I arrive at work. Ty blows in a few minutes later, and I assault him before he even has his coat off.

"Sean says the FBI is running a big investigation into the counterfeit Blast-Masters. You need to call their tip line and tell them everything you know about the guy in Hillside." I keep talking as he opens his mouth to protest. "Sean says not to worry. People who bought the fakes aren't getting into any trouble. The FBI is only interested in finding out the source of the counterfeit toys."

Ty fixes me with the prison death stare.

"Seriously, Ty—you need to help them catch these guys before even more people get scammed." I fumble with my phone. "I'm sending you the FBI contact info right now."

"In what universe would I *ever* be an FBI informant?"

"Do it for the little kids," Donna chimes in. "Your help could prevent more Christmas morning disappointment."

I know Donna meant well, but she said exactly the wrong thing. Ty's face flushes a muddy maroon as he thinks about a BlastMasterless Lo on Christmas morning.

"Imma find those lowdown snakes myself. I don't need the help of no fancy-ass Federal agents with wires in their ears."

Argh! Pleading and threatening will never work. I need a new approach. "Maybe if you talk to the FBI, you can learn something from them."

Ty sits at his desk and turns on his laptop. "They're not going to tell me anything about their investigation."

"No, not intentionally. But maybe if you tell them what you know, you'll learn something from watching their reactions. Maybe you can tell how close they are to cracking the case."

Ty purses his lips and studies his email inbox with great concentration.

"It's worth a try," I cajole. "I'll go with you."

He looks up. "Whoa, whoa—What makes you think they'll want to talk to me in person?"

"Maybe they will, maybe they won't. Sean says they screen the calls and if you have significant information, they might want to talk to you. Shall I call and just give them the basics and see what they say?"

Ty bangs his fist on the desk. "Why do you have such a bug up your—" He takes a deep breath and lowers his voice. "Why are you so determined to make me talk to the FBI?"

"Because I'm worried about you, Ty. I don't want you to get in trouble for tracking down the guy who scammed you and messing him up."

"I wouldn't actually hurt him," Ty mutters. "I just want to scare him. Let him know I'm pissed. That he scammed the wrong guy."

"Oh, and that couldn't possibly go wrong?" My voice escalates in a challenge. I feel Donna watching us like we're in the final volley at the US Open. "What if he pulls a knife or a gun on you? Then what are you going to do?"

Ty flings himself back in his desk chair. "Fine. Fine. Call the damn FBI tip line."

"Great!" I smile cheerfully and whip out my phone before he can change his mind. Before long, I'm speaking to an agent who is clearly reading from a list of questions. I provide my profile data as Ty pretends disinterest while listening to the conversation on speakerphone. We go through a few more queries to establish our BlastMaster is definitely fake, and I explain that it belongs to my employee, not me. This doesn't seem to concern the FBI agent until we get to the next question: when and where was the fake purchased? As soon as I tell him June in Hillside, I hear his voice change from bored to intrigued. He wants me to describe the encounter. I tell him the man seemed to have a Ukrainian accent.

Now Ty is fully engaged. He wants to tell his own story and approaches the phone lying on my desk. Before long, he's telling the agent the story of his fake BlastMaster acquisition.

"I believe Supervisory Special Agent Magee will want to interview you in person regarding this encounter, Mr. Griggs. You can expect a confirmation call later today."

We hang up and Ty lays his head on the desk. "Why did I let you get me mixed up in this, Audge?"

Chapter 25

I leave the office before four to head to Min Wei's clinic for my weekly appointment. My obstetrician smiled indulgently when I told her that acupuncture is what succeeded in getting me pregnant, but she doesn't object to my continuing treatment as long as I don't miss any of my traditional pre-natal appointments. Min Wei is treating my lower back pain and swollen ankles. Plus, her huge recliners are a great place for a pregnant woman to take a nap.

After an hour, I wake from my treatment and my nap feeling so energized that I decide to walk to my father's place for a quick visit before I go home. I haven't seen him since before Thanksgiving as he and Natalie spent the holiday with her son in Boston.

When I arrive, I allow them to fuss over me as I provide an update on my health and the development of their future grandchildren. Then the conversation turns to my maternity leave and the latest news at Another Man's Treasure. I fill them in on Ty's BlastMaster catastrophe.

Natalie scratches her head. "I forget—what took him to Hillside in the first place?"

I recap the story of *Your Move* and how it ended up in storage despite our efforts.

"The story of that painting is fascinating," Dad says.

"Yes, I'd love to see it," Natalie agrees. "How tragic that we probably never will."

"You can see a photo of it," I say, pulling out my iPad. "Not quite the same, but it will give you a sense of Thurman's style.

Dad and Natalie crowd around me as I call up the photo of *Your Move*. I show them the full image, then zoom in on the details I like best. "Look at the expression on the old woman's face as she leans out the window, watching the girls jump rope. And this is the figure that got blacked out. Thurman knew the young man personally. And see the intense concentration on the faces of the chess players? Look, Dad—I know you recognize the opening they're playing."

My father pulls the iPad from my hand to study the players and the board between them. He lets the device drop into his lap as he stares at the ceiling, biting his lower lip.

"What's wrong?"

Dad taps the screen. "I know that fellow. Played him in a tournament years ago."

"Really? You're sure?" If one or both of the chess players are real people who are still alive, maybe we can finally get some information on the meaning of the painting.

"I'm sure that's the man I played. See, he has half of his left middle finger missing. And he moves the pieces with his left hand. That's why I remember him."

"Wow!" I enlarge the player's hand until it fills half the screen. Dad is right—the middle finger is amputated above the joint. "I never even noticed that tiny detail."

Dad cradles his chin in his hand. "Now, if I could just remember his name. Clarence? Clyde?" Dad sits bolt upright. "Clive! Clive Lorriss. He was ranked 75th in the United States back in the eighties. We played a tournament at Princeton."

Dad beams, clearly proud of this feat of memory. "I wonder where he is now? He was a few years older than me." Dad gets a dreamy look in his eye. "A very iconoclastic player. I wouldn't mind playing him again."

"You should reach out to him, dear." Natalie pats Dad's hand. She's always encouraging him to widen his social network to keep his mind sharp.

"Want me to see if he's on Facebook?" I offer.

"Pah! I don't need that nonsense," my father scoffs. "The man was once a ranked player. I can find him through the International Chess Federation."

I give my father a peck on the cheek as I prepare to leave. "I'm glad my visit put you on track to find an old friend."

Dad responds with a crafty smile. "Clive is an old opponent. It remains to be seen whether he'll want to take up the challenge again."

Chapter 26

Ty arrives at the office early the next morning with the news that Supervisory Special Agent Magee will be visiting us shortly. He'd called Ty last evening to say that he would be in our vicinity conducting interviews today and suggested he could come to Ty's apartment.

Ty countered with an offer to meet him here.

Or not at all.

As Ty tells it, "No freakin' way was I lettin' a crew of Feebiees into my *home*."

"Donna will be sorry she missed it," I say with a laugh. "She's off running errands."

Ty points a long finger at me. "Don't you plan on leavin'. I want some support here."

I wonder if Magee will be okay with that, but we'll see how it plays out.

Minutes later, Magee and his assistant arrive. The two of them are straight from Central Casting—painfully short hair, squinty eyes, chiseled chins. If it weren't for the rainstorm of Biblical proportions going on outside, I'm sure they'd both be wearing mirrored dark glasses.

"Is there some place we can speak privately?" Magee asks Ty.

Ty spreads his hands to encompass the one-room chaos that is the AMT office. "What you see is what you get."

Magee scowls as he looks at me in all my pregnant glory and at the pelting rain outside the window. Then his gaze zeroes in on the broken down faux Japanese folding screen in the corner.

"We can unfold the screen," I offer sweetly. I've kept it in hopes that I'd one day need it for breast-feeding privacy, and I was right.

Magee's assistant sets the screen up between my desk and Ty's, and I make a show of typing industriously. Me, nosey? Never!

Of course, we all know that I can still hear everything, but I guess Magee is reassured that I can't send Ty furtive warning glances or hand signals, even though I have no reason to. As useless as the screen is, I suspect setting it up allows Magee to assert his control over the interview.

Magee begins by re-asking all the questions the guy manning the tip line asked. Then he moves into new territory. "So, Mr. Griggs, you live and work in Palmyrton. What took you to Hillside?"

"That's a long story," Ty explains. "I was looking for a guy connected to an estate sale we were working on. And while I was looking for him, I met the BlastMaster dude."

"And who was this guy you were looking for?"

"He's got nothing to do with the BlastMaster. He once worked for our estate sale client."

I can tell that Ty doesn't want to drag poor Eugene into the FBI investigation, but his caginess is making Magee press even harder. After more back and forth, Ty starts at the beginning and explains the sale, the visit by Eugene and Thurman's relatives, the damage to *Your Move*, and our desire to get some help from Eugene to persuade Pearl to let us sell it. Periodically, I remember to type a little so I sound busy, but I'm listening to every word.

Through Ty's long soliloquy, I can hear the steady scratching of a pen on paper and the rapid flip of pages as one of the agents takes notes. Ty concludes by saying he tracked down Eugene by asking around various neighborhood bars in Hillside, and that's where he encountered the BlastMaster con man.

"And this painting—who owns it?" Magee asks.

"Pearl Aronson, our estate sale client."

"She bought it from the artist?" Magee clarifies.

"No, her husband, Irv Aronson bought it. But he's dead now." Ty pauses. "Why you askin' about the painting?"

Magee ignores Ty's question and continues his inquiries. First, he clarifies that Eugene used to work for Irv when Irv own the factory. Then he continues, "Did the man who offered to get you a BlastMaster hear you asking about Eugene Caldwell?"

That's an odd question. I roll my desk chair a couple of inches and position myself so I can see through a small tear in one of the panels of the screen. I can make out part of Magee's face in profile. He's leaning forward, looking at Ty with intense interest.

"Uhm, I dunno, probably." Ty scrunches his face in thought. "I was asking people standing at the bar—there were only six or seven people in the whole joint. Then someone further down the bar mentioned they wanted to buy a BlastMaster but couldn't find one. Then I said, 'yeah, me too—you got any leads on what stores have them?' And that's when the con man came up to me and the other guy who wanted a BlastMaster."

"What is the name of this establishment where you met?" Magee asks.

"I wouldn't call it an establishment. It's a hole-in-the wall dive bar. Doesn't have a name that I noticed. Just a couple neon beer signs out front." Ty grins at the agents. "You two wanna visit there, you better find a brutha to go with you."

Magee stares fiercely at Ty, unamused by the advice. "And did you ultimately get the information on Eugene Caldwell's location from someone at this bar?"

"Why you so interested in Eugene?" Ty challenges Magee assertively. "He's got nuthin' to do with this BlastMaster con. He's a nice, retired grandpa."

Magee didn't come here for opinions. He wants the facts, and nothing but the facts. He repeats the question.

"Yeah—it was like a twofer. I located Eugene and got a chance for a Blast-Master." Ty answers with a peevish edge in his voice. "Except the second half turned out to be not such a good deal, as you know."

Next Magee peppers Ty with questions about the appearance of the con-man who approached him, his words, and his accent. Ty tells him the man had light brown hair, pale skin, and light gray eyes. He spoke with an accent that Ty insists is Ukrainian. The FBI agent reviews the information several times, I suppose to see if Ty will remain consistent.

He does.

Ty is getting restless. I can tell from the long squeak of his desk chair that Ty is shifting and stretching his long, lean body. "We about done here? I got work to do today."

Magee stands. "We appreciate your assistance, Mr. Griggs. One last question. How close was this unnamed bar to the factory once owned by Irv Aronson?"

"Couldn't really say. Hillside's not that big a town, and the streets are like a rat maze. Probably not too far."

I hear the door open. "Thank you. We may be back in touch."

"Wait!" Ty says. "How close are you to breakin' up this ring? Is the guy who scammed me goin' down?"

"We have several promising leads. I'm confident of a good outcome." The door slams behind the two agents.

Instantly, I pop out from behind the screen. Ty stands scowling at the door. "That's a bullshit answer."

"Oh, they never reveal what they've got until after they make the arrests," I reassure him. "I thought the interview went well. He didn't give you a hard time about anything."

"Hmmph. How come he was sniffin' around Eugene? I don't want that poor old dude gettin' hassled because of me."

"I agree, Magee's interest in Irv, his factory, and Eugene came from out of left field." I do a few of my pregnancy stretches to help my sore back. The effects of yesterday's acupuncture treatment have already worn off. "Do you think there could be a connection between Irv's factory and the BlastMaster con?"

"Those agents were definitely interested in what took me to Hillside." Ty chews on his lower lip as he thinks. "Maybe you were right, Audge. I did learn something from those Feds. I think Hillside might be ground zero for the Blast-Master scam."

Chapter 27

"Dear, I want to thank you for showing your father that painting." Natalie's soothing voice greets me when I answer my phone later that afternoon. "He's been having the best time reconnecting with Clive. They've been playing chess for hours today, and they plan on playing again tomorrow. In between games they reminisce about old players they both knew and famous old matches. The experience is very energizing for your father."

In the background, I hear a howl of protest from my father and then two peals of laughter, one his, one belonging to another man.

"Will Clive be there for another half hour?" I'd love to talk to the man. And Sean can't complain about me working too hard and coming home late if I'm visiting my father.

Again.

"Oh, he'll be here for a while. They just started another game."

"I'll be right over."

I enter Dad and Natalie's condo to find my father making the final move in a chess game.

"Checkmate." It's unseemly to shout out your victory in chess, but Dad looks pleased with himself. His partner smiles and accepts defeat graciously.

Clive Loriss is a wiry Black man wearing a bright red Rutgers sweatshirt and sharply creased khaki slacks. His face is remarkably like the face of the chess player on the right side of the board in *Your Move*. And, just as in the painting, the middle finger of his left hand is missing above the joint.

The two men look up as I enter.

"You didn't tell me you were about to have a new grandchild," Clive says to my father after taking in my baby bump. "Grandchildren are one of life's greatest blessings." He tugs on his sweatshirt. "My grandson is studying accounting at Rutgers. He bought me this sweatshirt."

I explain that I'm having twins and Dad expresses the hope that he'll live long enough to see them enter college. Then Clive takes over the conversation. "Roger told me how he decided to look for me after you showed him Nathaniel Thurman's painting. Can I see it?"

"Of course." I invite Clive to sit next to me on the sofa and pull out my iPad. His face scrunches with deep concentration as he looks at the full painting, then zooms in on the two chess players. "I never saw the finished painting," Clive says. "Nathaniel would come to the park with his sketch pad and draw us as we played. He'd draw the folks on the sidewalk and the kids jumping rope. Then he'd go back to his studio to make the drawings into a painting."

"Did you ever visit his studio?" I ask.

"Only once. He invited me to see a different painting, one that he painted before this one. He didn't like anyone to see what he was working on before it was finished."

"Did you know that he was putting you in this painting?"

"Oh, yeah. I was honored. Couldn't wait to see what he did with my ugly puss." Clive chuckles, then the smile fades. "But Nathaniel disappeared before I got a chance to see the painting. I never knew what happened to it. I asked his sister and she said there wasn't a painting of chess players in his studio when the police searched the place."

Had Irv Aronson bought *Your Move* and taken it to his home before the artist had a chance to show it to anyone? Or could Irv have taken it away in that period of time when no one realized Nathaniel was gone?

Could Irv have stolen the painting?

Surely not—Eugene knew it was hanging in the Aronson's dining room.

I hadn't given much thought to what happened to Nathaniel's studio after he disappeared. That's a good question for Ty to ask Eugene when he sees him again. Ty called Eugene after the FBI agents left us just to warn the old gentlemen, and Eugene asked Ty to come see him again. He implied he had some information to share.

Right now, I turn my attention back to Clive. "Who's the other chess player in the painting?"

Clive taps the screen to zoom in on the other player. "Heh-heh, this guy's kind of an inside joke, not a real person. You only see him in profile, not his full face. But there's little clues in there about who Nathaniel was pokin' fun at."

My ears prick up. "Oh? Who's that?"

"That basketball player who became an actor—Rennie Pike. See, the chess player is wearing basketball shoes, and he's got a big 'fro like Rennie had in the movie where he played a Black Panther. And then Nathaniel painted this branch hanging down over his head. That's a reference to that crazy action movie Rennie was in where he was getting swept over a waterfall and saved himself by grabbing onto a tree."

I laugh. I've never seen the entire movie, but the scene is iconic, immortalized in memes whenever people want to show they're hanging on by a thread. "Why did Nathaniel want to poke fun at Rennie Pike?" I ask Clive.

Clive blows air through his lips. "Who knows? Nate was peculiar that way. He'd decide a person wasn't up to his standards, and he'd try to bring him down a peg or two."

Interesting. I scroll over to the figure of Darnell Peterson, stretched out and staring at the sky. "Did you know him?"

Clive nods and frowns. "The boy was always hangin' on the corner, waitin' for trouble to find him. Small surprise he came to no good." He makes eye contact with me. "Your father told me the painting was damaged by a vandal. This is the figure that was blacked out?"

"Yes. Do you have any idea why? Do you think it could be related to Darnell's gang affiliations?"

Clive snorts. "Nate painted this almost seven years ago, right? People livin' the gang life don't last that long. They end up dead or in prison. A few are smart enough to get out and move away. There's probably still gangs in the neighborhood, but it wouldn't be the same members. Darnell is long forgotten."

"Do you still live on that street, Clive?"

"Nah. I moved out of the neighborhood a year or two after Nate disappeared. Wanted to be closer to my daughter in Somerville. Don't have to worry about gangs there."

Clive continues to study the painting. His finger joints are swollen with arthritis, but his hand is steady as he zooms in on Darnell.

Not his face, but his chest.

"Huh," Clive muses. "Look at what clothes Nathaniel painted for Darnell."

I squint at the iPad. Blown up this big, the photo is blurry. Darnell appears to be wearing a long-sleeved, pale blue shirt with a gold and red insignia on the chest. "What's so special about his shirt?"

"I think that's supposed to be the kind of shirt made in Irv's factory around the corner. Those shirts are very expensive, so it's not likely a street kid like Darnell could afford one. And if he had one in real life, he sure as hell wouldn't be layin' on the ground in it."

"So the artist was making some social commentary by dressing the figure that way?" my father enquires.

Clive chuckles. "You could call it commentary, or you could call it flippin' the bird to The Man."

This is an intriguing change in perspective. "You're saying Nathaniel Thurman didn't approve of Irv Aronson? I thought they were friends."

"I wouldn't say they were friends. Not sure Nathaniel had real friends—he always held himself apart. But he and Irv liked to trade stories, that's for sure."

"Did Nathaniel criticize Irv for making these shirts in his factory?" I ask. "Is it because the people who made them couldn't afford to buy them?"

As Clive shrugs, Natalie interjects. "But Irv Aronson didn't own the brand, correct? He was just carrying out the manufacturing of the product. Why condemn him for being elitist?"

Clive leans back on the sofa, holding his hands out in mock self-defense. "I can't explain it. All I know is, Nathaniel's paintings always had a message." Clive chuckles. "Sometimes no one understood the message but Nathaniel himself."

Chapter 28

I open my eyes and struggle to roll on my side to check the time on our bedside clock.

9:07! How did I sleep that late?

Then I remember—I was up twice in the night to pee, and then couldn't fall back asleep because my back hurt. I vaguely recall Sean creeping around trying to get dressed and eat breakfast without waking me at seven. I must've fallen back into a deep sleep after that.

I feel well-rested, but of course, I desperately need to pee.

Again.

With that taken care of, I waddle down to the kitchen, checking my phone once I've got the decaf coffee brewing.

The first thing I see is a text from Sean.

Made it to work safely. The roads are TERRIBLE!!

We are not the kind of married couple who checks in with each other all day long. We each assume the other is fine unless specifically notified of disaster. I suspect what Sean is up to with this text. He wants me to stay home today but knows better than to issue an ultimatum. Hence the "I barely survived the trip to work" message.

I look out the window and see that the patio and driveway are indeed covered with an inch of frozen slush, and the low grey clouds threaten to dump more of it shortly. I turn on the TV in time to catch the soliloquy of the local weatherman, a man so melodramatic he should star in Mexican telenovelas. "The dreaded wintry mix is HERE! We've already got three inches of frozen slush on the roads and another storm system is headed our way, ready to drop a mix of freezing rain and wet snow all across northwestern New Jersey. When temps drop, we'll see lots of BLACK ICE!" He flails his arms at the arrows and maps behind him. "Stay at home folks, so this doesn't happen to you." The camera then switches to a film of vehicles strewn across the Garden State Parkway like Lo's Matchbox cars abandoned after a rough-and-tumble game. I pound the remote to shut up Mr. Doom and Gloom.

For consolation, I turn to Ethel, who sits beside the back door whining. When I open it for her, she recoils at the first stinging sleet hitting her snout and returns to her favorite family room chair.

All right already. I get the message. I won't go out.

Looks like I'm in for a long, lonely day of solitary confinement. I pat my belly. "You know, you guys really aren't much company right now. I can hardly wait to meet you face-to-face."

Obligingly, one of them kicks me in the kidneys.

Even infants screaming in stereo would be better than the tomblike silence of this house. I put on some lively music—Lake Street Dive, Sharon Jones, Tina Turner—and turn to my computer for distraction.

I pass by all my spreadsheet files. No entertainment there. Both my business and personal finances have been balanced, analyzed, budgeted, and projected. Every bill is paid, every investment finalized.

I scroll through my own social media accounts, but the photos of skinny friends drinking cocktails at holiday parties are too depressing.

Next, I check the social accounts for Another Man's Treasure, where Donna is doing a bang-up job generating interest for our first sale in January. She's already posting pictures of some cool vintage jewelry and a huge custom doll-house too elaborate for a child to play with. While I'm on Instagram, I get pulled down the usual internet rabbit hole, jumping from #vintagestyle to #whatIwore to #streetstyle.

And there in the stream of street style photos, I see a picture of Rennie Pike. The actor grins audaciously at the camera, a young starlet hanging on his arm. He's rocking a sleek tuxedo on his tall, muscular frame as he prepares to enter some hot LA nightspot. Rennie shows up over and over in other photos tagged #menwithstyle. It seems the actor and former NBA star has added fashion icon to his list of accomplishments.

I hop over to Rennie's own account to see what he's up to these days.

I find tons of sultry poses of Rennie wearing a big gold watch and not much else. It seems he's now the spokesman for a brand of luxury watches too new to show up at estate sales.

In my opinion, Ty is every bit as handsome as Rennie Pike. I giggle at the thought of Ty as a brand spokesman. He'd probably be quoted saying something like, "You need your head checked if you're spending twenty grand on a watch."

Is this why Nathaniel Thurman was making fun of Rennie Pike—for promoting needless extravagance?

I switch over to read Rennie's Wikipedia bio, which paints a picture of a wholesome success story. Rennie Pike grew up in a happy home in suburban Ohio, was a high school and college basketball star, and got drafted to play in the NBA. To make his parents proud, he completed his college degree and encourages other young athletes to do the same. Here, the bio shows photos of Rennie playing college ball and then dressed in a cap and gown holding his diploma and flanked by his happy parents. Good for him. Kids could use more role models who value education.

I keep reading and discover that while he was an NBA star, Rennie was recruited to be the spokesmodel for Founders. I'm no fashionista, but even I know that brand. The styles are classic, high quality, and very pricey. The name is a reference to America's founding fathers and mothers, and part of their brand identity is that all the clothes are made in America from American-sourced materials. They started out in menswear, but soon women were wearing their boyfriends' Founders shirts, and the company branched out. I'm pretty sure if Sean ever spent $250 for a shirt, he wouldn't let me borrow it to wear over leggings. This part of the bio shows Rennie in a crisp pinstriped shirt worn with trendy ripped jeans.

The next paragraph of the bio grabs my interest. "In an example of art imitating life—or commerce—Rennie Pike appeared in so many Founders ads under the headline "American Made" that Hollywood producer Dirk Bogard created the action movie *American Made* about three homegrown American heroes combatting a terrorist network. Rennie Pike was cast as one of the leads." Here, the bio shows an intense Rennie with his two co-stars as they battle their way out of danger.

The bio concludes with a paragraph explaining that after the enormous success of *American Made* and its many sequels, Rennie Pike quit basketball in favor of acting and fashion. It goes on to list all his film credits and the different brands he's been associated with over the years.

The "made in America" slogan piques my interest. Irv's factory features a patriotic sign with a flag, and Ty says Irv kept his garment factory going by catering to brands that wanted to position themselves as made in America. Did Irv's factory manufacture Founders clothing when *Your Move* was painted? Does it still manufacture that brand?

I skip over to the Founders website to learn more about the brand. The website shows that their high-end 100% cotton shirts begin life in a cotton field in Mississippi. Their 100% wool sweaters come from fluffy sheep grazing in Vermont. And their leather accessories come from good ol' Texas cattle rounded up by American cowboys.

I roll my eyes—these guys really lay it on thick!

Next, the materials are sent to factories across America to be sewn and woven and knitted by all-American workers. The photos depict smiling men and women operating high-tech equipment in clean, modern factories, none of which look remotely like Irv's gritty location in Hillside. Virtually all the workers depicted are blond-haired and blue-eyed, and they all have perfect teeth. Sheesh! Do you have to show your membership in The Daughters of the American Revolution to get a job here? No, wait—I take that back. There's one black guy in one of the shoe manufacturing photos. Of course, he's got great teeth, too.

None of this looks like it could be happening in Irv's factory. But these are probably stock photos like the kinds used on college websites that show happy, wholesome students with no tattoos, piercings, or hangover symptoms. Branding is all about creating a mythology for your customer to believe in.

My gaze travels to the Founders logo at the top of each website page: a stylized red and gold eagle. Then I flip to the photo of *Your Move* and zoom in on the figure of Darnell Peterson. The insignia on his shirt is visible only as a blurry blob of red and gold, but I'm pretty sure it's the Founders' eagle.

What does it mean? Is there some significance in the fact that poor, gang-banging Darnell wears the Founders shirt while stretched out on the dirty front stoop?

Does it mean anything at all? Or is it simply an inside joke from the mind of an artist who struggled with bipolar disorder and saw the world through his own unique lens? Or maybe it's the product of my own over-active imagination reacting to my house arrest.

Outside, pellets of freezing rain ping against the family room window. If I were at the office right now, I could discuss the significance of the figures in the painting with Ty. I guess I could call him although Ty hates having long phone conversations.

Then in an act of telepathy, my phone beeps with a text from Ty.

I need to go over some deets on the client I'm going to see tomorrow. Can I come over?

Chapter 29

"Sorry to bother you," Ty says fifteen minutes later, shaking sleet from his shoulders in my foyer.

"You're not bothering me. I'm still working, remember."

I lead Ty to the kitchen. It's only eleven, but I've never known the man to turn down food. And eleven is time for my post-breakfast, or my pre-lunch, depending on the menu.

We settle on some of Natalie's cranberry orange bread slathered with cream cheese, with a side of cantaloupe to keep me virtuous. Ty pulls out a list of questions that a client has emailed him after his first visit to her home. She's not willing to commit to Another Man's Treasure until all her objections have been overcome. I'd be happy to write a long, detailed email response, but she has requested a follow-up visit.

As we go over the list of questions, Ty grows impatient. "I know all these answers. I think I'm worried that I won't be able to stay friendly when I'm talking to her. I do best with old people who don't want to have a sale at all, not people who think we're not good enough to handle their sale."

"Ah, Ty—salesmanship begins when the customer says no. Let's do some role-playing." I assume a querulous voice. "Ventura Estate Sales guarantees they can sell all my furniture."

"Huh. Sure, go with them if you want a jackleg who can't tell an antique from an Ethan Allen knock-off."

I giggle. "Now, find a way to say that nicely without rolling your eyes."

Ty takes a deep breath. "With our expertise and connections with antique dealers, we will be able to secure the best prices for your Empire armoire, your Early American cherry rocker, and your rustic pie safe. But we have to be realistic about your contemporary china cabinet. Many homes today don't have the space for such a, er, magnificent piece. But even if we don't sell the china cabinet, you'll end up making more overall with Another Man's Treasure."

I clap my hands. "Bravo. Try not to choke on 'magnificent' and you'll win her over."

"That's a challenge. It's a big, ugly-ass china cabinet circa 1975 filled with crap no one uses in the 21st century." The smile fades from Ty's face. "Making sales calls for Another Man's Treasure is a big responsibility, Audge. I don't want to screw up and lose jobs that you coulda nailed."

I put my small, pale hand over his large dark one. "Ty, I appreciate what you're doing for me and for my business while I'm on maternity leave. I don't expect you to land every job. I've had some spectacular failures. Remember Mr. Wesselman?"

Ty chokes on his cranberry bread and has to drink a big swig of tea before he can speak. "That house seemed totally normal until you opened the spare room door."

"Screaming 'that's disgusting' wasn't my finest moment of customer relations," I reply. "But geez, he could have warned me he was a retired anatomy teacher who kept his collection of specimens floating in jars of formaldehyde. Maybe I could have sold them with a little research. But I never got the chance."

Ty gathers the list of questions from the nit-picky prospective customer. "I can do this, Audge. I think I just needed a little pep talk."

"I'm happy to provide it." I slide off the bar stool and clear away our dishes. "As long as you're here, I want to show you something related to the Thurman painting. I give him a quick recap of my conversation with Dad's friend, Clive the chess master. "See this shirt Darnell is wearing? It's a Founders shirt."

Ty squints at the blurred photo of the painting. "You sure? Those shirts are *fine*." He rubs his thumb and forefinger together, imagining the silky feel of the fabric. "They start at $250 and go up from there. How would a poor street kid like Darnell be wearing one of those?"

"According to Clive, Nathaniel Thurman wasn't always painting reality. He filled his paintings with subtle messages—sometimes so subtle that he was the only one who understood them. What if Darnell was blacked out of the painting as a response to one of Nathaniel's messages?"

Ty's right eyebrow shoots up, his standard "don't mess with my head" response. "You're saying Thurman and someone else are trading messages through the painting?"

I close the dishwasher and lean against the counter. "Mmmm, maybe. Let's say it's a theory that fits the facts. It would explain why Pearl suddenly put the painting in storage."

"To stop the convo." Ty cradles his chin in his hand. "But that would mean the person who was intended to get the message is only getting it now, seven years after Thurman finished the painting."

"Exactly. Clive said he knew Thurman was painting him playing chess because Thurman came to the park and sketched him." I move into the family room to lie on the floor and perform my back stretches. "But after Thurman disappeared, Clive asked about the final painting, and Thurman's sister said no painting of chess players was found in the studio when the police searched it."

Ty follows me and plops onto the sofa. "That means Irv must've bought *Your Move* right before Thurman disappeared."

"Or he knew about the painting and moved it out of the studio and into his dining room in Palmyrton before anyone realized Thurman was gone."

"Irv stole the painting?" Ty's voice squeaks with incredulity. "You think he had something to do with Thurman's disappearance?"

I can tell Ty wants to keep on liking Irv, the friendly old gentleman who talked to people in the neighborhood and offered jobs to the locals. "Another possibility is that Irv moved the painting to conceal the message it contained."

"So what's the message of Darnell lying on the dirty stoop wearing a fancy shirt? I feel like I'm back in English class, with all the symbolism in the poems going—" He zooms his hand over his head. "The bird means this, the fire means that. Geez, just come out and say it."

"I feel your pain—interpreting symbolism is no easier for me. I was a math major, remember?" I shut my eyes, trying to open my logical mind to new possibilities...the Founders' eagle...the dirty concrete....

Ty snaps his fingers. "Maybe we're trying too hard to think of artistic symbolism. Maybe the message is literally about the shirt. What if Founders shirts are still made in Irv's factory and there's something sketchy about that, and Irv wanted to conceal it?" He jumps up. "And what if that's why the FBI agent was asking me whether the bar where I met the BlastMaster con man was near Irv's factory?"

I get on my knees and arch my back like a cat. "Maybe that factory is already on the FBI's radar for some reason."

Ty paces from the sofa to the bookshelves. "But why? Why would the FBI care about a clothing factory?"

"If Supervisory Agent Magee routinely supervises counterfeiting operations, then maybe his team has an eye on that factory because it makes knockoff Founders shirts."

"For seven years, and they're just catching onto it now? And if the FBI cares about knockoff clothing," Ty asks, "how come you can buy a plastic Louis Vuitton purse or a polyester Burberry scarf on every street corner in Manhattan?"

"I don't know the precise rules and regulations, but I think if you make a close copy but don't try to pass it off as the real thing, that's not a crime. So, for instance, you can make and sell a beige and black and red plaid scarf as long as you don't sew in a label that says 'Burberry.'"

"That makes sense. My fake toy box says BlastMaster and it even says 'made by Sonic Boom, Inc.', so they were trying to pass it off as real. If Irv's factory is making really good fakes, why doesn't the FBI shut it down? It can't be that hard to prove."

"TV makes it look easy. They just kick down the door and raid the place. But in real life, law enforcement has to have evidence of a crime to show the judge in order to get a warrant," I explain, showing off my cop's wife knowledge. "Maybe they're building their case."

Ty waves his hand. "I don't care what they're making in that factory. I just wish we could get *Your Move* out of storage."

"I know. But maybe criminal activity at the factory is the reason Pearl got scared and hid the painting even better than Irv did."

"She doesn't own the factory anymore" Ty points out. "Why would she care?"

I look at Ty sheepishly. "I guess that's where my theory falls apart, eh?"

"I'm going over to Eugene's house on Monday," Ty says. "I'll be sure to ask him about what goes on in that factory."

Chapter 30

I can no longer see my toes.

Simple acts of grooming, like trimming my toenails, are a thing of the past. I guess it's time to pay a visit to the only nail salon that doesn't intimidate me, the painfully double-entendre House of Nails.

The salon, located in a strip mall on the outskirts of Palmyrton, is utterly without pretension—just a row of manicure tables and a row of footbaths presided over by a stern Korean woman and her husband who were probably rocket scientists back in their home country. No appointments are required, so Sean drops me off on the Saturday morning of Lydia Eastlee's girls-only Christmas party. He's on his way to Home Depot. We've finally settled on a color for the nursery, and he's eager to get started painting and installing shelves. He can work all day and into the evening since I'll be out.

I rarely get a manicure since my work is a nail-destroyer. But after months of no box lifting, van loading or attic exploring, I actually possess enough nail to paint. And since I can't wow the ladies at Lydia's with my high fashion (my maternity frocks all look like they came from Party Tent Rental), I might as well impress them with my holiday manicure. Once inside The House of Nails, I commit to the mani-pedi special.

"You pick color," the owner barks, pointing me toward the display of polish bottles beside a crooked, fake Christmas tree.

I waddle over in my flip-flops, immediately overwhelmed by the range of choices. Do I want a tasteful pale pink or an audacious poinsettia red; a funky holly green or a downright weird steel gray? I watch to see what the two teenagers ahead of me choose, and peer at the gnarled hands of an old lady in the first chair. That helps me rule out three colors, leaving me sixty other options. I paint a few sample strokes on the nails of my left hand and study the effect.

Finally, the petite young manicurist waiting to work on me takes pity. "That a pretty color," she offers shyly, pointing to the deep rose on my ring finger.

Sold.

I struggle to clamber into the pedicure chair, a big Barca lounger with a sink for my feet. The husband of the owner rushes over to help haul me up, and I land like a giant catfish on a fisherman's dock.

Despite the salon's tinny Musak renditions of "Jingle Bell Rock" and "Frosty the Snowman", the warm water, gentle hands of the pedicurist, and vibrating back massage of the chair combine to relax me to the edge of sleep.

Then the big bleach blonde in the chair beside me pulls out her cellphone.

First, she calls her sister and discusses the stupidity and inconsiderateness of her husband at top volume. She pauses to yell at the pedicurist for cutting one toenail too short, then dials her husband to discuss the rudeness and cluelessness of her sister, also at a decibel range rivaling a leaf-blower. Foolishly, I forgot my earphones, so I have no choice but to listen to all her family drama. When her husband hangs up, we have a few moments of blessed silence until her phone bursts into the opening bars of "You Give Love a Bad Name," and she begins a new conversation.

"Did you get it?" she shouts into her phone. "Are you sure it's real, not like last time?"

After listening to the answer, the blonde continues, "I'm not paying you for the fake one. You should have known better than to go to a sewer like Hillside to buy a toy on the street."

I tense up. Suddenly, I'm no longer trying to tune her out. She's clearly talking about a fake BlastMaster, and it seems someone she knows procured one in Hillside, just as Ty did.

"All right. Bring it to the house at four." She shifts her broad beam in the lounge chair. "I'll have the five hundred bucks for you." She clicks off and switches gears. "Make sure you remove all the callus on my heel!"

I make sympathetic eye contact with her beleaguered pedicurist and figure I'll be doing the poor woman a favor by distracting this customer from hell. "So, I couldn't help but overhear that you seem to have finally found a real BlastMaster," I say to her with a smile. "Congratulations!"

The loud blonde twists in her chair to look me over. "You're lucky your kids aren't born yet, or you'd be paying through the nose for this piece of shit toy, too."

Will I? Will childbirth release some hormone that makes me go crazy over toy procurement? Because, honestly, I'm not feelin' the BlastMaster frenzy now.

I smile at her and respond. "My friend got carried away trying to get a BlastMaster for his nephew and ended up with one of the fakes. He bought it in Hillside."

Like a lot of loud people, the blonde has no clue that I heard every detail of her conversation. She jumps on my remark as if it's a total coincidence that I brought up Hillside. "Get outta town! My husband's idiot drinking buddy got us one in Hillside. I took one look at it and told him it was obviously a fake. You can't put one over on me!" She points at her chest with one long, gel-manicured talon. "So now he claims he's got us a real one. We'll see."

She bends forward to study the neon orange polish the pedicurist is applying to her toes. "What do you think of this shade?" she asks me.

"A very fun color," I reply, summoning my inner Isabelle.

"I think so, too." She settles back in satisfaction. "I'll wait until Christmas week to do red. Or green."

Now that we're best buddies, I push the envelope, acting fast before her phone rings again. "Do you think your husband's buddy could get a real BlastMaster for my friend? He'd be so grateful."

"Sure, you can try." She winks at me. "Joey's one sketchy dude, you know what I'm sayin'? And he's got rocks for brains. But here, I'll share his contact info. Tell your friend to say that Lorenzo and Victoria sent him."

Seconds later, a contact labeled "Joey P" pings into my phone, and Victoria the blonde bombshell launches into a loud call with her best friend over the pain she's feeling in her breast implants.

Relaxation is now off the table, so I close my eyes and contemplate what I intend to do with the Joey P contact info that I impulsively procured. Should I pass it along to Ty on the off chance that this guy can get him a real BlastMaster? Do I want to aid and abet Ty in a quest I don't even approve of? One that, if successful, will serve to tick off Charmaine?

But Ty keeps nosing around Hillside, looking for the dude who swindled him. When Ty is restless and disgruntled, I worry for his safety. And since I haven't been going into the office every day, I can't ride herd on him. Maybe acquiring an authentic BlastMaster will appease him, and he'll let go of that mission of retribution. If so, I could anticipate the holidays without anxiety.

On the other hand, Joey P is, by the blonde's admission, a sketchy dude with rocks for brains. He could try to scam Ty again. And that wouldn't end well for either of them.

The pedicurist nudges me, indicating that my pedicure is complete, and it's time for me to move over to the manicure station. Even with my legs extended in the special chair, I can't see the job she's done on my toes, but I trust that they've got to look better than they did when I sat down.

A crane would be handy to get me out of the pedicure chair, but I settle for the help of two tiny Asian ladies. I settle in my new location and extend my hands. The manicurist frowns but quickly regains her composure and sets to work, leaving me free to return to my speculation. What if this Joey P person is affiliated with the original scammer? Granted, Joey P, friend of Victoria and Lorenzo, doesn't sound like he would be Ukrainian, like the man who scammed Ty back in May. But what makes Hillside the epicenter of the BlastMaster underground market? Maybe there's a way to use the Joey P connection to get to the bottom of what's going on there.

I shoot a stealthy look at big, blonde Victoria, now haranguing her manicurist. The problem with calling the FBI tip line to report Joey P. is that Victoria has my cellphone number from sharing her contact with me, so my snitching could come back to haunt me. I don't want to be on the wrong side of that broad!

She's supposed to be getting her real BlastMaster this afternoon. Maybe I'd better wait a few days before I call the tip line. I suspect that once Victoria gets her BlastMaster, she won't care what happens to Joey P. And if the man tries to stick her with another fake, she'll want him to go down in flames.

With my decision made, I return my attention to what's happening to my hands. Amazingly, my stubby, unevenly shaped nails and ragged cuticles have been transformed into perfect rose ovals.

I beam at the woman who pulled off this miracle and give her a big tip.

She folds the bills into her smock pocket. "You look pretty now, mama."

"Thank you." I may be a whale, but at least I'm a well-groomed whale.

Chapter 31

While I'm sitting under the nail dryer in the salon's front window, I see Victoria pull out in her gargantuan white SUV with glitter-framed vanity plates: Hot Mama2.

That implies there's another woman in New Jersey with Hot Mama1. I look down at Thea and Aiden and assure them I'll never embarrass them as Hot Mama3.

Shortly after Victoria leaves, Sean pulls up outside. I'm eager to talk to him and ready to be gone from here, so despite the dire Korean/English warnings of the staff, I leave with not entirely dry nails.

In the parking lot, I gesticulate at Sean until he gets out of the car and comes around to open the passenger door for me. "What's up, Princess Di? You need a full-service chauffeur now?"

"Take my coat and open the door. My nails are still sticky, and I don't want to smudge them."

Sean rolls his eyes and does as he's told. "You know I married you because you're a woman who's not afraid to get her hands dirty," he complains as we drive off. "What kind of bait and switch is this?"

I hold my hands out and wiggle my fingers. "A princess locked up in a tower gets the consolation of pretty nails. I think it's safe to say that once the twins arrive, my hands will be plenty dirty."

Sean grins and pats the bump. Then he launches into a blow-by-blow description of his interactions with the Home Depot paint and carpentry department staff. I let him lecture on the benefits of eggshell versus semi-gloss finish for children's rooms. When he breaks for air, I start my own tale. We're back in Palmyrton sitting at a stoplight by the time I finish my saga of Victoria, Joey P, and BlastMasters from Hillside.

Sean rests his head against the steering wheel. "Geez, Audrey—I leave you unsupervised for one hour and this is what you get into."

"I plan to report it to the FBI tip line," I assure my husband. "I just wish there was some way to use this information to help Ty. He's obsessed with finding the guy who scammed him, and I'm worried he'll get himself into a jam."

Sean sighs and shoots me an exasperated look. "I didn't want to tell you this, but some of the guys at work who bought fake BlastMasters have been running their own off-the-books investigation."

"Oooo! Tell me more."

Sean points the car towards home and keeps talking. "Local cops never play nice with the Feds—there's a natural rivalry, and the Feds always think they're smarter than God. There are cops from a few departments in Palmer County who don't want to admit that they got caught up in something that they should have realized was illegal. That's why they don't want to give their BlastMaster evidence to the FBI. But they're all ticked off that they got scammed, and they want to break up this counterfeit ring."

"So you want to give them the lead instead of giving it to the FBI tip line?" Frankly, I'm surprised that Sean doesn't want to play this strictly by the book.

He keeps his eyes on the road. "W-e-l-l-l, we could give it to the locals first. Let them get a head start."

"What about the blowback from snitching? Loose lips sink ships, and all that?" Ty has always been so adamantly anti-snitch that his ethos is wearing off on me.

"Yeah, we'll wait until tomorrow to keep the Victoria connection on the downlow." Sean purses his lips and squints his right eye, which means he's strategizing. "You say Victoria is meeting this Joey P. guy this afternoon? Too bad we can't watch her house, see who turns up."

I perk up. "Wait! I saw her license plate number—HotMama2. Run it and then we can go on a stake-out."

"We? I think not, my dear." Sean makes the turn onto our street. "I'm dropping you off at home. You have a party to get ready for, remember? I'll follow up on Victoria and Joey P, and we'll see what plays out. But there's not much time."

As I exit the car, Sean squeezes my knee. "Good work, Sherlock. I'll keep you posted."

Chapter 32

At home, I pace around the house feeling like the one kid in third grade who didn't get invited to the popular girl's birthday party. This despite the fact that I've been invited to Lydia's party, an event I've been looking forward to all week. But now I want to be at Sean's party. The one where he tracks down the BlastMaster scammer and busts open the counterfeit ring. How can snowman cut-out cookies and eggnog compare to that?

It's four-thirty. What is Sean doing? Has Joey turned up? Will Sean follow him after he drops off the BlastMaster, or call other cops for backup? There was no time to grill him on his strategy before he had to take off.

I really want to text him, but obviously if he's screwing around answering me, he might miss something important happening at Victoria's house. So I restrain myself. Sean will call me when he can.

I drift around the house in search of a productive activity that won't destroy my nails and will keep me occupied until it's time to leave for Lydia's party. After all that effort, it would be nice to preserve them for at least one day. Scrubbing the bathroom is out, as is breaking down cardboard boxes for recycling. I finally settle on clearing out soggy items from the vegetable crisper drawer.

Just as I toss a baggie of green sludge into the trash, my phone rings. I lunge for it, but the call is from my friend Roz, not Sean.

"I'll pick you up at five-thirty," she tells me. Roz has offered to ferry me to and from Lydia's party.

"I'll be ready. I've got a bottle of wine and my Secret Santa gift. Do you think I need to bring a hostess gift as well?"

"If you do, I swear I'll throw you out of my car with my secret ejector button," Roz says.

I laugh. Roz is so down to earth, definitely not one to worry about Miss Manners niceties. "Good, because I had enough trouble with the Secret Santa gift."

"Tell me about it," Roz agrees. "I think the gift I bought can work for any of us. Except Isabelle. I really hope she doesn't get mine."

"I've been thinking the same thing about mine." I bought a funky, bohemian style scarf that I can easily picture Roz or Lydia wearing. Madalyn might be a stretch. Isabelle is a hard no. "If it's any consolation, Isabelle was also really struggling last week with buying her Secret Santa gift."

"Why do we torture ourselves like this? Next year, we'll do a Hanukkah party at my house," Roz grumbles. "Light a candle and move straight to the food."

"Sounds good to me! See you at five-thirty, Roz."

By the time Roz and I arrive at Lydia's house, I have received one brief, cryptic text from Sean. *Interesting developments. Can't talk now. Everything fine—don't worry.*

Yeah, right.

But Lydia's brightly decorated house, the plump tree twinkling in the corner of the living room, and the scent of pine and mulled cider in the air drive out my BlastMaster concerns. Despite the Secret Santa gift pressure, I've been looking forward to this party, and I intend to have fun.

"Audrey! Oh my god—look at you!" Lydia hasn't seen me in a few weeks, so I allow her to fuss and pat my huge belly. She's never had kids, and I can see by the look of suppressed horror in her eyes that she's happy with her decision.

Madalyn is next in the baby bump examination line. She has four young adult kids, and I suspect my condition is sparking a nostalgia for a time before she had to deal with drinking and pot-smoking and tattoos. "You're glowing!" she declares.

"Just a hot flash." I bypass the hot cider and take a cold sparkling water.

Roz removes her coat, revealing the most hideously hilarious Christmas sweater ever: four reindeer playing poker on the roof while Santa flounders in the chimney. "Jews like to play cards," Roz explains. "I thought it was a good bridge between cultures." All the laughter brings Isabelle out from the kitchen looking festive yet tasteful in an ice blue cashmere sweater beaded with tiny snowflakes.

Roz and I exchange a glance as we put our Secret Santa gifts under the tree. "We gotta find a way to rig this," she mutters in my ear.

After half an hour of mingling, my back is killing me, and I sink into Lydia's sofa. Isabelle comes to sit beside me. "I need to talk to you."

Given that we've all been talking nonstop since we arrived, this seems like an odd opening. "Sure. What's up?"

"Honestly, I'm not quite sure. Have you heard from Pearl Aronson lately?"

"Me? No. Why would I?"

"I knew it was a longshot, but with the painting connection...." Isabelle twists a champagne-swilling elf cocktail napkin in her hands. "I'm worried about her, Audrey."

I shove a cushion behind my back and lean forward with interest.

"The new owners of Pearl's house are doing some remodeling. They knocked down a wall between the smallest bedroom and the hall bathroom, and they found a fairly new, locked fireproof box," Isabelle explains. "They figured it must be important, so they contacted me. I went over and got it, but I've called and left several messages for Pearl, and she hasn't responded. So I called the lawyer who handled her closing, and he hasn't been able to reach her either. I'm at a dead end. And now I've got this big, heavy box in my condo, and I don't know what to do with it."

I smile because I know Isabelle prides herself on helping her clients with everything and anything, but she's a neat freak. The buck stops at cluttering her own home with her clients' junk. "Pearl mentioned some nephews—do you have their contact info?"

"No." Isabelle's smooth brow furrows. "I don't even know their last names."

"Oh, that's easy to find out. They'd be listed in Irv's obituary." I immediately begin googling.

"You're so clever." Isabelle leans over my shoulder to see the results on my phone. "I knew you'd have ideas."

Irv Aronson's obituary fills my screen. It's quite long, listing his achievements and affiliations. We skim to the paragraph about the survivors. In addition to Pearl, two nephews are listed with their full names and cities.

"Why are you two huddled over your phones?" Lydia scolds. "Put that away. It's time for Secret Santa, and then we'll sing some Christmas carols."

I stash my phone, and Isabelle gives me a hand up from the sofa. "Thanks, Audrey. I'll look up the obituary again tomorrow and reach out to Pearl's relatives."

"Let me know what happens."

The Secret Santa game involves answering funny questions and then picking a number which correlates to a hidden number Lydia has affixed to each gift. There's a lot of hilarity around over-ruling one another's answers to the questions, but finally we each end up with a gift that isn't the one we brought. Roz gets my scarf and immediately sheds her ugly sweater to try it on. Everyone agrees the jewel tones compliment her dark, curly hair. Whew! My gift was a success.

Madalyn receives two popular new novels which I suspect came from Roz. "I've been wanting to read these! Now that I'm off the night shift at the hospital, I can finish a book without falling asleep on page two." Another winner.

I receive a cute teapot big enough for two cups and a selection of gourmet teas. "Perfect!" I exclaim. "I'm drinking a lot more tea since I've had to give up wine."

Lydia receives a small Japanese-style vase called an ikebana that allows for arranging three perfect stems. "I love this! It's just right for small, garden flowers."

All eyes turn to Isabelle. Of course, Isabelle will be gracious no matter what she receives. And no one is better than her at maintaining an upbeat demeanor. But I'm keenly aware of her vocabulary of euphemisms. All I can hope is that she doesn't declare her gift precious (small and cheesy), or worse yet, highly original (downright weird).

I sense we are all holding our breath as Isabelle removes a small box from underneath the tissue paper stuffing of a gift bag. Uh-oh—jewelry. I've never known Isabelle to wear anything other than pearls, gold hoops, or small diamond studs. She removes a pair of dangling earrings. They're light as air—drops of crystal and silver. I nearly blurt out, "Those are gorgeous," but restrain myself, waiting for her reaction. She carefully removes her gold hoops and puts on the gift earrings, then crosses to the oval framed mirror on Lydia's living room wall. "I love them," she says softly, tucking her blond hair behind her ears. She straightens her already impeccable posture. "I've become too predictable. I'm going to leave my pearls at home and wear these every day on my vacation."

"Too wild for work?" Roz teases her.

"One should make a distinction between special occasions and the everyday. I'll wear them on dates."

We all howl and start pumping her for information on who she's dating. But Isabelle offers only a sly smile.

———————◆———————

On the drive home, Roz and I do a post-mortem of the party. We agree that the spinach artichoke dip was to die for, and that the Secret Santa exchange, despite our grousing, was fun.

"Gift-giving is so fraught with peril," I say. "I only have one more hurdle to clear—a gift for my mother-in-law."

"Is she fussy?" Roz asks.

"No, she's ultra-practical. If you buy her anything that isn't strictly utilitarian, she puts it aside for a special occasion. Except nothing she does is ever special enough. Last year, Sean's brother bought her a new raincoat when he noticed hers had frayed cuffs. She loved it, but the next time it rained, she was still wearing the old one. She told Brendan she didn't want her nice, new raincoat to get wet."

"Jews don't go crazy on Hanukkah," Roz explains. "Warren and I have agreed not to give gifts, and I try to avoid my cousin Wendy at this time of year."

"Roz, can I ask you something about Judaism?"

She laughs as she makes the turn toward downtown Palmyrton. "I'm not a very good Jew, Audrey. I only go to temple for funerals and bar mitzvahs."

"My question isn't deeply theological." Isabelle's concern for Pearl's whereabouts has made me think about Irv's death and how it may have affected his widow. "Do Jews believe in heaven and hell?"

"Not hell. And not a heaven that's a gated community to which you can be denied admission." Roz offers a wry grimace. "I guess we've been turned away from too many country clubs to believe in a place where God picks and chooses."

"So even bad people get to go to heaven?" I ask.

"The way I remember my childhood rabbi explaining it, the worst thing that can happen to a Jew is to be a person who renounces God, faith, and morality in this world and then gets cut off from his family after death."

I nod. "That sounds like a bad fate."

"Even though Jews believe in an afterlife, we're not so focused on that. Mind you, this is reform Judaism I'm talking about," Roz clarifies. "I can't speak to what the ultra-orthodox believe. Instead of worrying about eternal rewards, we're more concerned with having a positive impact in this life so we can live on in the lives of others who come after us."

"That sounds like a good philosophy. So, for example, raising your kids to be good people?"

"Yeah, but it doesn't have to be only your kids." Roz gestures with one hand while steering with the other. "I can live on in the lives of my students if I have a positive influence on them. The falling leaf fertilizes the ground for a new tree to grow. An oak could fertilize a maple."

"Hmm. I like that."

"See, you woulda made a good Jew, Audrey." Roz slaps my knee. "Why are you so interested in Jewish ideas of the afterlife?"

"It has to do with a client Isabelle and I have in common. She told me something tonight that got me thinking."

I gaze out the car window at the riot of Christmas lights on the houses we pass. Irv and Pearl never had kids. Could they possibly be worried about not being reunited in the afterlife because Irv had a bad influence on someone? I keep coming back to the significance of the boy, Darnell Peterson, who was blacked out of the painting. Could Irv have led him astray in some way? Or maybe turned him away when he needed help?

Soon, the lights I'm gazing at belong to my own house. Roz pulls into my driveway, and I give her a hug good-bye.

"Thanks for the ride, Roz. And the mini-immersion course in Judaism."

Chapter 33

When I enter the house, Ethel charges to greet me. I can tell by her frantic behavior that she's been alone the entire time I've been at the party.

It's ten o'clock and Sean still isn't home.

Officially time to start worrying. And texting.

Where are you? What's happening?

Long minutes tick by before Sean answers. *Ty and I are on the way to our house. See you in ten.*

Ty? How did he pair up with Sean? Now I'm bursting with curiosity. I settle in my favorite chair and wait for the action to start.

In less than ten minutes, Ethel announces the arrival of Sean and Ty. I hear them banging around the kitchen getting drinks and snacks, but I don't bother getting up. Soon enough, they enter the family room looking tired (Sean) and disgruntled (Ty).

"What happened? How did you two run into each other?"

Sean pops open his beer and stretches out on the sofa while Ty paces restlessly around the room. "I sat outside Victoria's house with another cop from Morris Plains. At four, a car pulled up and a guy got out carrying a large box covered with a cloth."

"The BlastMaster delivery, just as Joey P. promised." I'm delighted that my lead panned out.

"He wasn't in the house more than five minutes before he came back out again with the box. Victoria stood at the door screaming at him to get lost," Sean says.

"He tried to stick her with another fake? Man, that takes some nerve!"

"So we ran the plates on his car and started following him. Once he got on Rt. 78, we were pretty sure he was leading us to Hillside. The guy's name is Joseph Perigno, and he's got a record of misdemeanors—drunk and disorderly, public nuisance, traffic violations."

"A sketchy dude—I guess Victoria was right about him." I glance over at Ty. "Where do you fit in all this?"

He scowls. "Sit tight. Sean's gettin' to that part."

"Joey eventually arrived at a boarded-up row house in Hillside. He carried the box around the back. I followed him while my partner stayed in the car and watched the front of the house. And guess who I met in the backyard?" Sean glares at Ty.

Uh-oh. "How did you know to watch that house?" I ask my assistant.

Ty jams his hands in his back pockets. "I've been going to Hillside, askin' around, makin' connections. I finally got a lead on this house. I was there in the back yard, waiting for the dude to show up. Instead, I get five-oh on my case." He scowls at Sean.

I can tell the two men in my life have already been around and around on this point before they arrived here. Sean does not bother to reprimand Ty any further. But I feel queasy. This encounter could have gone wrong, very, very wrong. What if Sean's partner had come around and found Ty in the back yard? I shudder at the possibilities.

"So neither one of you went into the house?" I ask.

"Joey put the box in the house and left," Sean explains. "I told my partner to follow him, and I stayed with Ty."

"To stop me from finding out what I need to know inside that stash house," Ty raises his hands to the heavens. "Oh, no—we can't go in. We need a *warrant*. Wouldn't be no warrant if...."

He doesn't finish, but we both know what he's thinking.

If the dude was Black.

"We need the evidence to hold up in court, Ty," Sean explains patiently. "It's not just about getting back your cash."

"And I told you," Ty wags an index finger at my husband, "I don't care about the money. I want to meet the man who scammed me. I wanna let him know there's consequences to ruining my nephew's Christmas."

Revenge. Pure and simple.

Sean and I exchange a glance. I'm not sure what else I can say about Lo. He's the happiest, sunniest little kid I know. It's crazy to think he'll be disappointed on Christmas morning if he doesn't get a BlastMaster. He'll be thrilled with every gift he gets, even the socks and underwear. This obsession is all about Ty, but he refuses to admit it.

"So what's the next step?" I ask briskly to move past this awkward moment.

"My partner followed Joey to his home. No more action there. I'll pass the information along to the FBI," Sean says. "And Ty will stay out of Hillside."

Ty says nothing.

Again, I work to move the conversation along. I don't want these two to get into a power play about who's calling the shots. "Guess what I learned at the Christmas party tonight? Isabelle Trent says that the new owners of Pearl's house found a lock box when they knocked down a wall during renovations. Isabelle wants to return it to her, but she's having a hard time connecting with Pearl."

For the first time since he arrived, Ty drops his belligerent attitude. "A hidden lock box that Pearl didn't know about? Irv must've hidden it."

"That's what I'm thinking. Isabelle says the box looks new, so it's not something they hid years ago and forgot about. Irv died suddenly, so maybe he didn't have time to tell Pearl about it."

"Or maybe he didn't want her to know about it," Sean says.

"I thought they were such a happy old couple, but maybe they had secrets." Ty sits down across from me and rests his elbows on his knees. "I keep coming back to Darnell Peterson. Why is he the one who got blacked out of the painting?" Ty makes eye contact with Sean. "Do you know exactly how Darnell died? Eugene never said specifically—just made it seem like the kid got caught up in gang violence. Did he get shot? Did the cops ever arrest anyone? Or did they just figure 'another gangbanger dead, so why bother'?"

It's taken years, but Sean has learned to not let Ty's resentments against law enforcement get under his skin. "When I get into the office on Monday, I'll look up the case. Maybe there's something more to Darnell Peterson's death that no one realized at the time."

"Let me know what you turn up. I'll be visiting Eugene on Monday night."

Chapter 34

"Audrey, you won't believe this." Isabelle's voice is breathless over the phone on Monday morning. "I called Irv's nephew and he said he hadn't heard from Pearl apart from a few emails, but he wasn't concerned because they didn't talk regularly. He got in contact with the super of her Florida condo, and when they entered, there was no sign that Pearl had been there. The fridge was empty, and her suitcases weren't there. No one in the building has seen her since she left for New Jersey months ago. All her Florida friends thought she was in New Jersey, and all her New Jersey friends thought she was in Florida."

"No one has seen the old gal since June, but they didn't get worried about her?" I'm astounded because Pearl seems like the kind of woman who has lots of friends. Wouldn't some of them be concerned even if the nephews weren't?

"They all got emails from her," Isabelle explains. "But when they started comparing notes, the friends and relatives realized that the emails were very vague, and that Pearl didn't always respond directly to their questions."

"Weird. Could it be that someone else is controlling her email account? What about the lockbox?"

"The nephew says he'll come and get it. But Audrey, now I have doubts." Isabelle's voice grows tense. "Maybe I shouldn't give it to him. I told him I thought we should report Pearl missing to the police, but he seemed reluctant to do that. He brushed me off. Said he'd handle it. It's none of my business, but...."

"You want me to talk to Sean about it?"

I hear her relief through the phone. "Yes! Would you mind?"

When I call Sean, he has news for me, too. "Darnell Peterson's death was definitely a homicide—stabbed through the heart with a thin knife. No witnesses. Weapon never found. Kid bled out on the street half a block from his front door. Mother thought her son was asleep in his bed."

I feel my eyes tear up. Since I've gotten pregnant, I notice I'm more emotional. I get weepy at Hallmark card commercials and lost dog posters. The pregnancy book says this is common—caused by the extra hormones circulating in my system. I rest my hand on my belly. Even though I haven't met Aiden and Thea yet, I can feel the horror of thinking your child is safe in his bed while in reality he was bleeding to death just outside your door.

"I called the Hillside detective who investigated seven years ago," Sean continues. "No one denied Darnell had gang affiliations. But when the detectives talked to the rival gang, they noted that those guys seemed genuinely surprised Darnell was dead. They swore they had no beef with him. The implication was Darnell wasn't important enough to kill."

"So Ty was right—Darnell's case went into the files as another unsolved murder of a young, Black man."

Sean sighs. "Yeah, I'm afraid so."

"Do you think it's possible Darnell's murder and Pearl's disappearance are linked?"

"I think it's worth looking inside that lockbox. And if an eighty-five-year-old rich woman has disappeared, I think a judge will let us do it. Give me a few hours."

"What should I tell Isabelle?"

"Tell her not to answer any calls from Irv's nephew and sit tight on the box."

When I hang up with Sean, I tell Ty what Sean said about Darnell. "So maybe he wasn't killed because of gang activity."

Ty grimaces. "Guess it came in handy for whoever did kill him to make it seem like a gang retaliation."

Nothing in police work ever goes as quickly as planned, so by the time Ty is ready to depart for his visit with Eugene, we still haven't heard any news on the lockbox. Sean has texted me that he'll be working late on this.

So I'm sorely tempted.

"Can I come with you to Eugene's?"

Ty cocks his head and squints his left eye. "Why?"

"I'm worried about Pearl." This is not a lie, but neither is it the complete truth. I'm more worried about Ty. There are multiple threads here: Irv's factory, Nathaniel's disappearance, Darnell's murder, and the BlastMaster con. Each thread seems to be connected to another one, but I'm not certain they're all connected to one another in a single piece of fabric. If Ty discovers more information from Eugene, will he follow that thread into a place where he shouldn't be, a place connected to another thread? The encounter between Sean and Ty in the dark backyard of an abandoned house in Hillside haunts me. The more I think about it, the more terrified I get.

Ty has come so far. I can't bear to think of him dying in a confused encounter where neither side understands what the other is after. If I go along on this visit, I can keep Ty on a short leash.

I hope.

Ty is still scrutinizing me with suspicion. "I thought by now, the police would have taken possession of the lockbox as evidence in Pearl's disappearance," I explain. "But since they haven't, maybe I should see if Eugene has any ideas about where Pearl could be."

"Nice try." Ty grabs his coat. "You just worried Imma get in trouble while I'm in the vicinity of Hillside."

I should know that Ty can see right through me. I heave myself out of my chair and tag behind him to the door. "Yes, you're right. I keep thinking of Darnell bleeding to death when his mom thought he was safely sleeping in his bed. How could I ever face Grandma Betty and Charmaine and Lo if something like that happened to you?"

"I'm not a stupid kid like Darnell." Ty says with his hand on the doorknob.

"Smart or stupid doesn't always matter. The safest driver in the world is toast if a drunk runs a red light. You need someone to watch your back."

My words hang in the air.

"I've always had your back," I whisper.

Ty hands me my coat with a huff. "Fine. Have it your way."

Chapter 35

Our second visit to Eugene's house unfolds differently than the first. When Ty rings the bell, we can hear someone moving inside the house for a full minute before the door opens a crack.

"Hi, Eugene," Ty says in a loud, cheerful voice. "I brought Audrey along with me. Hope you don't mind."

I hold up a tied box from the Swiss Chalet Bakery, a last-minute inspiration that struck on our way out of Palmyrton. "I brought us some treats to enjoy!"

Eugene opens the door as far as it will go on the chain.

"You remembered I was coming today, right?" Ty says, surprised by the old man's suspicion given how warmly he welcomed us on our last visit.

"Anybody follow you here?" Eugene asks. "Look around."

We look up and down the quiet street, but it's already dark. Anyone could be in the shadows.

"Seems okay," Ty answers. "What's wrong?"

Eugene slides back the chain and urges us inside, then quickly locks the door behind us.

"Someone been hasslin' you, Eugene?" Ty asks.

In the bright light of his small front hallway, the man we recall as jovial looks small and diminished. Something is definitely wrong.

"My niece told me it was a mistake to let you come," he says.

Ty and I trade a glance. Why would Eugene's niece Gloria have anything against us?

"Well, we're here now," I say brightly. "Let's sit in the kitchen. I'll put on the tea kettle, we'll eat some cookies, and you can tell us all about it."

We make our way back to the kitchen, and Eugene sits down heavily. "I wish I never told anyone about that painting," he begins.

"How did it come about that you and your great-nephews came to Pearl's sale?" I ask, hoping to get him to begin at the beginning.

"Pearl sent me a note." Eugene gestures to a basket of mail on the counter, and I hand it to him as I fill the kettle with water.

He pulls a small, hand-addressed pink envelope from the basket. "When Irv owned the factory, Pearl always sent cards and notes to the longtime employees. If ever there was a birth or a death or a graduation or a sickness in your family, Pearl would send a card." Eugene hands the card to Ty, and I read it over his shoulder.

Dear Eugene,

Now that Irv has passed, I have decided to sell the house in Palmyrton and move to Florida full-time. I'm selling the Thurman painting, too, as it is too big to move. I thought you might like to come and see it one last time and say good-bye—to the painting and me. I'll be at the house all day on Friday during my estate sale. Hope to see you there.

Best wishes,

Pearl Aronson

The note seems straightforward enough although I suppose it's a little odd that a wealthy widow would be reaching out to one of her husband's former employees. "Were you surprised to get the note, Eugene?"

He shakes his head. "No, Pearl sent me a real nice card when my wife died. And also when my grandchildren were born."

"But had she ever invited you to her home before?" I press. "Do you stay in touch on a regular basis?"

Do you know where she is now?

"No, we don't talk on the phone—nuthin' like that." Eugene smiles. "Pearl's friendly, but it's not like we run with the same crowd."

"Why did she think you'd want to come and say good-bye to her and the painting?" Ty asks.

"Well, that's the odd part, see? I think up until the sale, I was the only person who ever saw that painting finished. Gloria and her sister both told me they never saw it."

"When did he show it to you?" Ty asks.

"Nathaniel didn't actually show it to me. I kinda stumbled into it. See, sometimes after work, I would stop by Nathaniel's studio for a visit. He'd get real caught up in his painting, and my wife worried that he didn't eat right, so she'd send me with home-cooked food for him." Eugene breaks apart one of the cookies I brought but doesn't move to eat it. "One day right after I retired, I showed up with food, and Irv was there. Nathaniel was putting the finishing touches on *Your Move*. They both kinda jumped when I walked in."

"Why?" Ty asks. "Was the painting supposed to be a secret?"

Eugene shrugs. "I didn't notice that painting when I came to the studio a few weeks before, but it could've been covered up. Or maybe he painted it fast, between one visit and the next. Anyway, Nathaniel started talking kinda loud and fast. He said that Irv wanted the painting and was going to hang it in his house in Palmyrton and wasn't that great. He said something like, 'This painting is going into the Irv Aronson *collection*.' Kinda sarcastic, know what I'm sayin'?"

Eugene massages his neck, as if the weight of these thoughts pains him. "Nathaniel seemed agitated, and that worried me. I thought he might be heading into one of his crazy spells."

Nobody says aloud what we are all thinking: Nathaniel disappeared shortly afterwards, so Eugene was right to be worried.

I set the tea mugs down and sit across from Eugene. "And how was Irv behaving?"

Eugene squirms in his chair. "At the time, I didn't think he was acting strange. He sorta laughed and nodded. Then Nathaniel turned to me and said, 'Don't nobody else need to know about this, not even my sisters, hear?'"

"How did you respond to that?"

"I told him, sure, whatever. Then Nathaniel got right up in my face and made me promise not to tell them. So I did." Eugene taps his teaspoon on the table. "Lately, I've been going over and over that day in my mind."

That sounds intriguing. "Why are you thinking about it now?"

"'Cause all kinda strange things been happening lately, and I don't know what any of it means."

Eugene looks imploringly at Ty, so I hold my tongue. Clearly, the old man trusts Ty.

"What strange things?"

"First, someone left a pile of dog dirt on my front porch with a note stuck in it." Eugene wrinkles his nose. "It said, 'forget you ever saw the painting, or you'll be sorry.'"

"Those were the exact words?" I ask. "Do you still have the note?"

"Words to that effect. I didn't keep it." Eugene looks at me like I'm crazy. "It had shit on it!"

Hmmm. A great way to ensure your target destroys the evidence of your threat.

"So back when you walked in on Nathaniel and Irv and the painting, did Irv seem like he was happy to be buying a piece of art that he loved? Did he mention Pearl?" Ty asks. "Because the house is filled with stuff that she picked out."

Eugene shakes his head. "No, they were both acting shifty. I felt like I walked in on two people having a conversation they didn't want to let me in on. So after Nathaniel made me promise not to mention the painting, I dropped off the food and left."

"And you never saw the painting again until you went to Pearl's estate sale?" I ask.

"Nope."

"What happened to Nathaniel's studio after he disappeared?" I ask.

"The police came and looked around after Gloria reported Nathaniel missing. Eventually, when he didn't return, Gloria took all his stuff outta there. She didn't want the bums and addicts to get to it."

I lean closer. "Eugene, recently I met one of the chess players in the painting. His name is Clive Loriss. Do you know him?"

Eugene frowns as he thinks. "Clive? Doesn't ring a bell. I don't play chess myself. I didn't realize the chess players were based on real people."

I launch into Clive's theory that the painting contains a message, possibly related to Darnell. "He's wearing an expensive Founders shirt in the painting. Did you make that brand in Irv's factory?"

"Yes—Founders was our biggest customer. Still is, I think." Eugene bites into a cookie and chews thoughtfully. "No way would Darnell be wearin' one of those expensive shirts in real life. If ever a shirt didn't pass the quality inspection, it had to be destroyed. Founders wouldn't allow the seconds to be sold, like some brands do. Said it would undermine their reputation."

Ty rolls his eyes. "Don't want their clothes to be associated with poor folks, I guess."

"But what about Clive's idea that the shirt was a message inserted into the painting," I ask.

Eugene gazes around his homey kitchen: the snapshots and class photos of grandchildren on the fridge, the calendar from the local Chinese restaurant on the wall, the souvenir pitcher from a trip to Niagara Falls on the shelf. "I loved Nathaniel, but I sure never understood him. If there were messages in his paintings, I don't know what they are."

Ty brings the conversation back to the here and now. "What other strange things have been happening to you?"

"This is crazy." Eugene takes a gulp of tea to fortify himself. "The FBI left a message on my answering machine saying they wanted to talk to me. When I told my niece Gloria, she about hit the ceiling. She told me to keep my mouth shut and not answer the message. But keep my mouth shut about what? I don't know nuthin' of interest to the FBI! And what if they come here? What am I supposed to do?"

I feel sorry for the poor old gentleman. He looks so confused and distraught.

"I can help you with that, Eugene," Ty says, and proceeds to explain the BlastMaster investigation and how, in the course of explaining to the FBI what brought him to Hillside, Ty had mentioned Eugene.

"BlastMaster? That toy they've been talking about on TV?" Eugene looks even more perplexed than before. "What would I know about that?"

"The FBI wouldn't give me any information on where their investigation was headed," Ty says, "but the agent got very interested when I told him about Irv Aronson and the factory."

Eugene's hands grip the tea mug. He gazes into the liquid looking like he wants to dive in and swim away.

"What do you know about the new owners?" I ask. "Could they be involved in something illegal?"

Eugene stares at us for a long minute. "I sure hope not. That factory has provided good jobs for a lot of local people for a long time. Of course, a lot of the old timers I knew are gone now."

I recall that his niece Gloria, who we met on our first visit, still works at the factory. Could this be the reason she told her uncle not to talk to us? Does she know something sketchy is going on at the factory? "But you said things are different there now." I nudge him. "What do you know about the new owners?"

"I enjoyed my job, and I woulda kept working as long as I had the energy." Eugene shakes his head. "But when Irv sold the factory, he told me there would be changes. He said old dogs like us don't like to learn new tricks. Told me it would be best if I retired. Offered me a big bonus for my years of service and threw me a real nice party."

But Eugene doesn't look happy at the memory. He continues to stare into his tea, lost in thought.

We let the silence hang for a while. Finally, Ty speaks. "You think Irv was tryin' to get you outta the way?"

Eugene looks up at us. "I managed the whole shop floor. Knew every piece of material that came into the factory. Knew every finished item that shipped out. Knew every worker on the floor."

Ty laces his fingers. "Sounds like maybe you knew too much."

Chapter 36

Ty and I walk away from Eugene's house, both lost in thought. The evening is raw with a damp, cold wind. We had parked my car in the only available spot halfway down the street. When we reach it, Ty takes my keys from his pocket since he drove us here and will drive us back. Sitting behind the steering wheel is becoming increasingly uncomfortable, so I'm happy to let him drive. We could've taken his car on this junket, but I figured I'd have more leverage to veto side trips in search of the BlastMaster conman if we were in my car.

"So what do you think?" I ask to break the silence once we're on the road.

"I think there's something going on at that factory. I think it started with the new owners. But I think Irv knew about it." Ty leans forward to peer at the small street signs on the corners in Hillside. "And I think Nathaniel knew what was going on there, too."

"What about Gloria," I ask? "Why is she warning Eugene to keep his mouth shut?"

Ty frowns as he navigates down a narrow street lined with parked cars. "She's the only one in this group who still works there. Maybe she's caught up in the action at the factory and doesn't want her uncle to find out."

That seems plausible. But the theory doesn't make me happy. Gloria seems like a nice person. She cooks for her uncle and cleans out his fridge and has sons who go to college even if they're not particularly enthusiastic about art. But as Sean likes to remind me, not all criminals are slimeballs.

And not all slimeballs are criminals.

"And she took everything that remained in Nathaniel's studio," Ty continues. "Maybe she and her sons planned the defacement to bring attention to Nathaniel's work and drive up the value of the paintings they must have."

"Would they know enough about how the art world works to do that?" I ask.

Ty doesn't answer. He's concentrating on turning left at a tricky intersection. If my mental map is correct, the entrance ramp to the highway is in the other direction. "Where are we going?"

"Relax. I just wanna drive past the factory. I'm not getting out of the car."

We make a few more turns on the narrow streets and suddenly the hulking four story building appears ahead of us, the rows of narrow windows impenetrable to our eyes. A spotlight shines on the rooftop sign that says I A Industries with the picture of the big American flag. "I don't know what you expect to see," I grumble. "Whatever might be going on inside, you can't tell from out here."

Ty says nothing, his lips pressed in a hard line. He drives down the street, then turns on the intersecting side street. From this angle, we can see the short side of the building. He stares for a while, then points. "Look up there. There's lights on in the last six windows on the top floor."

I twist my head to see. "Okay, maybe someone forgot to turn them off. Or maybe that's the office and someone's working late. Although I sure wouldn't want to be all alone in that big, creepy building."

"Neither would I."

We drive away from the factory, and in a few minutes we're on the highway heading toward Palmyrton. Ty turns on the wipers as a sleety drizzle hits the windshield. His hands look tight on the wheel. "Is the road getting slick?"

"A little. I wish that guy wasn't riding my ass."

Bright headlights shine into our car. Ty adjusts the rearview mirror and scowls. "Why is he tailgating me? He could pass me if he wants to go faster."

I twist to look behind us. A big SUV is right behind us in the middle lane, even though the left lane is totally clear. Ty signals and moves into the right lane to get away from the car riding our bumper.

The SUV also moves into the right lane. What's going on?

Then the car ahead of us slows down dramatically as he hits a huge puddle of slush. I grip my armrest thinking we're going to be crushed between the speeding SUV behind us and the slowpoke in front.

In a skillful maneuver, Ty pulls onto the shoulder and the SUV surges forward, nearly clipping the bumper of the car ahead before moving across to the left lane and tearing off into the night.

Ty's hand shoots out to protect me as we skid to a stop on the shoulder. "You okay?"

"Yeah," I answer shakily. "Good defensive driving, Ty. What's wrong with that jerk?"

Ty pulls cautiously back onto the highway. "I think he mighta followed us from Eugene's house."

"Really?" Up to that moment, I hadn't taken Eugene's paranoia in opening the door seriously. "You noticed him back there for a long time?"

"I noticed we passed a big SUV when we pulled away from the factory. I didn't pay much attention to it until that SUV started tailgating us. I think it could have been the same one."

Either we're both as paranoid as Eugene, or something sinister really is going on here. "Let's get back home, Ty. I think we need to turn all this over to the police and the FBI."

⎯⎯⎯◉⎯⎯⎯

Ty picks up his car at the AMT office and tells me he'll see me tomorrow. I arrive home shortly before eight.

"Where have you been?" Sean asks as I enter the kitchen.

"Hello to you too, dear." I kiss him on the cheek.

He frowns. "I was worried when I came home to an empty house. Why didn't you leave a note or text me?"

How would I have phrased that text? *I'm off to Hillside on an escapade with Ty. See you later.* That would've prompted an immediate command not to go. And an argument from me. I react to Sean's over-protectiveness about as well as Ty reacts to mine.

I give Sean a chipper smile and hang up my coat. There's no way I'm mentioning the road rage incident on the highway, but I can't lie about my whereabouts. "Ty and I went to see Eugene. We had a very interesting visit."

Sean crosses the room and stands in front of me. "What? Why would you two go there alone at night?"

"It's not night. We went there right after work."

"Don't split hairs, Audrey." An angry flush appears on his fair cheeks, making his freckles stand out. "You and Ty went off freelancing. My god, you're just as reckless as he is."

Now my back is up. "We were not reckless. We just went to Eugene's house and talked to him. Ty wanted to explain that Eugene's name came up during his interview with the FBI."

Sean pulls his phone from his pocket and waves it under my nose. "Has Ty never heard of this device? A simple heads-up phone call would have sufficed. You two went there on a fishing expedition."

Of course, this is true. Not for nothing that my husband is a detective. "I wanted to keep Ty out of trouble."

"Stop worrying about a grown man and start worrying about your babies." He kicks Ethel's dog toy and sends it flying. "Audrey, you're nearly seven months pregnant. This isn't about just you anymore. You're responsible for the lives of two children. *Our* children. You don't have the right to put them at risk."

Our children. Reflexively, my hand moves to cradle my belly. It never dawned on me that this trip would be dangerous for them. A wave of guilt and remorse hits me as I think of how close we came to a terrible crash. I run my hands over my belly and shudder imagining the airbag slamming the twins full force. I can never admit this to my husband. "I'm sorry, Sean," I whisper. "You're right."

Sean is taken aback by my quick concession. Not sure what to do with his anger, he turns away from me and lets the dog out into the backyard for a brief potty stop.

I scrounge in the kitchen for a snack while he heads down the hall and upstairs. Knowing it's best to give him some space, I pick at my leftovers with a hopeful Ethel at my feet. "Will I ever get this motherhood thing right, girl?"

She lays her snout on my knee and offers one slow swish of her fluffy tail.

Ethel forgives everything: late meals, missed walks, stepped-on paws. Will my children be as resilient?

I have a half-silly, half-terrifying vision of super-dog Ethel pulling the twins back from the edge of a cliff and blocking their path into a raging river while I'm pre-occupied with some puzzling conundrum. "Will you help me with this motherhood gig, Ethel?"

She gives a short, sharp bark. Signing on for duty or impatient for the last bite of my chicken? I give her the treat and head upstairs.

Sean is reading his science fiction novel in bed

"So, what happened with Pearl's box," I ask cautiously as I load my toothbrush with paste.

"We finally got it open this evening. Kind of anti-climactic. It contained a receipt for *Your Move*. Irv Aronson paid Nathaniel Thurman $50,000 for the painting."

I stop brushing and spit. "Fifty thousand dollars! No way was it worth that much seven years ago. Ty thought we could get twenty-five grand for it now, after all the publicity surrounding Thurman's disappearance."

Sean places his bookmark as I get into bed. "I guess Irv was a patron of the arts."

From what I've heard, Irv was generous but drove a hard bargain. And why hide the receipt in a special locked box instead of filing it with the rest of his business transactions? But now is no time to be questioning the conclusions of my husband and his colleagues. I keep my doubts to myself and snuggle alongside Sean.

He reaches out and pulls me into his arms. "I love you, and I can hardly wait to raise these kids with you."

I snuggle into his embrace. "Me too."

All thoughts of Irv, Pearl, Eugene, and the painting slip away.

Chapter 37

Saturday morning dawns crisp and sunny. A fine dusting of snow has fallen overnight—real snow, not that horrible frozen slush. Just enough to make the world seem festive and fresh, but not enough to clog the roads or throw out the backs of sidewalk shovelers. Over breakfast, Sean and I make plans for the day.

"Let's go get our Christmas tree this morning," I say. "And we can decorate it later today after we finish our other errands."

I want to start and end the day with something fun because the middle is going to be a chore. We've been nominated to select for Sean's parents the big "family gift" from all the siblings. The siblings have agreed in principle that this should be two matching chairs to replace the worn-out brown velour BarcaLoungers in the Coughlins' family room. But the wrangling isn't close to being over. Terry and Alison, perpetually broke, will want the cheapest possible models, while Brendan and Adrienne will want to up their parents' style quotient with something on the cutting edge of fashion. But since "power recline" is one of the must-have features, I think we're out of the race to be spotlighted on HGTV. Everyone agrees that Sean and I are the shoppers most likely to bring home chairs Joe and Mary will actually sit in, but I anticipate lots of texting and photo exchanges before the deal is sealed.

Sean agrees to the agenda, and after breaking the news to Ethel that she can't come along on this jaunt, we set off.

As we pass the Palmyrton Garden Center, I cast a wistful look at the rows of lush Christmas trees on display. I've long contended they have the best selection of super-fresh trees, but Sean insists we get our tree at the lot run as a fundraiser by the Police Benevolent Association. Last year, our tree's needles all dropped by New Year's Eve, but I guess that's a small price to pay to support the good works done by the PBA.

The intoxicating scent of balsam and spruce and fir greets us as we exit the car. The trees lean against wooden frames, organized by type and size, with the small, spindly balsams destined for the homes of apartment dwellers separated from the towering Fraser firs that will reside in cathedral ceiling family rooms. I hook my arm through Sean's, basking in the glow that I no longer qualify for the Charlie Brown Christmas tree of my single-girl past.

The cops running the lot immediately hail Sean as one of their own. After some backslapping and introductions, we get down to brass tacks. "What can I show you?" a burly off-duty cop in a Carhart coat and a stocking cap asks.

"A Fraser." I speak with authority. If we're shopping here, we're going top-of-the-line. "Seven feet."

The cop grins. "The lady knows what she wants." He winks at Sean. "The wives always do." Sean joins him in "whattaya gonna do, bro" laughter.

I choose to ignore the silly sexism in his remark. We head for the row of Frasers, and I see Sean wince at the seventy-dollar price tag. But sexism works both ways. I know my husband won't balk at the price in front of his colleague.

The cop chooses a tree and pulls it out, banging its stump on the ground to make the branches fluff out.

"That looks good," Sean says.

It *is* a nice tree, but we've just begun to shop. "We can't buy the first one," I say. "Let me see that one," I point out another tree, and the cop dutifully pulls it out.

I circle the tree looking for flaws while Sean stands with his hands in his coat pockets. "That one's nice and full, too," he says to encourage me to decide.

"It's got a hole on this side." Rejecting the second tree, I head further down the aisle. Behind me, I can feel Sean and the cop rolling their eyes and shaking their heads. But I won't be denied my tree shopping experience. I stop in front of another tree. "Let's see this one."

The cop pulls it out, staggering under the weight. This tree is a good two feet taller than my six-one husband.

"This is too tall, Audrey. You'll never fit the angel on top."

Reluctantly, I must agree. "Okay, forget that one." I smile at our salesman. "You don't mind showing me another tree, do you?"

"Nah, you gotta find the right tree," he assures me. "How about this one?"

I back up and study it from a distance. No holes, but the bottom branches are droopy. Those could be trimmed, however. "This one's in the running. Let's look at it next to the first one."

Sean sighs and pinches the bridge of his nose as he follows us back to the first tree. No doubt he'll be the butt of some jokes in the office next week.

I study the two trees side-by-side. "The one on the right. Definitely."

"That was the tree we started with!" Sean protests.

I smile sweetly. "Yes, but now I'm positive it's the right one."

The cop salesman drags the tree to the payment area where he makes a fresh cut on the trunk and runs the tree through the gadget that binds the branches. While this is going on, another customer arrives, and he and Sean greet each other. I recognize him as a fellow detective that I've met briefly before. After we all say hello, he starts talking shop with Sean. I'm busy pointing out our car so the tree can be loaded, but I hear the name Pearl Aronson pass between my husband and the other detective.

Once we've paid and Sean has double-checked to make sure the tree is securely tied to the roof, we pull out. We're barely into the road before I start. "What was that about? I heard him mention Pearl."

Sean glances heavenward. "Don't worry about it."

"C'mon, Sean. I like the old gal. She was a client. I want to know if you guys think she's dead or alive."

Sean points the car toward Route 10 where we plan to visit some furniture stores. "The nephew has been cooperating. They got access to Pearl's bank records. She withdrew ten grand right before she disappeared and there hasn't been any activity on her accounts or her credit cards since."

I take a sharp breath. "That sounds ominous."

Sean rolls his shoulders as he drives. "It's interesting, for sure. Could be someone pressured her for money then killed her once they got it. But ten grand isn't all that much for a woman like Pearl. If someone is blackmailing her, why not go for more?"

"True. But what other scenario would explain the large cash withdrawal and the disappearance?"

Sean shoots me a sideways glance. His cop instinct is to withhold information, but his spouse instinct is to talk it over with me.

The husband instinct prevails. "Maybe she got a supply of cash and went into hiding somewhere."

Chapter 38

When we pull onto Route 10, home to every big box store known to American shoppers, traffic is at a standstill.

"Oh, geez—look at the gridlock!" Sean pounds the steering wheel. "Every person in northern New Jersey is shopping here today. We should've come here first to beat the crowds."

"We're in no rush," I remind him. "We just have to go to two furniture stores and Target for some extra tree lights. Think of the slow traffic as a way for us to spend more time together."

"You have a point," Sean says. "Since you're trapped in this car with me, why don't you tell me all about your visit with Eugene last night."

So I relate to Sean all that transpired in Eugene's kitchen, and all Ty's and my theories. I even tell him that we drove past the factory and saw lights on the top floor. The only detail I leave out is our near collision on Route 78 on the way home.

Because that had nothing to do with Eugene or the factory. Just because Ty thought he saw a big SUV near the factory doesn't mean it was the same SUV that tailgated us on the highway.

New Jersey is full of SUVs.

Right?

My husband listens attentively, asking only a few questions. At the end of my story, he says, "I think I need to call the FBI on Monday. There are a lot of strange loose ends all leading back to Hillside. Maybe Agent Magee is aware of them and was playing his cards close to the vest with you and Ty. But just in case he's not as sharp as he thinks he is, I'd better share this with him."

As we're talking, Sean starts waving at the people in the car crawling along in the lane beside us. It's our neighbors from down the street. I smile and wave, too. "Boy, you weren't exaggerating when you said everyone in the state is on this road."

Sean cranes his neck. "I think the furniture store is at the next intersection."

Soon we're off the road and circling the parking lot for a space. "I'll drop you off at the front door and park in the back. You can do some preliminary reconnaissance."

Miles of silver and gold garland festoon the huge furniture store. An artificial Christmas tree stands guard in every department as "I'm Dreaming of a White Christmas" blares over the sound system. I make my way through Dining Rooms and Bedrooms until I find the line-up of behemoth recliners in the back of the store. They're all ugly. My job is to find the least offensive one.

And then buy two of them.

Sean arrives fifteen minutes later after I've already tested and rejected three chairs. "Don't even look at those—they're out of the running. Which of these two do you like best?"

Sean reclines and I take some action shots to send to his siblings.

"If they don't vote in the next five minutes, they don't get to vote at all," Sean warns. "I'm not hanging around here all day waiting for Adrienne to weigh in."

The siblings vote and the decision is unanimous. They even agree on the sage green upholstery instead of the murky hides-the-dirt beige Mary and Joe would have chosen if left to their own devices.

"That's a freakin' Christmas miracle," Sean mutters as we flag down a beleaguered salesman and close the deal. "Now we don't have to go to the second furniture store."

"Next stop—Target. And then home to decorate. We can go to the Panera drive-through for a little sustenance on our way."

Fortified, we enter Target ostensibly to procure two strings of white lights and some picture hooks. But once inside the sprawling store, we both think of a dozen other things we need. "I'm going to Hardware and Kitchen Supplies," Sean says. "I'll meet you in Christmas Decorations."

We part ways, and I quickly find the lights we need from the fast-emptying shelves. I decide to head over to Home Accessories to see if I can find some nice throw cushions to match the new recliners. On my way across the store, I greet a former client and nod to a familiar-looking man who might be a volunteer at the Parks Center.

As I stand evaluating throw cushions—bold or traditional?—I overhear a woman barking orders at a young man who's a foot taller than she is. "Put those towels in the cart and come tell me which lamp you want—black or silver?"

"Aw, Mom—I don't care. Let's finish up and get outta here."

"We drove to this Target because it has the best selection. I don't want to forget anything."

Feeling holiday camaraderie, I smile and prepare to speak. My eyes meet the woman's, and we recognize each other in the same instant.

Gloria, Eugene's niece. And the young man is her son, the older of the two who came to the sale.

Gloria's eyes widen. "You," she says in a harsh exhale. "You need to stay away from my family." She heads down the pillow aisle toward me. I keep my big, red shopping cart between us. Gloria is a statuesque woman—taller than me and broader in the shoulders. In my current condition, we're about the same weight, but I have no doubt she could knock me flat if she chose to.

"I don't know—"

Gloria places her hands on one side of my shopping cart. "Don't you play dumb with me. You and that young man you run with and old Pearl Aronson are looking to make money off my brother's painting. And then you have the nerve to cause trouble for me at my job and upset my poor old uncle."

Her stream of accusations comes at me so fast and hard, I can barely process the words. "I'm not—"

She shakes the shopping cart. "You leave us alone, hear? I worked hard my whole life to support my sons, to keep them off the streets. I won't let anyone take what I've earned, earned with my hard work, away from me." Gloria's eyes narrow to slits. "You stay outta my bizness."

"Mom, c'mon." Her son tugs at her arm. I can't decide if he's simply embarrassed by her outburst or worried that she's digging herself into a deeper hole.

Gloria takes one step backward, but she's not done yet. "This here is your world," she lifts her hands to the gleaming suburban Target store. "You don't know nuthin' about life in Hillside. You need to stay away from there or you'll be sorry."

"Mom!" Her son places a hand on each of her shoulders and pulls her backwards. "Let's go right now."

Another shopper is trying to get down this aisle, so with a final scowl, Gloria rolls off.

By the time Sean tracks me down in Home Furnishings, the tremor in my hands has ceased. "Let's check out," I say. "This place is overwhelming."

We join the end of a long, snaking check-out line. I don't see Gloria and her son anywhere in the crowd, and I want to keep it that way. I'm afraid if I tell Sean about the encounter, he'll go off looking for the woman who assailed me.

And I'm not up for prolonging this encounter. My back hurts and my feet hurt and I have to pee (again). I want to get home and relax—maybe take a nap before we tackle decorating the tree.

I can tell Sean about Gloria tomorrow, before he talks to Agent Magee.

"You okay?" Sean asks as I gaze out the window on the ride home, thinking about Gloria's outburst. She's suspicious of me and I'm suspicious of her. Why did she say I was causing trouble for her at her job? Was she playing tough to scare me off? Or is she herself scared, worried that I'm going to make her situation worse?

"Just tired all of a sudden." I pat his knee. "I'll get a second wind when I see the tree set up in the living room."

As we approach our house, we can see three more packages have been delivered to the front porch in our absence. Up ahead, an Amazon van disappears around the corner. "Man, these deliveries are nonstop. Those guys work from sunrise to late at night, seven days a week during the holiday season," Sean marvels.

When we get inside, he goes to retrieve the packages while I flop down on the sofa. Man, it feels good to be horizontal!

Sean returns, handing one box to me and keeping two for himself. I accept the Amazon package—a game for one of Deirdre's kids—with a frown. "Still nothing from that Etsy vendor. I bought a bracelet for Natalie on Black Friday and it still hasn't come."

"Maybe tomorrow," Sean assures me. "I'm expecting a big one for you, so don't go opening anything that comes while I'm out."

I feel my eyelids flutter. "Do you need me to help you bring the tree into the house?"

"Nah, I can manage. You rest."

When I wake up, it's dark outside and the tree is glittering in the corner. Sean is adjusting the final strand of bulbs. "You did the lights," I murmur groggily.

"I figured you wouldn't mind. I saved the ornaments for you. Did I get the lights evenly distributed, captain?"

I sit up, refreshed. I don't know how Sean managed to get the tree in the stand single-handedly. I've missed the annual argument about which side of the tree should face the room and whether the screws in the trunk are holding the tree straight. Yet the tree looks perfect.

All that's left for me is the fun part: hanging my collection of vintage Shiny Bright ornaments, each on precisely the right branch. Sean extends his hand and helps me off the sofa. We study the tree together, his chin resting on the top of my head, his hands cradling our babies.

I take a red and silver ornament with a starburst pattern from its nest of tissue paper and reach out to hang it.

This is going to be my best Christmas ever.

Chapter 39

"I'll be home by three-thirty to go to your doctor's appointment with you." Sean kisses me good-bye on Monday morning and heads off to work.

I stare glumly at the clock on the oven as I shovel cereal into my mouth. Seven-thirty. I have eight long hours with nothing to do before the "excitement" of a doctor's visit.

I suppose I can write a few more Christmas cards. In the past, I've been pretty hit-or-miss with card-sending. But this year I had cards printed up with a photo of me and Sean proudly displaying the baby bump. This should surprise a few of my far-flung college friends. But the concept of sharing our happy news is more appealing than the actual work of writing a short note and hand-addressing the envelopes.

Every time I seal an envelope, I'm reminded of the *Seinfeld* episode where George's fiancée poisons herself by licking the envelopes of her wedding invitations. To distract myself, I search for the clip on YouTube. This leads me down the rabbit hole of watching other priceless *Seinfeld* clips, including a few featuring George's father, played by the hilarious Jerry Stiller. And watching Jerry Stiller reminds me of...someone...someone I know...

Irv Aronson.

The resemblance is only passing—the smile and the mustache—but Jerry Stiller reminds me of the photo of Irv that appeared in his obituary. And thinking of Irv makes me think of Pearl. And the factory. And Gloria. And *Your Move*.

I realize that in the Hallmark glow of decorating the tree last night, I never did tell Sean about my encounter with Gloria. I suppose I should do that before Sean talks to Special Agent Magee. I text my husband to call me when he gets a chance. I add, *Don't worry. Not a problem,* to diffuse pregnancy-related worries.

Then I go back to thinking about Pearl. Where is she? Is she alive or dead? And why is no one knocking themselves out to look for her?

I remember that Pearl planned to donate the proceeds of the estate sale to charity because Irv's nephews—their only relatives—had enough money.

Maybe the family feels some resentment over that, which reduces their desire to find the old gal. In my experience, having more than enough doesn't stop people from wanting even more.

And maybe Pearl has too many friends. If she had one, single best friend, that person might feel compelled to take charge of a search. Ironically, having scores of friends diffuses responsibility. Each person thinks someone else will handle it.

In addition to Pearl's neighbors, there was a contingent of friends from her synagogue who showed up at the estate sale. I wonder if they might have useful information without realizing it. I look up Irv's obituary to refresh my memory. The Aronsons were members of Temple Shalom in Palmyrton. I hop over to the temple's website.

The photo of the rabbi at Temple Shalom depicts a stylish woman in her forties with a friendly smile. I'm pleasantly surprised; I guess I was expecting a solemn, bearded Talmudic scholar. Then I reprimand myself. Who's to say Rabbi Sheila Hirsch isn't a Talmudic scholar, albeit a fashionable one? But the fact that she looks similar to me and my friends makes it easier for me to cold-call her with a strange question: *Do you have any idea where Pearl Aronson might be hiding?*

To which she most likely will reply, *"What's it to you?"*

Before I dial, I mentally prepare my explanation. But I'm finding it a challenge to come up with a cover story for the truth: I'm a bored, lonely, perpetually curious pregnant woman and Pearl was my likable, intriguing client who started behaving weirdly after her painting was defaced while in my care. And I don't think the police, or anyone else, is doing enough to find her.

Finally, I decide there's no way around it—I'm going to have to tell the rabbi a little white lie.

Or three.

I call Rabbi Hirsch and introduce myself as a volunteer at the Rosa Parks Community Center. So far, so true—I do help my dad with the children's chess club there. I tell her Pearl has made a generous gift to the center, and the kids would like to invite her to one of their performances given her enthusiasm for the arts.

This could be true. I wouldn't doubt that Pearl and Irv donated to the Parks Center.

"She told them she'd love to see their work someday. But we haven't been able to get in touch with her," I tell the rabbi. "Pearl hasn't acknowledged our invitation one way or the other, which is very unusual for her. She's a very gracious person."

"Indeed, she is," Sheila Hirsch replies. "But why are you reaching out to me?"

"We were worried about Pearl. And she always spoke so highly of you and the Temple Shalom community. I just thought..." I trail off. "Well, I knew it was a long shot, but I thought if anyone would know how to reach Pearl, it would be you."

There's a period of silence before Rabbi Hirsch speaks. "Several of Pearl's friends here have expressed concern to me that Pearl has been out of touch." She doesn't say more. I sense she's waiting to see how I'll respond. You don't get to be rabbi of a prosperous temple by blabbing about your congregation members to total strangers on the phone.

"Maybe we could all put our heads together," I suggest. "I know Pearl was involved in a mahjong group. Would that be a good place to start?"

The fact that I know Pearl well enough to know about the mahjong group seems to reassure Rabbi Hirsh. "The ladies meet today at one for their weekly game. Feel free to drop by if you wish."

My day is looking up!

Surely, Ubering across town to visit a bunch of game-playing old ladies doesn't qualify as over-exertion. And I can be back home well before my doctor's appointment. I eat lunch and change into my dowdiest maternity wear. Who can mistrust a pregnant lady?

I arrive at the Temple Shalom, a modern building with a glass-walled front entrance, and a receptionist directs me to a large room containing three tables with four chairs each. Each table contains mahjong tiles, and the ladies are getting themselves positioned to play. They all look to be in their seventies and eighties. Some have silver hair, but others have resolutely clung to the shades of their youth: jet black, Titian red, platinum blond. They all look up and contemplate me with suspicion.

Before I can speak, Rabbi Hirsch arrives, apparently notified of my arrival by the receptionist. She introduces me to the mahjong players, and they all begin talking at once. Their voices rise in agitation as they talk about who saw

Pearl last, what she said to each of them, and what might possibly explain her absence. The theories range from cancer treatment to plastic surgery to a late-life romance with an old flame.

"She might have connected with a man from high school on the Facebook." A mournful woman shakes her head in disapproval. "And maybe they decided to get back together to rekindle the flame and don't want anyone to know."

A cheerful lady wags her finger at her dour partner. "Now Esther, that's the kind of talk that Pearl always warned against. She always said not to long for the past, but to look ahead to the future, even at our age."

"Hmmph," the other lady says, snatching away some tiles from her opponent.

But the cheerful lady's comment reminds me of something Pearl said on the day of the estate sale. "Pearl told me she used to perform on the Borscht Belt. She said those were happy times, but that those old resorts don't exist anymore."

"Ach!" the crabby lady laments. "Our whole family would leave Brooklyn every summer to spend two months at The Concord. The ladies and kids spent the whole summer, and the men would come for the weekends."

"The Concord's been closed since the nineties," a lady with black hair declares. "I think they tore it down."

This jibes with what I recall Pearl saying—that many of the old resorts were now closed. But she also said some had been repurposed. Could there be....

"I don't recall that Pearl ever performed at The Concord," a bossy lady slams her tiles on the table. "They got all the really big acts there in the Fifties. I remember seeing Buddy Hackett once."

A quieter lady nods in agreement. "I think Pearl performed at some of the smaller venues."

"She met Irv at Grossinger's, that I know for sure," a lady in a sky-blue pant suit asserts.

"She did," the quiet lady replies. "But I remember her telling me it was pure luck their paths crossed because normally she performed at another place, a smaller place. Now what was it called?" She tilts her head back and closes her eyes.

The game and the conversation move on without her.

I hear the tiles clicking as the ladies' hands dart across the tables taking tiles from a wall and discarding tiles from their hands. When someone discards a tile, she announces what it is, so there's always a low buzz of sound. They seem to have forgotten about me and Pearl as the play intensifies. Maybe it was a waste of time coming here. I'll wait a little longer and see if an opportunity arises for me to ask more questions.

Suddenly the quiet lady shouts, "Mortenson's!"

Is that part of the game? Surely not.

The others turn to stare at her.

"Mortenson's is the name of the small resort where Pearl once performed," the lady clarifies. "I knew it would come to me. It's still in business, too. Mountain bike trails is what they offer these days."

The lady with the jet-black hair frowns. "It's your turn, Lucille. Are you playing, or walking down memory lane?"

Chastened, Lucille draws a tile.

I pat her shoulder as I leave. I think I've learned something here.

Chapter 40

I make it back home well before three-thirty. Surprisingly, Sean never did call me back. "Don't tell Dad I was out investigating," I warn Ethel as I return to my computer to do more digging. I quickly find the Mortenson's website and read the introductory information on the homepage.

Mortenson's Resort has been owned and operated by four generations of the Mortenson family. Once one of the grand Borchst Belt hotels, Mortenson's now offers a range of recreational opportunities to modern families, including tennis, water sports, mountain biking, and our recently added zip-lining course.

My heart quickens as I look at the main chalet-style lodge surrounded by individual bungalows, all out in the woods miles from nowhere in rural New York. Four generations of family ownership means that one of Pearl's contemporaries might still be around even if he doesn't manage the place. This could be it. Wouldn't Mortenson's be the perfect place for Pearl to lie low until whatever is going down at the factory is resolved and she feels it's safe to emerge?

When I hear the garage door go up, I quickly log off my computer. Sean enters the dining room and smiles at the array of cards, envelopes, and stamps spread across the table. "Wow—haven't you been busy, Santa's helper! Our cards might actually get delivered before Christmas this year."

I raise my cheek for a kiss. "I'm embracing my inner elf."

Assuming some elves are assigned to tracking missing persons.

I haven't decided how I'm going to share my theory about Pearl's whereabouts with Sean—maybe I'll confess my trip to the synagogue or maybe just claim a flash of divine inspiration—but I know I'm not getting into it now, right before the doctor's appointment.

Sean is always more nervous about these appointments than I am, worrying that every calamity outlined in the *What to Expect* book will befall me. Once we saw the twin heartbeats on the first ultrasound confirming that there really was something alive inside me, I've been pretty chill about this pregnancy. As far as I'm concerned, the hard part—conceiving—is over, and we're now coasting to the finish line. Apart from some lower back pain and heartburn, I feel great.

I follow Sean back into the car, and he is quiet on the short ride to the doctor's office. Once we arrive, we take seats among the crowd of expectant parents. I leaf through a parenting magazine—sleeping issues, weaning, solid foods. Same articles I read last month. Sean sits beside me with his hands tightly clasped.

We quickly progress to the examining room. Dr. McLaughlin enters with her usual calm good cheer. Before beginning the exam, she asks if we have any concerns.

I say no. Sean whips out his detective's notebook and begins peppering her with questions. She answers each one patiently, assuring him that despite the plan to deliver the twins at thirty-six weeks, they'll be fully cooked when they arrive.

She turns to examine me, and I expect the usual pat on the back and "keep up the good work, mom" I get every month.

Instead, she frowns when she takes my blood pressure.

Sean immediately keys in to her expression. "What's wrong?"

"Audrey's blood pressure is a little high."

"Pre-eclampsia?" Sean's voice quivers with worry. This is the mother of all complications.

The doctor shakes her head. "It hasn't risen to that yet. Were you rushing to get here? Anything stressful happen today?"

"No," Sean answers for me. "She was home all day writing Christmas cards. But yesterday, we spent the day shopping and decorating. That must've been too much exertion."

Sean and the doctor both stare at me, but I keep my eyes focused on the fetal development poster on the wall. Geez, did my foray into investigative work cause this uptick in my blood pressure?

"Okay, don't worry." Dr. Mclaughlin squeezes my hand and smiles at Sean. "Just take it easy. Spend a couple hours every day with your feet elevated. And I'm going to want to see you once a week for these last four weeks before delivery."

"I don't see how I can possibly take it any easier and not be in a coma," I grouse as we leave.

"Audrey, you have to listen to the doctor," Sean scolds. "We're going home and you're putting your feet up. I'll make dinner."

I can't argue with a home-cooked meal. But it's clear to me I'd better not share my theories on Pearl's whereabouts over the dinner table. And forget about the encounter with Gloria.

On Tuesday morning, I log in for a Zoom chat with Donna and Ty at the office.

Donna reports that she's updated our website, purged our mailing list, and scheduled social media posts for every day between now and our next sale in January.

Ty reports that he's dispatched to the dump or to charity every unsold item hanging around the office or the back of the van.

"We rented a shampoo-er from Lowes and cleaned the office carpet and I put fresh shelf liners in the supply closet," Donna adds.

The two of them stare at me expectantly through the screen. "Great work, team. We've never been this caught-up before the holiday break." I bite my thumbnail. "I guess I should stay home more often."

We laugh, but one fact remains: my employees are looking at a week with nothing to do. I shift my weight on the sofa. "So, how would you two feel about an unconventional assignment?"

Ty rolls his eyes. "This oughta be good."

I fill them in on my visit to the synagogue. "Why don't you take a road trip to Mortenson's tomorrow and find out if Pearl is there?"

"Why don't you just call and ask?" Ty counters.

Donna makes a face. "If she's hiding, they're not going to put our call right through to her."

"I'm willing to drive," Ty says, "but I don't wanna hang around to see what happens when a big black dude shows up in cow-town looking for a little old Jewish lady."

"I'll do the talking," Donna volunteers. "I'll think of a cover story. It'll be fun. We can stop at the outlet mall on our way home and finish our Christmas shopping."

Ty's face registers some interest in that agenda. I think he still hasn't found the right "wow" gift for Lo to replace the BlastMaster. "If we find Pearl, what do you want us to do?" he asks.

"Good question. I don't want to scare her and make her feel she has to run and hide again. But I'd feel better knowing she's alive. Then if we figure out the connection between the factory and the painting and...." I scratch my head, not sure where I'm heading with this. "Well, it would be good to know where she is, right?"

They both seem to see this journey as a way to humor me while occupying themselves during this dead pre-holiday time in the estate sale business. It will take about two hours to drive to the Catskills, so they agree to leave at nine tomorrow and report in after lunch.

Ty ends the conversation with a request. "You mind if I leave the office a little early today, Audge? I want to go into the city to see a gallery exhibit, and I don't want to be on a rush-hour train."

"No problem. What's the show?" I ask.

"No one famous," Ty says. "It's a group show of hyper-realist paintings at a gallery in Washington Heights owned by one of Carter's friends. He thought I might like to see some of the stuff."

"Ooo—Mr. Art World!" Donna teases. "Are you going to drink champagne and meet the artists? What are you going to wear?"

Ty waves off her mockery. "That's why I want to get there early. I can look at the paintings in peace before the art snobs show up. And maybe I'll swing by the tree in Rockefeller Center on the way back to the train."

"Sounds like fun," I say wistfully. Sean and I love going into Manhattan during the holiday season, but the journey is off the list this year. Elbowing through crowds of tourists requires speed and agility I don't currently possess.

I sign off with Ty and Donna, accepting that they're going to have more fun over the next two days than I am. Then Thea and Aiden turn a few somersaults to remind me that I'm a lucky woman. I decide to spend the rest of the day sorting through the many hand-me-downs bestowed upon me by my sisters-in-law. "Your cousins and aunts love you, guys—and so do I."

Chapter 41

When Sean gets home from work, he finds me cross-legged on the nursery floor, sorting through boxes and bags of used baby paraphernalia bequeathed to us by the Coughlins. I point to three piles. "I've divided this into stuff we'll definitely need, stuff we might need, and stuff that's ridiculous." I hold up a baby-sized headband with a gargantuan pink bow attached. "I don't care if Thea is bald as a cue ball for two years—no daughter of mine will ever wear this."

Sean laughs at the mounds of crib sheets, onesies, sippy cups, and changing pads. "To think my Irish grandmother raised eight babies in County Cork without a Diaper Genie or a Snugli."

His expression softens as he picks up a yellow duckie blanket with frayed satin edging. "I remember this from when Deirdre's oldest was born. It's been passed down to every Coughlin baby since."

My eyes prick with sentimental tears. "It'll reach the end of the line with Thea and Aiden. They'll be the last of their generation."

A baby kicks, and Sean notices the movement beneath my stretchy top. "One more month guys, and all this will be yours."

"We've been cleared to give away anything we don't want. Help me box up this pile of rejects," I say. "I can have Ty take it over to Sister Alice."

As we work, Sean brings up his conversation with Special Agent Magee. "I had to call twice and leave two messages before he got back to me," my husband complains. "And when I told him how Irv and the new factory owners seemed to want to get rid of Eugene, he grunted."

"That's it? A grunt?"

"Mmmm. It seemed like a significant grunt. Like I was confirming something he already suspected."

"You think he's onto something sketchy at that factory?" I hand Sean a scratchy looking lace dress guaranteed to make any infant scream.

"Could be. But he's sure not sharing it with me." Sean shoves a loaded box with his big foot. "These Feds are so territorial. They won't share an iota of information."

I've been a little weak on information sharing myself. I decide to tell Sean about my encounter with Gloria in Target. In the days since it happened, Gloria's fury has receded in my memory, and I decide to present it to Sean as an odd interaction in which Gloria was a bit cold and rude, rather than threatening. "She seemed to imply our conversations with Eugene were causing problems for her at work," I conclude after I tell him the modified story.

Sean puzzles over some sort of swaddling contraption before shoving it into the donation bag. "Why didn't you tell me this sooner?"

"I was tired and cranky by the time we left Target, and so were you. I texted you to call me yesterday, but you never did."

Sean looks guilty. "Sorry. I meant to call, but then I got busy. You said it wasn't an emergency. You could've told me when I got home."

"I forgot about it until now."

Sean gives me a skeptical look, suspecting this is an approximation of the truth. "I'm not sure it's worthwhile for me to call Magee back with this. The man doesn't seem to want local assistance."

"The factory and the BlastMaster investigation belong to the FBI. What about the Palmyrton PD effort to find Pearl?"

"Nothing new happening there," Sean admits.

I toss the smallest sized baby clothes into a laundry basket to be washed. "I've had a little brainstorm about where she might be hiding," I say with my back to my husband.

"Have you now?"

I tell him about Mortenson's, implying that Pearl herself mentioned the place during the estate sale and that I just remembered it. "So Ty and Donna are going to drive up there tomorrow."

"Audrey! That's crazy." Sean snatches a tiny Boston Red Sox t-shirt from my hand and deposits it in the donation bag. Our children will be Yankees fans.

I defend my staff assignment. "It can't hurt for them to enquire—it's not like it's dangerous. And the lead is too flimsy for your guys to follow up." Sean continues to glare at me with his hands on his hips. "Besides, Mortenson's is not that far beyond a big outlet mall they both want to visit. Ty still needs a good gift for Lo."

Sean ties up the donations bag. "Fine. Let me know if they miraculously find Pearl."

Chapter 42

The next morning, Donna texts me to say they're on the way to Mortenson's. I wait anxiously for them to report in after the visit, but one o'clock and two o'clock pass with no call. Finally, I can't endure the suspense any longer and text her.

What happened at Mortenson's?
We have A LOT to report.
You found Pearl?
Could be. It's too complicated for the phone. Can we come to your house?
Of course. When will you get here?
One hour.

I pace around the house, bursting with anticipation. My Mortenson's hunch must have paid off. But it seems Ty and Donna didn't see Pearl.

I take Ethel for a walk to kill some time. Shortly after we return, my staff members burst through the back door.

"I'm starving," Donna declares. She kicks off her shoes in the back hall and heads straight to my kitchen to fix herself a cup of tea and a snack.

"Don't you want something?" I ask Ty.

"I'm good. Went through the Mickey D's drivethru right near the outlets, but Donna wouldn't eat that."

"Ah! And how was the shopping portion of your trip?"

"Fantastic!" Donna squeals as she helps herself to yogurt from my fridge. "I got a gorgeous designer purse for my sister—40% off. And Ty got the most awesome toy for Lo."

"Alien Invaders Space Station." Ty says with a notable lack of enthusiasm. "It's no BlastMaster, but I guess he'll probably like it."

"He'll love it!" Donna punches Ty's rock-hard bicep. "They had a Space Station set up in the toy store and three little kids who didn't even know each other were playing with it together. I told Ty it was a great toy for a four-year-old."

"Sounds like a perfect gift for Lo," I agree. "BlastMaster is a thing of the past. Your Christmas shopping is all done. Stop obsessing."

Ty grimaces but stays quiet.

Food in hand, Donna hops on the stool at the kitchen island and starts talking about their investigative mission. Ty paces around, working out the kinks from a long day of driving.

"We decided I should go in alone and Ty would wait in the car in the parking lot," Donna begins. "The place is open, but hardly anyone's there because it's a week before Christmas. I decided to tell them I was looking for a spot to hold a college friends reunion. That we were all athletic and wanted to hike and do cross-country skiing."

Ty shakes his head. "They believed that coming from her."

Donna is undeniably fit, but she wouldn't be caught dead in hiking boots. And her big hair wouldn't fit under a ski hat.

Donna runs a manicured hand through her mane. "Anyway, since business was slow, they got the Director of Group Sales to show me around. She was about my age and her name was Rebecca Mortenson."

"Wow. Part of the fourth generation to run the place, huh?"

"Exactly. I got her talking about the history of the resort as she was showing me the dining room and the great room with the huge stone fireplace and the games room that had a stage where she said they did karaoke." Donna grins. "It actually did look like fun. She kept assuring me the place is usually really hopping with activity except this is the slow time of year. All the while I was keeping an eye peeled for Pearl, but I didn't see any guests at all."

"She was gone forever," Ty gripes. "Good thing I brought a book to read."

"Then I asked to see some guest rooms and one of the guest bungalows. And while we were doing that, I said I had an old family friend who had once performed at Mortenson's and Grossinger's and some of the other old resort hotels. And Rebecca said her grandfather, Ralph Mortenson, used to book all the talent back in the day. I asked if he was still alive, and she said he was retired and lived in a special suite on the property. He loves to walk around and talk to the guests and make sure everyone is happy."

"So you think Pearl would have known him and stayed in touch?"

Donna sits up straight and taps a long nail on the countertop. "I'm sure he knows her. After I finished the tour with Rebecca, I asked if it would be okay if I strolled around on some of the trails through the property. She said sure, so I set off on my own to do some snooping."

"She texted me to say she was still alive," Ty adds. "I was gettin' antsy."

"I walked up a hill behind the main building and there was a house back there similar in style to the guest bungalows, but bigger. There was smoke coming out of the chimney, and on the front porch there was a tray, like a room service tray, with dirty dishes on it. And the coffee cup had *coral lipstick* on the rim."

Donna pauses for dramatic effect.

I frown, about to object that Pearl is not the only woman on the planet to wear coral lipstick. But Donna cuts me off before I can speak. "A-a-a-and, on the doormat was a pair of ladies red snowboots with faux fur trim." Donna holds her hands apart to indicate the small size. "I'm sure Pearl was in there visiting with old Ralph. I bet she's staying in one of the other bungalows."

Not one hundred percent conclusive, but it does seem plausible. It would explain why Pearl hasn't needed to use her phone or credit cards. Ten grand in cash would be more than enough to cover her minimal expenses at Mortenson's. "She can't stay there forever," I say. "It's like she's waiting for something to happen that will let her know it's safe to come out again."

"It's a good hideout," Ty concedes. "Far away from her friends and family and the dudes in Hillside. I'm glad the old gal is alive, but I don't see how this helps us figure out what's going on with *Your Move*."

"What if we wanted to get in touch with her in case something breaks in the case with the painting? How would we do it?" I ask.

"We could contact old Mr. Mortenson by email or snail mail. Let him know information to share with Pearl," Donna suggests.

I nod. "Better not do that until we're sure it really is safe for her to come out of hiding."

"Which brings us back to the painting itself. When you think about it, *Your Move* is also in hiding," Ty says. "And the reason why has to be in the painting itself. You know, spending time with Carter yesterday at the gallery taught me something. The man really knows how to look at a painting, how to see every brush stroke."

Ty glances into my family room. "Let's cast the photo of the painting up onto your TV screen. That way we can study every detail blown up really big."

I hand Ty my iPad and let him handle the electronics. Soon, the characters of *Your Move* fill the wide screen on my family room wall, almost as big as they were in real life.

"There has to be more of a message in the painting than just Darnell lying on the pavement in a fancy shirt," Ty says as he moves past the figure of Darnell and zooms in on the two ladies pushing strollers down the sidewalk. "That's too, too...."

"Subtle," I supply the word he's searching for.

"I don't see anything unusual about those ladies," Donna says. "They look like average moms to me. But I'm no art critic."

"You don't have to be an art expert to find these clues. More like a mystery book reader." I give Donna a reassuring hug. "Let's start at the top and look at every square inch of the painting," I suggest.

Ty scrolls past the empty blue sky in the top left-hand corner of the painting and moves toward the truncated factory in the opposite corner. Blown up this big, the lines of the painting are blurry. Ty tilts his head and narrows his eyes. "Is that supposed to be the sign with the American flag that's on the real factory? Because the colors here aren't red, white and blue."

"This sign is yellow and blue," Donna says. "What does that mean?"

Ty presses his lips together and thinks. He points at Donna. "Google the Ukrainian flag."

She does and her face lights up. "It's blue and yellow horizontal stripes. You're so smart, Ty!" Her face clouds. "But what does that mean? Why did Thurman put a Ukrainian flag on the factory in the painting? I mean, I know the new owners are Ukrainian, but you told me they've still got the American flag sign up there in real life."

"But Thurman doesn't paint reality," Ty says. "He paints his own vision."

I make a note of the flag detail. "Let's keep looking for clues and analyze them all together when we're done."

Ty scrolls down to the next level of the painting and squints. "Thurman has painted just a few of the windows on the top floor of the factory. It looks like...." Ty crosses over to the TV screen and points to a tiny, unclear detail. "Do those look like bars on the windows?"

"Yeah, there are certainly intersecting lines." I make a note of that, too.

We continue scrolling down. We already know the significance of the chess players, so I write "Rennie Pike spokesman for Founders" on my list of clues.

Then we get to the figure of Irv entering the bodega. His face is depicted in profile, so part of his mustache is visible. He's smiling and has one hand raised as if in greeting. "Seems like a nice portrayal," I observe.

Ty scans down. "Whoa, whoa—look at this by the door of the bodega, peeking out from behind the trash can."

Donna gets up close. "It's an animal, a little animal."

"A rat!"

We scroll through the rest of the painting but don't find anything else of interest. Everyone gathers around me to look at my list:

Darnell Peterson wearing a Founders shirt while lying on the dirty stoop.

Rennie Pike spokesman for Founders.

Founders brand is famous for being made in America.

Founders shirts are made in Irv's factory, but Thurman shows a Ukrainian flag instead of American.

Windows on factory seem to have bars on them.

Rat is painted by Irv's foot as he enters the bodega.

"I dunno." Donna sits back and rubs her eyes. "I don't get it. I'm no good at puzzles."

Ty and I continue to stare at the list. Ty strokes his chin, his eyelids at half-mast. "When we drove past the factory after we visited Eugene, we saw lights on in the top windows. Those would be the same windows as shown in the painting with bars on them."

I pick up the free associating. "What if someone's living up there?"

"A prisoner?" Donna says.

"Workers," Ty jumps back in. "Workers who maybe aren't literally locked behind bars, but who can't leave their job."

"Because they have nowhere to go," I add with rising excitement. "Because they're in this country illegally, and the new owners of the factory make them work for peanuts."

"So Founders shirts may be made in America, but they're not made by Americans. They're made by desperate poor people from other countries who came here looking for a better life," Donna says, catching on.

"And instead they get locked up in that factory by Yuri and Lev." Ty thumps his right fist into his left palm. "I wonder where Rennie Pike fits in all this?"

I ponder that question for a moment. "I'd guess he doesn't know anything about it. After all, his whole career has been based on those *American Made* movies. It would ruin his reputation if it came out that he was the spokesman for a brand that took jobs away from Americans and exploited poor immigrants at the same time."

"So the owners of the factory wouldn't want Rennie to know how the clothes are really made, right?" Donna grabs her phone. "I'm going to follow Rennie Pike on Twitter and see if he ever talks about how Founders shirts are produced."

She glances from me to Ty. "It seems like you've figured out what Nathaniel Thurman knew and how he showed he knew it in the painting. But what was he trying to achieve by selling the painting to Irv?"

"Okay, okay." Ty sits with his elbows on his knees and his head bowed like a student praying the answer to a test question will come to him.

Donna and I watch him.

After a full minute Ty lifts his gaze. He begins to recite a timeline. "Eugene accidentally walked in on Nathaniel and Irv making the deal on the painting and he said they were both actin' shifty. Irv paid Nathaniel four times as much as the painting was worth at that time. Irv took the painting to Palmyrton. Nathaniel disappeared."

I pick up the story. "And everything was fine for nearly seven years until Pearl decided to sell the painting and move. We spread the word about *Your Move* on social media. Pearl invited old friends to the house to say good-bye. Eugene and his great nephews showed up, and they both told Gloria what they saw."

"We'd better take notes again." Donna picks up my pen and yellow pad. "I'm having a hard time holding all this in my head."

"Write this down," Ty commands. "Nathaniel knew what was going on at the factory under the new owners. And he knew that Irv knew. So he painted *Your Move* as a bargaining chip."

Donna's eyes light up. "The painting was Nathaniel's opening move, and he was saying to Irv, 'now it's your move.'"

"Exactly," Ty confirms. "Nathaniel was telling Irv there was a price to pay if Irv wanted him to keep quiet. And the price was paying Nathaniel fifty grand for the painting."

"If the painting was incriminating, why didn't Irv destroy it instead of hanging it in his dining room?" I ask.

Donna doodles on the pad as she thinks. "Maybe Irv brought it home intending to get rid of it. But Pearl saw it and liked it and wanted to keep it. Irv could never say no to her."

I like this insight. "Especially if Irv didn't want Pearl to know the truth about what was going on at the factory. He'd have a hard time destroying the painting without telling her why."

"And did Nathaniel use the money to run away and never come back?" Donna pauses with her hand poised above the pad. "Or did Nathaniel get killed for what he knew?"

Chapter 43

It's getting dark outside as I wave good-bye to Ty and Donna. Sean has texted me that he won't be home from work until seven. Ty has committed to babysitting Lo tonight while Charmaine goes to her office Christmas party, and Donna is expected at her parents' house for dinner. We agree to think about all we've learned and touch base tomorrow with an action plan.

I stretch out on the sofa to think and soon feel myself drifting off.

Ethel's hysterical barking awakens me. I don't know how long I've been dozing, but I must've been aroused from the deep phase of sleep because I feel groggy and befuddled. "Is Dad home, Ethel?"

The dog continues barking without leaving my side. If Sean were coming in, Ethel would be greeting him by the garage door.

Ethel and I hear footsteps on the porch and the dog flings herself at the front door.

No doubt another package has been delivered. I stumble to the front door and open it.

There's no box. A black-hooded figure lopes down the sidewalk, disappearing into the dark, but I don't see the lights of a delivery van anywhere on the street.

I get ready to close the door when I smell something. Ethel smells it too and pushes onto the porch to investigate.

The motion-detector light has come on, and now I see there *is* something on the porch.

A big, stinking pile of dog doo.

Ethel, of course, has stuck her nose close to determine the identity of this brazen invader. As I pull her back, I notice something in the pile that definitely wasn't left by a canine.

It's a note. I reach for it, but then pull back. My groggy brain fog has lifted. Eugene received a similar message...a threatening message. He read it and threw it away. I won't be so careless.

I go back in the house and find the box of latex gloves Sean keeps in the bathroom and grab a roll of clean paper towels from the kitchen. I return to the porch and remove the note, then carry it through the house to the garage where I place it on a strip of paper toweling on Sean's workbench.

Not until I have the evidence safely preserved do I actually read the note. It's printed in black marker on cheap, white paper.

Stay away from Hillside. Stay away from Eugene Caldwell and Pearl Aronson.

This is your only warning. you're going to end up like Darnell Peterson. Blacked out. For real.

It's signed with a black square made by pressing so hard, the paper is torn.

My knees feel weak. Reflexively, I cradle my belly. What have I done, endangering my babies like this? I must be insane.

I scurry back into the house and double-check that all the doors are locked. Then I call Sean and tell him what happened. He doesn't bother to ask questions.

"Stay in the bedroom. I'll be there in five."

And he is, followed by three patrol cars, lights flashing.

Sean finds me and Ethel huddled in the bedroom, where I've pushed a chair in front of the locked door. Not that a wingback would slow down a thug hell-bent on killing me.

I rush into his arms, comforted by his solid embrace. But I sense a stiffness in my husband.

Sean is angry.

He steps back from me and looks me in the eye. "Why did this happen today?"

I tell him about Ty and Donna's visit after their trip to Mortenson's. I tell him about everything we deduced from examining the painting.

He listens with his mouth ajar, his breathing heavy.

When I finish, Sean is silent for a long moment. When he speaks, his voice is low and even. "Audrey, this has to stop. Right here, right now. You are endangering your life and the lives of our unborn children. There's no justification for that. None."

He's right. I have no defense. I brought this upon myself because I'm curious and bored and I'm used to being busy and challenged all day, every day. Sitting at home waiting for the babies to be born is tedious, but that's what I have to do.

That's what I will do.

"I'm sorry, Sean." I lift my hands in surrender. "I'm dropping it right now. I don't care what happens to Pearl and *Your Move.*"

"You can't stay alone in this house. Until arrests are made, you're going to have to spend your days with your father and Natalie. Their building has a doorman. You should be safe there."

I'm in no position to argue. Look on the bright side, Audrey—at least Sean didn't suggest I spend all day with *his* parents. A knock on the bedroom door interrupts our tense encounter. "Sean, Agent Magee is here. He wants to talk to you and your wife."

Chapter 44

It was nearly midnight by the time I finally got to sleep last night, so I remain in bed until nearly eight. Even though I've slept in, I arise feeling achy and unrefreshed. Sean would normally be off to work by now, but he's determined to escort me personally to my father's condo. As I eat my breakfast, I note there's a patrol car in our driveway keeping watch over the house.

I attempt to engage my husband in some light conversation. "I guess one positive outcome of last night's incident is that Agent Magee is finally sharing some information with you, eh?"

Sean has already eaten and is banging away on his laptop. He doesn't look up from his work. "That's of no concern to you."

I try again. "Is the dog poop gone from the front porch? We'll probably be getting more deliveries today."

"Bagged for evidence," Sean snaps.

"I think I'll take Ethel with me to Dad's place."

"Fine. But you can't walk her. Your father or Natalie will have to take her out."

House arrest. I'm surprised I don't have to wear an ankle monitor. I'd better pray they make an arrest soon.

My father and Natalie are delighted to shelter me and Ethel for the day, and I'm glad to be in the presence of people who aren't mad at me. Dad looks like he might scold when I tell him about the events that have led me here, but Natalie shoots him a hushing look.

She really is the world's best stepmother.

I help Natalie bake some cookies in the morning, then Dad invites me to play a game of chess. "Clive is coming this afternoon and I need to warm up."

"Beating me ought to be good practice," I say with a grin.

As Dad sets up the pieces, my phone rings with a call from Ty.

"Audge, my phone is blowin' up! Agent Magee wants to talk to me and Donna. And I got a message from Carter sayin' he's heard some talk that Nathaniel Thurman is comin' back."

"What?!"

"He texted me, but when I called him back, his line was busy so I gotta wait. In the meantime, why is Magee after me again?"

I fill Ty in on what happened last night. "Tell Magee everything. And watch your back, Ty. Stay close to home. These guys mean business."

"Me? You're the one who better watch out. This stress isn't good for you, Audge."

His concern is sweet, but I'm really getting tired of this delicate flower stuff. I want to tell Ty to call me about whatever he discovers from Carter. But no. I'm off that line of inquiry now.

I hang up and try to concentrate on the chess match. But my mind is spinning with the possibility that Nathaniel Thurman has reappeared, and Dad beats me in fifteen moves.

"Sorry I wasn't much of a challenge," I say. "I'm a little tired."

Dad encourages me to rest, so while Natalie walks the dog, I retreat to the spare room, put my feet up, and read a book. Once horizontal, I discover that I am tired, and my eyelids droop. In the murky haze of napping, I hear Clive arrive and the low murmur of his and Dad's voices as they play chess. Eventually, hunger drives me out to the kitchen for a snack, and I stop to say hello to Clive.

His face lights up when he sees me. "You know, I was thinking about you the other day."

I smile, thinking he's going to mention the progress of my pregnancy. Instead, he veers in a different direction.

"I was back in the old neighborhood last week, visiting a friend. We were trading stories about the old days and folks we used to know. Got to talkin' about the Peterson family." Clive rolls a captured pawn between his fingers. "Couldn't neither one of us remember what ever became of Darnell's mother and his younger brother and sister. His mother was a good woman who lost two sons to the streets—one boy murdered, and one a gangster. It was bad enough when her older son started runnin' with the gangsters. But when Darnell died, it about killed her."

I nod and look sympathetic, but I'm not sure why this story reminded Clive of me.

"My friend and I couldn't remember when's the last time we saw Teresa Peterson. But then I recalled that Nathaniel Thurman once painted a picture of Teresa. He sketched her while she was watching her boys play basketball. Then he turned it into a painting in his studio." Clive tips his head back and looks at me. "That's when I thought of you because you showed me that painting I was in."

"Ah, I see. And did you ever see the painting he did of Darnell's mother?"

Clive nods. "I surely did. It was small—a portrait. Nathaniel showed it to me before he gave it to Teresa. He wanted to know if I thought she'd like it. I told him of course—a woman's going to be pleased when you make her look real pretty like that." Clive smiles at the distant memory. "I think Nathaniel mighta been a little sweet on Teresa."

Dad taps his knight impatiently and they return to their game.

Absolutely unable to resist texting Ty, I go back to the spare room and pull out my phone. But when I ask him what's happening, he doesn't reply. Maybe he's in the middle of being interviewed by Agent Magee.

I turn to Twitter and search for any mentions of Nathaniel Thurman.

There are scores of tweets. I scan the first few:

Strange similarities noted between work of #NathanielThurman and New Mexico artist #JustinClay.

Are #NathanielThurman and #JustinClay the same artist?

Has #NathanielThurman been hiding in plain sight in Madrid, NM all these years??

Then Ty calls. I start talking before he can say a word. "Ty, have you seen Twitter? Is this what Carter was talking about? Nathaniel has been painting under a new identity?"

"Seems to be. Someone bought a Justin Clay painting in New Mexico, then decided to sell it in New York. The gallery owner noticed the similarity to Thurman's work. So he started digging, looking for more Justin Clay paintings and comparing them to Thurman paintings."

"Wow! Has anyone been able to get in touch with Thurman? Or should I say Clay?"

"Word on the street is he's going to make an announcement on Twitter tonight," Ty says.

I tell Ty what I've learned from Clive. "Maybe Nathaniel and Teresa used the money from Irv to run away together to New Mexico."

"Mmmm. Still doesn't explain why he's stayed quiet all these years."

I'm intrigued by the possibility of a tragic love story. "I hope having his cover blown doesn't ruin Nathaniel's happiness with Teresa."

"How 'bout you focus on your own safety," Ty reminds me. "I gotta say, the action at your house seems to have lit a fire under the FBI. I think they're sending agents up to Mortenson's to get Pearl. I know you already told him about the clues in *Your Move*, but he made me go over it again. And he seemed to be taking it seriously. Especially the part about the windows on the top floor."

"So our theories were right! Did you pick up any information from Magee? Will the FBI raid the factory?" I pace back and forth in Dad's spare room. "Because Sean won't tell me a thing, and I'll risk World War Three if I even ask."

"Magee was tight-lipped, as usual. But he took a call while he was interviewing me. Sounds like something big's about to go down."

Chapter 45

My house arrest at Dad's condo lasts only one day. By the time Sean comes to pick me up, the evening news is bursting with news about a joint task force raid in Hillside. We all gather around the TV as one breathless reporter after another tells the story of what's been going on at the I A Enterprises factory since Irv Aronson sold it to Yuri and Lev Aksamit.

We start watching Channel 4, where a grim-faced reporter stands in front of the factory.

"The FBI, INS, local, and state police today conducted a raid on this factory in Hillside, NJ. Inside they discovered more than forty men and women from Romania, Albania, and Serbia being forced to work without pay. Authorities say that human traffickers brought them to this country and confiscated their passports."

"Scum!" My father growls at the TV. "You suspected that was what was going on in there, Audrey?"

"Not this. There were clues in Nathaniel Thurman's painting that something wasn't right about the factory, and we passed them on to the FBI."

Natalie's brow furrows. "But I thought Immigration and Naturalization investigated human trafficking, not the FBI."

"The FBI was after one thing and the INS was after another." Sean switches channels, where the headline crawling across the screen is, "BlastMaster Counterfeiting Operation Busted."

We come in on the middle of an interview with Special Agent Magee. "Yes, most of the factory was used to manufacture clothing, but one hidden assembly line was devoted to producing counterfeit BlastMaster toys."

"The counterfeiters were taken down right before Christmas!" the reporter says gleefully. "How did the FBI manage to break this case?"

"We are grateful for the many useful tips from the public which were instrumental to the success of our operation. Ultimately, we received the go-ahead for the raid when we suspected workers in the factory were being exploited."

"Grateful," Sean scoffs. "You'd never know it from the way he treated me." He rolls through more cable channels until I grab his hand to stop him. "Look, there's Rennie Pike being interviewed."

"Who's that fella?" Dad asks as Rennie's handsome face fills the screen.

"A movie star, dear." Natalie leans forward to hear what he's saying.

"I had no idea what was going on in that factory," Rennie says to an interviewer sitting across from him in a studio somewhere in California. "Founders has always assured me that the clothes I endorse are made in state-of-the art factories by well-paid American workers."

The interviewer, acting as if he's a hard-nosed investigative journalist instead of a hack on the celebrity beat, continues to quiz Rennie on his involvement with a company that uses slave labor to produce luxury goods. "I feel sort of sorry for the guy," I say as I check my phone. "Founders pays him to look good in their shirts, not inspect all their factories." Sure enough, Twitter has turned on Rennie Pike with a vengeance. The *American Made* action movie series has probably died today.

Sean taps my knee. "C'mon, Sherlock—we'd better get home."

"Are you sure it's safe?" Dad asks. "Did they arrest the man who threatened Audrey?"

"Yeah, he's a local tough guy the Ukrainians hired to do their enforcement. They verified it's him because he used his own dog's dirt to hold his messages."

Dad frowns. "Not a very smart criminal."

Sean clips on Ethel's leash. "It's the little details that bring the bad guys down every time."

Chapter 46

Three days after the raid, Special Agent in Charge Magee has called us together to provide some final details that will help him close out his investigation of the BlastMaster counterfeiting scheme and the illegal workers at the factory. When Ty, Sean and I arrive at the FBI field office, Pearl Aronson is already there, bright plumage intact. With her green eye shadow, coral lips, and lavender nails, she's clearly rebounded from her months in hiding.

Pearl jumps up to hug Ty, a hilarious sight given that her head is barely above his belly button. "You're my hero, young man. Thank goodness you helped me out of the fix I was in."

Agent Magee, stone-faced as always, waits for this flurry of emotion to subside before directing his attention to Pearl. "Mrs. Aronson, can you explain to me please how your husband came to own the painting *Your Move* by Nathaniel Thurman?"

"Irv bought it from Nathaniel to keep it out of the public eye. I didn't realize it at the time. I thought he bought it because he liked it. And because the artist put Irv in it."

Magee frowns. "But the painting was displayed in your dining room, correct?"

Pearl nods. "When Irv brought *Your Move* home, he intended to hang it in a room upstairs, but it was too big to be carried around the turn in the staircase. That upset him. But I loved the painting as soon as I saw it and wanted to hang it in the dining room." Pearl looks down at her clasped hands. "Irv never could say no to me. We were still debating where to hang it when—"

Her voice quavers, and she pauses to regain her composure.

"Take your time," Magee says with surprising gentleness.

"Irv collapsed at home, right after dinner. Said he felt like a boulder was on his chest. I knew it was a heart attack. I rode with him in the ambulance and stayed with him, holding his hand, in the emergency room. The whole time he kept saying, 'I don't want to be separated from you.' I kept assuring him I was right there, that I wouldn't leave him alone. He died in my arms."

Pearl wipes her tears. "I realize now Irv didn't mean he didn't want to be alone in the hospital. He meant he didn't want to be alone for eternity. He realized he'd made a deal with the devil when he sold the factory to Yuri and Lev. And Nathaniel realized it too, and he painted *Your Move* to challenge Irv to do something about his mistake."

"But Irv was afraid to turn the new owners in to the authorities?" Agent Magee asks. "Even when he realized they were human traffickers making people work long hours against their will?"

"Irv didn't care about himself. You see, my husband worried he would die before the business was sold. He wanted to provide for me. Didn't want me to have to deal with a sale. So he took the first offer he got. And then those people caused him nothing but heartache."

Pearl twists her crumpled tissue. "I think he was afraid those awful men would find a way to have me killed. Irv spent the months between the sale of the factory and his death doing as many mitzvahs as possible. The scholarship fund, the refugee assistance program—" Pearl sighs. "I realize now he was trying to atone."

"And the money he paid Nathaniel for the painting?" I ask.

"That was another mitzvah."

Ty picks up the story here. "The money wasn't for Nathaniel Thurman. It was for the family of Darnell Peterson so the mother could move away from Hillside with her remaining younger children. Nathaniel helped them get resettled in a new town, far away." Ty gestures with his hand. "Madrid."

Agent Magee looks confused. "She went to Spain?"

"No, Madrid, New Mexico. It's an old mining town that became a ghost town and then got reborn as an artist's colony. It's about as far away from Hillside—physically and psychically—as you can get," I explain.

"And then Teresa Peterson fell in love with her rescuer, and Nathaniel decided to stay in New Mexico," Ty volunteers. "He's been painting out there under the name Justin Clay and selling his works in local galleries for the past seven years. A dealer I know made the connection when he saw one of the New Mexico paintings in a gallery in New York. The style was so similar to *Your Move* and Thurman's other New Jersey paintings that the art world had to find out who Justin Clay was. Didn't take them long."

"Doesn't sound like Thurman was trying too hard to hide his identity," Magee says.

"Nathaniel never intended to disappear forever," Ty says. "According to the statement he made, he thought he'd go out West and get Teresa settled—take a break and come back. But then he liked it so much, he stayed. He liked being away from the New York art scene and all the competition for attention. He was selling his paintings and Teresa was working and it was cheap to live there, so why leave?"

"What about his family? Didn't he feel bad that they were worried about him?" I object. "He could've let them know he was okay."

"True. But he was mad at Gloria for continuing to work for Yuri and Lev even though she knew what they were into." Ty holds his hands palms up. "Nathaniel...Justin...is definitely a quirky guy."

Magee grimaces. "I believe there was more to his secrecy than his anger at Gloria. Our investigation into the I A Industries factory and the BlastMaster counterfeiting scheme also turned up some information that allowed local Hillside police to solve a cold case murder."

"Darnell Peterson?" I guess.

"Yes. Darnell was killed by the local man that Yuri and Lev Aksamit used as their enforcer." Magee glances my way. "The same man who threatened you. He graduated from being a gangbanger to working for Ukrainian mobsters. Both Teresa and Nathaniel had good reason to fear him."

Ty shifts uneasily. "Is it someone I ran into when I was nosing around Hillside?"

Magee pulls out a mugshot of a dead-eyed Black man in his late thirties. "Do you recognize this man?"

Ty nods. He was drinking in the bar that night when the guy approached me about buying a BlastMaster. What's his name?"

"Keith Peterson, Darnell's older brother."

Pearl gasps. My hand rises to my mouth.

"He killed his own brother?" Ty asks. "Why?"

"From what we've been able to piece together, Darnell liked to show off and bask in the notoriety of his older brother. But he talked too much to too many people on the street. Keith's Ukrainian bosses gave the command that Darnell had to be silenced. So Keith killed him."

Ty hangs his head. "That's cold. Ice cold."

I feel sick to my stomach. A man this ruthless wouldn't have hesitated to kill a pregnant woman.

"People in the neighborhood were terrified of Keith," Agent Magee says. "But once he got arrested for his involvement with the Aksamit brothers, the Hillside police started getting lots of tips tying him to Darnell's murder. He won't see the light of day anytime soon."

"What about Gloria? Was she arrested in the raid?" Even though Gloria was aggressive toward me, I still feel bad thinking about a mother like her doing time in prison.

"Gloria is cooperating with us," Agent Magee says. "Yuri and Lev manipulated her by threatening her sons. And they knew she desperately needed a well-paying job, so they kept her doing their bidding. But if she testifies against them, she'll probably get off without jail time."

Magee turns his attention back to Pearl. "So after your husband died, you hung *Your Move* in your dining room?"

"Yes, the arguing was over." Pearl looks wistful. "But still, hardly anyone saw it. After Irv died, I lost my passion for entertaining. Just a few of my Palmyrton lady friends saw the painting, and they had no one to tell. Then, on the day of the estate sale, all hell broke loose."

"When you invited Eugene to come and say good-bye to you and the painting, you had no idea of the consequences?" Magee asks.

"None. I was feeling nostalgic. I knew I'd continue to see my best friends after I moved, but there were many neighbors and acquaintances I knew I'd never see again. Eugene was one of them. I always liked the fellow, and I knew he was the uncle of the artist who painted *Your Move*, so I reached out and invited him to come to the sale." Pearl blows a puff of air through her coral lips. "Hoo, boy! What a load of *tsuris* I brought down upon myself!"

"Walk me through the day of the sale and what happened afterward," Magee demands.

Pearl looks wistfully at me and Ty. "I was having so much fun that day. It was like being alive at your own funeral. People I hadn't seen in years kept showing up and telling me how much they were going to miss me. So I was very happy when, at the end of the day, Eugene and his nephews showed up. I was thrilled to see Eugene again and happy to meet the young men who were also related to the artist." Pearl pauses and sighs. "But once we went to look at *Your Move*, I didn't think the young men were so nice. They seemed to think *Your Move* wasn't an important painting, yet they were resentful I was selling it."

Ty nods. "That's how they acted. But now we know they were showing some attitude because Gloria sent them there to see what was happening with the painting. Eugene had extended the invitation to her, and she panicked. She and her brother had argued about her working for Yuri and Lev, and she knew he'd painted *Your Move* as a protest. But Gloria thought that painting was long gone."

Pearl throws her hands up. "If only we all understood one another!"

"So Gloria's sons came back and reported on the painting to their mother," I interrupt, eager to move the story along. "Who came to the house to deface the painting? When did they do the damage?"

"Gloria told us she didn't want Yuri and Lev to find out about the painting. She came to the sale herself on Sunday afternoon and slipped in without any of you noticing," Magee says. "Obviously, the painting was too big to be stolen, and slashing it was too risky, so she knelt down and blacked out Darnell's figure. Then she took a photo of what she'd done."

Pearl picks up the story again. "On Sunday afternoon, I got a text with that photo attached. The message said I'd be blacked out just like the boy if I sold the painting. It told me to put the painting in storage and not reveal to anyone where it was."

"Why didn't you ask us for help when we came to see you at your hotel that evening, Pearl?" Ty asks. "We would have protected you."

"Ach, you're a sweet boy!" Pearl pats Ty's knee. "I didn't want to bring nice people like you into this crazy mess. I knew the threat must have something to do with the people Irv sold the factory to. I always suspected they were no good."

Pearl rubs her eye, smudging her green eye shadow. "I remembered how nervous Irv was about that painting. How he'd wanted to hang it upstairs. So I decided there must be some bad luck attached to it. I decided to do as the text said and put the painting in storage." She nudges me with her tiny foot. "But then it turned out you people had already put pictures of the painting out on that Twitter nonsense, and I was getting more threats from those awful people."

"Despite Gloria's efforts, Yuri and and Lev learned about the painting," I say. "That's when things really got hot for you, right Pearl?"

"Yes. I decided it would be best for me to disappear for a while, so I invited myself to my friend Ralph's place, Mortenson's."

I have to smile at the plucky old woman. "That was probably the best place for you, Pearl."

"You found me, but not until it was safe for me to come out."

"So what's going to happen to *Your Move* now?" Magee asks.

"It will be restored by the artist himself." Ty rubs his hands together. "And then Pearl here plans to auction it off and give the proceeds to the workers held in bondage at the factory."

Pearl beams. "It will help them start new lives. I know it's what Irv would want me to do."

Chapter 47

Christmas Eve morning finds me sprawled on the sofa trying to wrap the last few small gifts in my lap since I'm no longer capable of getting down on my hands and knees with rolls of paper, scissors, and tape. Sean has gone into the office for a couple of hours to make sure every loose end on his open cases has been tied up, so we won't be plagued by messages tonight or tomorrow.

He assures me that Palmyrton's criminals take it easy on Christmas and that the low-seniority patrolmen on duty will be able to handle the family fights that tend to break out late on Christmas afternoon.

We are heading into two days of family time. Christmas Eve mass at four, followed by dinner for twenty-plus Coughlins at Deirdre's house, and a gift-opening extravaganza that will last well past midnight. Colleen's kids are the only ones young enough to still believe in Santa, so that family will get to go home early to await the arrival of the man in red. I pat my huge belly. These two will be our ticket to an early dismissal next year and for a few years to come.

Tomorrow, we'll spend a peaceful day with Dad and Natalie, eating canapes and listening to the ethereal voices of some English boys choir singing classic carols.

No *Grandma Got Run over by a Reindeer* for my father.

I look at our Christmas tree in the corner of the living room. The lights twinkle in perfectly distributed loops; the ornaments, many of them vintage, each hang on the branch that displays their beauty best. A few tastefully wrapped packages nestle underneath.

Enjoy perfection now, Audrey. Next year at this time, the twins will be crawling, pulling off the lights, chewing on the ornaments. We'll probably have to erect a circle of baby gates around the tree.

I grin. For the first time since my mother disappeared on Christmas Eve, casting her long shadow over the holiday for more than three decades, I am totally happy on December 24.

My phone buzzes with the arrival of a text from Ty.

It's a photo of an unfolded sheet of assembly instructions printed with diagrams, arrows, and paragraphs of warnings. The paper covers both cushions of Ty's sofa, and an array of plastic parts and tiny bags of nuts and screws cascade onto his rug.

His only commentary: *WTF??*

Clearly, the Alien Planets Space Station Ty bought in lieu of the BlastMaster came with the dreaded "some assembly required" caveat.

Bring it over here. I'll help you.

You da bomb, Audge. I'll be there in ten.

Ty watches me waddle from the front door into the living room. "You look like you grew since I saw you three days ago," he marvels. "How much bigger can you get?"

"Believe me, I ask myself that every day. I've got four more weeks until thirty-six weeks. That's when the doctor thinks I'll be ready to deliver. Hardly anyone makes it to forty weeks with twins."

One of the babies kicks and a little foot is briefly visible through the stretchy fabric of my maternity top. Ty shivers. "That freaks me out."

I laugh and collapse back onto the sofa. "It used to freak me out too, but it's amazing what you get used to when you're pregnant."

"You sure you're up for this?" Ty asks, dropping the space station box at my feet. "Maybe you should be takin' a nap or something."

"I can't sleep all day for the next month. This is a great activity for me. I can use my mind while you do the hands and knees work." I rub my palms in anticipation as Ty hands me the instructions. "I'm good at this. I loved playing with LEGO as a kid."

"I hated them muthas," Ty mutters as he pulls the pieces out of the box.

Ethel whines from the kitchen. I had to shut her in there—the last thing we need is a tiny part entering her digestive system and not reappearing until after Christmas morning.

"Okay, first we need the four side panels and the three connector doo-hickeys that look like tiny fly swatters," I instruct.

Ty laughs. "I probably coulda done this myself, but it's gonna be more fun with you."

Slowly, the space station takes shape on my living room floor. We have to disassemble one landing strip because it's facing the wrong way, but we work steadily with remarkably little cursing.

I shift on the sofa, and Ty catches me wincing. He drops his tiny allen wrench. "What's wrong? You hurtin'?"

"I'm fine. The babies just seem to be pressing on my back today." I hand him a red widget. "This goes on top of the tower."

As Ty screws it into place, I venture a touchy question. "Is your father coming to Charmaine's place tomorrow morning?"

Ty contemplates the space station control panel in his hand. "Yeah," he finally answers. "I realized I had to stop making everything about me and him. Christmas is about making Lo happy, and Lo wants his grandad there."

I reach out and squeeze Ty's shoulder. No one knows better than I do how hard it is to let go of past hurts, but what a relief it is when they're finally gone.

Ty snaps the control panel into place. "I tell you one thing—if I was puttin' this space station together with Charmaine and Marvin, there would be *blood*."

Finally, the space station stands before us in all its alien glory. We only have two screws and a small thingamajig left over. I call that a win. "Lo is going to love this, Ty. He can play with it by himself or with his little friends. He'll use his imagination to make the spaceships fly in and out, and he'll make the little alien mechanics do all the repairs."

Ty nods. "You're right—this is a really good toy for him. I dunno why I got so obsessed with the BlastMaster. I turned it into the cure for everything that was wrong in my childhood. But that's ancient history. My life is great right now, and that's all that matters."

My eyes well with tears, and one slips down my cheek.

"What's wrong?" Ty asks in alarm.

I shake my head, too choked up to speak. What pain awaits my children? Everyone wants their kids to have the perfect childhood, but no one ever achieves it. Disappointment...loss...disillusionment—all inevitable. But I don't want to go there with Ty. "Sorry," I manage. "I've got too many hormones circulating, that's all."

The great thing about men is they are always willing to let a touchy subject drop. Ty stands and opens my front door. He goes outside to open the trunk of his car before returning to pick up the unwieldy space station. "I think I can fit this in my car. Then I'll wait until Lo falls asleep to smuggle it into Charmaine's apartment." When he comes back to the house, Ty carefully folds the box that contained the space station. "I better save this. When Lo gets tired of playing with all his new toys, you know he'll go right back to playing with the boxes."

Ethel's whining in the kitchen becomes truly pathetic. "Let's have some lunch." I hold my hand out so Ty can help heave me out of the grasp of the sofa's soft cushions. I stagger to my feet, and a sharp pain lances my lower back.

I gasp.

"Audge, what's wrong?" Ty's smooth forehead furrows. "You wanna call Sean? The doctor?"

"No, I'm fine. I just felt a twinge from changing position after being stretched out for so long." I head for the kitchen. "Come on. I'll make you a sandwich."

The pain in my back continues, more a steady pressure now than a sharp stab. I've never felt this before, but every month of my pregnancy has brought some new, weird symptom. And every time I pull out my *What to Expect* book, I learn that millions of women before me have experienced the same thing.

No need to worry.

Sitting at the breakfast bar, we eat the ham and cheese sandwiches that I've made and talk about our holiday plans. Normally, I'm famished long before noon, but today I leave half my sandwich on the plate. "You gonna eat that?" Ty asks, and I push it toward him with a laugh.

I struggle off my stool at the counter and feel a gush of warm wetness on my legs. Did I knock over my tea mug?

I get my feet under me and look at the clear puddle on the floor. My mug and Ty's glass are upright on the counter. My maternity leggings are soaked.

Ty is staring from me to the floor, his eyes as round as saucers.

Another pain constricts my back and I clutch the counter. Ty swoops in to steady me.

"My water broke. I, I—this isn't supposed to happen now. It's too soon. It's only thirty- two weeks." I hear my voice getting shriller and shriller.

Ty's eyes dart from side to side. "Okay, okay, okay. We gotta be cool. Imma call 9-1-1."

I grab his hand. "No, you can't call an ambulance just because you're in labor." We had been warned about this in our childbirth prep class. With trembling fingers, I call my doctor. But of course, it's Christmas Eve and I get her answering service. *If this is a true medical emergency...*

Hell, yeah—it is. I leave a semi-coherent message, but I still don't know what to do.

Next, I call Natalie. Her phone rings and rings and finally rolls to voicemail. She's always available. Where could she be?

Ty watches with increasing nervousness. "Call my Grams. She'll know what to do," he suggests.

I can count on Grandma Betty to start praying, but I'd prefer some earthly guidance. I call my sister-in-law Deirdre.

Finally, I connect. "Hi." She starts talking rapidly before I can say a word. "The plan is to meet at the church at three-thirty."

"Deirdre, I—"

"I know it's crazy early, but Mom's worried we won't be able to sit together if—"

"Deirdre, my water broke."

"Huh?" I hear a sharp uptake of breath. "No."

Then nurse Deirdre, four-time mom Deirdre, takes over. "Don't panic, Audrey. You'll be fine. Have Sean take you—"

"Sean's at work. I haven't called him yet. Ty is here."

"Okay, good. Have Ty drive you to the ER. I'll tell Sean and your doctor to meet you there."

"Wait. What does it mean? What's going to happen to the babies?"

"They'll be fine. Just fine," Deirdre says briskly.

But I can hear the fear in her voice.

Chapter 48

The next two hours pass in a blur. I barely remember the drive to the hospital other than the death grip Ty had on the wheel as he navigated through Christmas shopping traffic in downtown Palmyrton. Once I clarified that Ty was not the father, he lifted his hand in a terrified farewell as the nurses put me in a wheelchair and rushed me away.

Unfamiliar nurses and doctors wearing jaunty elf hats and reindeer antler headbands ask me a million questions about my pregnancy and my current symptoms. They've put me in a hospital gown and taken me to labor and delivery, but I've managed to hang onto my phone. Fifteen minutes ago, I got a text from Sean saying he was on his way.

Where is he?

Can't he find me?

And why doesn't Dr. McLaughlin come, or at least talk to these people?

I fear I know the answer to that. Dr. McLaughlin is not on call today. Chances are, she's sitting in the same church as the Coughlins, waiting for mass to start.

I've heard every nurse I know say the same thing: never, ever get sick on a holiday. The hospital is understaffed, and those who are working are students or inexperienced doctors and nurses with low seniority.

Dr. McLaughlin assured me she'd deliver the twins because I'd most likely have a planned induction. Instead, the babies are arriving dangerously early with no one to help them into the world but a crowd of rank amateurs.

Two tears slip down my cheeks as another contraction wracks my body. But I'm not crying in pain. Fear is pushing those tears.

I've screwed up. I let my relentless curiosity put me in a dangerous situation. Maybe the stress of my threat from Keith Peterson precipitated my early labor. My recklessness caused this catastrophe. I should have known I'd never be able to pull off this motherhood thing.

Finally, the door opens and Sean rushes in. His face, always so calm and stoic, is contorted with anxiety. "Audrey—my God! What happened? Are you alright?"

"I don't know what's going on." I cling to him. "I don't know who's in charge here. Help me!"

"I will." He squeezes me tightly before letting go.

Sean opens the door and grabs the first nurse passing by. Panting through another contraction prevents me from hearing what they're saying out in the hall. The nurse enters and fusses with some monitors. "Dr. Rattanakosin will be with you shortly."

"Who?" My heart sinks. They're giving me a doctor doesn't even speak English!

She pats my arm. "He's excellent. Dr. R. has delivered tons of Christmas babies. He always volunteers to work the holiday since he's Buddhist."

I clutch Sean's hand as tears stream down my face. Not tears of physical pain, but mental anguish. "This is all my fault, Sean. I'm so sorry."

Sean wipes my tears with the ball of his thumb. "Hush. There's nothing and no one to blame. The babies are just ready to be born, that's all." But his face belies his reassuring words. Sean is scared.

Just like me.

Then Dad and Natalie arrive. My father's face is gray with worry. He looks ten years older than he looked last week. Natalie holds his hand tightly, her usual serenity replaced with a frown of concern. These three are my support team, but they're even more anxious than I am.

My next contraction comes wrapped in a cloak of dread. I'm in trouble. Big trouble. I must be.

Soon a thin man in his forties with kind brown eyes and dark hair enters. He shakes our hands and introduces himself as Dr. Rattanakosin. "I see you have twins insisting on being your Christmas presents this year."

I'm in no mood for jokes. "It's too soon. Can't you do something to stop this? They're not ready to be born."

"Sometimes when a woman's water breaks early, we can delay the onset of labor, but you are already four centimeters dilated. These babies are coming tonight." He's firm but unruffled in his assessment.

"Is this my fault?" I ask. "I had a shock a few days ago."

"No, no my dear." He squeezes my hand. "You have done nothing wrong."

I like him. I want to believe him. I glance over at Natalie, who can discern a good doctor through nurse's telepathy. She seems more relaxed.

Dr. R. continues to examine me as he talks. "I've spoken to Dr. McLaughlin and looked at your ultrasound images. The babies appear to be about three and a half to four pounds each—that's a good size for preemies. However, one is in the breech position. So I think it's safest to do a cesarean to deliver both."

Three and a half pounds? Lo was seven pounds when he was born, and I still remember being amazed by how small he was. Our babies are going to be tiny little aliens chained to incubators with tubes and wires and needles. I begin to cry in earnest. Why couldn't I hold onto them? Why couldn't I keep them safe until they were big enough to face this harsh world?

Why, oh why, did I ever keep pursuing the message contained in *Your Move*?

Dr. R takes my hand. "I know this is not how you imagined the birth of your babies. I know it's scary. But babies are unpredictable creatures. We must respond to their needs. And right now, these two are telling us they are ready to join us in Palmyrton. They will be in the very best of hands, I promise you."

"Will I be able to be there?" Sean asks.

"Of course, Dad." The doctor pats Sean on the back. "The anesthesiologist will be here shortly to give you an epidural. You'll meet your children before Santa comes down the chimney."

Chapter 49

Somewhere far, far away, I hear music.

I must know the song. I can anticipate the next note. La-a-a-a, la-a-a, la-la. La. La. La.La.

Joy to the world...let heaven and nature sing...let heaven...

My right eye opens. Then my left. I'm not at home. The bed is too high, the walls too pale, the fake tree in the corner too small and straggly. Where—?

I struggle to sit up, and a pain shoots across my midsection.

Sean springs from a chair at my bedside. "Hey, you're awake. How do you feel?"

"The babies! Where are they? Are they okay?" I'm pushing up, but there's a needle in my right arm and tubes tangle in the bedrail beside me.

"Easy, easy." Sean takes my hand. "Everything is fine. You held Thea and Aiden for a while last night. Then you fell asleep."

It's coming back to me now. Sean holding my hand in the delivery room. The screen that prevented us from seeing the doctor making the incision. No pain... just the sensation of something being removed from me.

A tiny, bloody creature.

Then a cry—outraged by the shock of arrival in this world. That was Thea. The oldest. The biggest.

Then the whole process again, and Aiden arrived.

The doctor and nurses were smiling. Pleased. Satisfied.

Sean got to go and watch as the nurse weighed and bathed the babies.

What about me? I want to see! I want to hold them!

But the doctor wasn't done with me. He disappeared behind his screen again to sew me up. Finally, they wheeled me back here and I was allowed to hold my babies. Slender Thea, with a thatch of black hair and rosebud lips. Aiden, even smaller, his head brushed with a fine red-gold down. Both so tiny, so thin.

"I want to hold them again," I tell Sean. "I want to count their fingers and toes. Are they hungry? I need to feed them, don't I?"

Sean laughs at me. "They're right here, Audrey. See—two isolettes. The doctor said they were just big enough to not need incubators. Thea is four pounds, four ounces and Aiden is four pounds even. They're both sleeping now, but probably not for long."

Right on cue, a baby whimpers softly.

Sean crosses over and peeks into the isolette. "It's Thea. Don't cry, sweetie. Mom and Dad are here."

"Bring her to me," I demand. But then I panic. I don't know what to do with her. I don't know how to nurse her or change her.

Sean is scared, too. "I don't think I'm allowed to pick her up. I'll get the nurse."

The nurse appears and picks up Thea as if she were a sack of sugar instead of a fragile, precious creature. She's a tiny little bundle wearing a jaunty pink cap that slides over her eyes. "Merry Christmas, darlin'! Are you ready for breakfast?"

"Wait—what time is it? What day is it?" I ask.

"They were born at 8:34 and 8:36 PM, Christmas Eve. Now it's Christmas morning." Sean explains.

The nurse places Thea in my arms. "Merry Christmas, mama."

Chapter 50

Christmas Day passes in a whirl of visitors: doctors poking and prodding, a special lactation nurse showing me how to breastfeed and pump, other nurses teaching Sean and me how to hold and change and dress our babies. In between all that, both sets of grandparents arrive and Deirdre, a nurse herself, talks her way past the woman who enforces the restricted visitation rules. Phone calls and text messages from friends and family increase as the news spreads. And the video chats! All the Coughlin cousins want to see the newest additions to their tribe.

By six, Sean and I are both exhausted although the babies are sleeping. "You'd better go home and get a good night's rest," I tell him. "This may be your last opportunity for the next few years to get eight hours of uninterrupted sleep."

"I don't want to leave you alone here," Sean protests, caressing my cheek.

"I'll be fine. The nurses will help me with the babies. Once we all come home, you'll be waiting on all three of us nonstop."

Finally, Sean accepts that sleeping in the lounge chair beside my bed is counter-productive in the long-run. He stands for a long while watching his children sleep. Then he goes home.

Alone with my babies in the dimly lit room, the reality of the past twenty-four hours sinks in.

I'm a mother.

I've given birth to two new humans, and they're relying on me for everything.

Am I up to the challenge? I nearly screwed up their birth. Can I do better—better than my own mother—with their lives?

As I lie here swamped by the hurdles that lie ahead, my phone chirps one more time.

A video chat from Ty.

When I answer, Lo's adorable face fills the screen. "Hi, Audee! Uncle Ty says you got two babies for Christmas. He showed me their picture." Lo dances up and down as he talks. "Can I play with them?"

"Not quite yet, buddy. They're still too little. But pretty soon you can show them all your favorite playgrounds and all your favorite toys."

"Okay." Lo disappears from view momentarily, and I see Charmaine in the background, vainly trying to pick up after the explosion of wrapping paper, bows, and packaging that detonated in her apartment today.

"Show her my toys," Lo directs, and Ty zooms the phone's camera on the array of unwrapped gifts under the tree.

"Wow, that's a lot, Lo! Santa was very good to you," I say.

Lo scoots back into the frame and smiles, his baby teeth perfect pearls. "Yes. I'm lucky. But my best gift didn't come from Santa."

"Oh? What's your best gift?"

Lo crouches before the Alien Invaders Space Station that Ty and I assembled together. Was that only yesterday? It feels like last year!

"Uncle Ty knows me even better than Santa does. That's why he got me the best gift." Ty picks up the alien spaceships and zooms them into the landing strip. "You and Sawn can come over and play with this, too, Audee."

"Thanks, Lo. We'd love to."

"Okay, say good night to Audrey, honey. She has to get some rest," Charmaine says.

"Good night, Audee," Lo calls.

Then the picture tilts. "Wait. I have one more thing to ask."

Lo's face fills the screen. "This was my best Christmas ever, Audee. Was it your best Christmas, too?"

The little boy's face blurs through my tears. "Yes, Lo—it really was."

<hr/>

I hope you enjoyed *Treasure Under the Tree*. Please post a review to help other readers find this book. I appreciate your support! If you'd like to receive periodic updates on my new releases, sales, and special events, please join my mailing list: http://swhubbard.net/contact.

Other Books by S. W. Hubbard

Palmyrton Estate Sale Mysteries
Another Man's Treasure
Treasure of Darkness
This Bitter Treasure
Treasure in Exile
Treasure Built of Sand
Life in Palmyrton Women's Fiction Series
Life, Part 2
Life, Upended
Life, at Last
Frank Bennett Adirondack Mountain Mystery Series
The Lure
Blood Knot
Dead Drift
False Cast
Tailspinner
Ice Jig
Jumping Rise

About the Author

S.W. Hubbard writes the kinds of mysteries she loves to read: twisty, believable, full of complex characters, and highlighted with sly humor. She is the author of the Palmyrton Estate Sale Mystery Series and the Frank Bennett Adirondack Mountain Mystery Series. Her short stories have also appeared in *Alfred Hitchcock's Mystery Magazine* and the anthologies *Crimes by Moonlight, Adirondack Mysteries*, and *The Mystery Box*. She lives in Morristown, NJ, where she teaches creative writing to enthusiastic teens and adults, and expository writing to reluctant college freshmen. Visit her at http://www.swhubbard.net.

Printed in Great Britain
by Amazon

32189731R10116